EVIL LURKS BENEATH

JENNIFER ANNE DAVIS

REIGN PUBLISHING

Cover Design by KimG-Design

Editing by Jennifer Murgia

Proofreading by Appalachian Proofing

ISBN (Paperback): 979-8-9864009-1-4

eISBN: 979-8-9864009-0-7

Library of Congress Control Number: 1-11881656841

For My Family

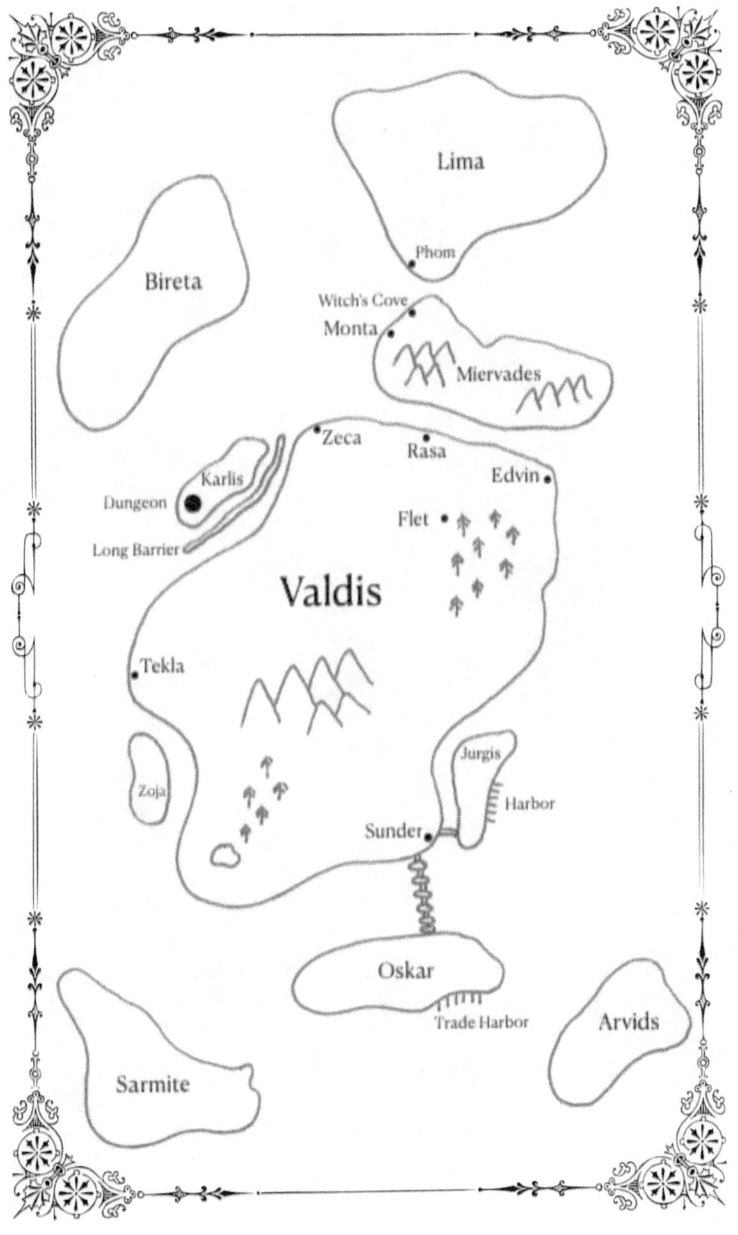

Lima
Phom
Bireta
Witch's Cove
Monta
Miervades
Zeca
Rasa
Edvin
Karlis
Dungeon
Flet
Long Barrier
Valdis
Tekla
Jurgis
Zoja
Harbor
Sunder
Oskar
Trade Harbor
Arvids
Sarmite

CHAPTER 1
MABEL

Fifty feet below the surface, Mabel Bakken sat shivering in the dungeon, her arms wrapped around her knees, trying to get warm. Soft footsteps echoed from somewhere down the corridor to her right, increasing in volume. The hair on her arms stood up, and she forced her mind to focus on what needed to be done.

A guard stopped before her cell. "I have your food," he said, his voice deep and raspy. He unlocked the door, then stepped inside.

When the man squatted to set the bowl on the floor, Mabel sneezed, momentarily distracting him.

"You're not getting sick, are you?" he asked.

"No, it's just the dampness of this place." She shivered. "What corridor am I in?" Her late father—she clutched her hands at the mere thought of him—had been a guard here in the dungeon, so she knew the layout.

"Your mum put you in the noble women's wing. No

murderers or thieves on this level." He patted her foot before standing. "I'll find a blanket for you since your mother asked us to take care of you until she returns."

Mabel didn't see how locking her up in the dungeon constituted safekeeping. Instead of voicing that thought, she asked, "What time is it?" Below ground, there weren't any windows, only a faint light from the torches in the corridor.

"Nearly midnight."

"Why are you feeding me now?"

He shrugged. "The cook is sick. No one got fed today. I made this for you and didn't want anyone to see me bringing it." He winked before exiting the cell. He shut the door with a *clang*, then headed back to the right.

Knowing she didn't have long until the guard discovered she'd swiped his keys when she pretend-sneezed, Mabel stood and went to the door. Not hearing anything coming from the corridor, she inserted the key into the lock, covered it with her hand to muffle the sound, and turned it.

Her mother had been gone too long. Since she hadn't returned yet, Mabel feared the royal family would send someone after her to finish the job that should have been done twenty-one years ago. While her mother might think the dungeon was the safest place for her, she knew otherwise. Right now, she needed to keep herself alive until she came up with a long-term plan. Later, when she was safe, she'd deal with what her father had revealed on his deathbed. But not now; she wasn't ready to face or acknowledge it.

She peered into the adjacent cell. It was empty. Slowly,

she made her way to the right, being careful not to jingle the keys or make any noise and alert the guards. Three cells down, she found a woman lying on the floor sleeping. The lines on the woman's face and the gray streak in her hair indicated she was much too old for what Mabel had in mind. She continued along, checking each person's face until she found a youthful woman who looked to be in her early twenties, sitting in the middle of her cell, crying. She was exactly what Mabel needed.

Mabel unlocked the door and entered. She knelt next to the woman. "I have food if you want it," she said gently.

The woman wiped her eyes. "I haven't eaten in two days."

Mabel nodded. "I know. That's why I want to help you."

"Thank you." The young woman's voice was barely above a whisper.

"Come with me." Mabel pulled the woman up alongside her. "You can eat in my cell."

The woman clutched onto Mabel's arm, never once questioning how Mabel had gotten in or why she was being so nice.

They slowly made their way to Mabel's cell. "Here," Mabel said, leading the woman into the tiny room. "Sit here and eat as much as you'd like. I'll go back to your cell in case a guard wanders by."

The woman dropped to her knees, grabbed the bowl, and started eating the contents without even looking Mabel's way.

"I'll return in twenty minutes." Mabel shut the door,

satisfied when she heard the lock click into place. She hurried to the woman's vacant cell, closing the door behind her. After tucking the keys into her bodice, she sat in the corner and waited.

Having grown up on the small island of Karlis that housed the kingdom's dungeon, she knew a thing or two about people's motives. It was only a matter of time. Most dark deeds happened in the dead of night. And tonight, her fifteenth night down here, meant something evil was going to happen at any minute. She was certain of it.

In the darkness of the damp dungeon, time could lose meaning. Mabel's father had told her it drove many people insane—even those who worked in the dark depths of this place. As a child, she'd visited countless times and could easily navigate the labyrinth of tunnels.

Mabel ran her finger along the hem of her dress, counting the stitches. It was a trick her father had taught her. He'd said when scared or anxious, she just needed to focus on one small thing to sharpen her mind.

The soft *clank* of a lock being picked echoed along the corridor. The dungeon had been designed to amplify all sounds. It made it harder for the prisoners to plan riots or attempt to escape.

The rough metal keys pressed against Mabel's skin. Her hands trembled, so she gripped the fabric of her dress as she listened.

"Mabel Bakken?" a soft, male voice asked from down the corridor.

"What?" a woman responded.

Mabel's entire body shook. She rested her forehead against her knees, her stomach turning sour. She'd had no choice. If she hadn't done it, she'd be the one in there right now.

A soft thump sounded, and then all went quiet. Mabel bit her lip to keep herself from screaming. She didn't even hear retreating footsteps. She squeezed her eyes shut. After counting to one hundred, she opened her eyes and forced herself to listen again.

The silence seemed to hum with anticipation. After waiting five minutes, she stood and exited the cell, heading back to where the young woman was, knowing what she'd find. When Mabel reached the cell, she peered inside, wanting confirmation. The woman lay sprawled on the floor, her throat slit, blood pooling around her lifeless body.

Mabel took a step back, gagging. Clutching her hands into fists, she inhaled a deep breath, releasing it slowly, trying to calm herself for what needed to be done next.

Standard procedure dictated that when a prisoner was found murdered, the guards would lock the dungeon and sweep the corridors. No one could enter or leave until the investigation concluded. Which meant Mabel had to slip out before somebody discovered the body. Once the guards identified who'd been murdered and they noticed a prisoner was also missing, it wouldn't take them long to deduce what Mabel had done. At that point, the island of Karlis would be closed to all ships, and she would be hunted like an animal.

At first, Mabel had assumed what her father revealed on his deathbed was some sick joke. He died before either she or her mother could question him. Her mother had seemed truly shocked by the revelation. Obviously, she believed what her husband had said since she'd dragged Mabel to the dungeon for safekeeping. Given that the young woman in Mabel's assigned cell had just been assassinated, Mabel's father must have spoken the truth.

A wave of nausea rolled through her body. To survive, she had to be strong. Mabel forced herself to take a deep breath. She shoved her insecurities aside and focused on what needed to be done. First, she had to get out of the dungeon. Then, she'd figure out what came next.

Years ago, her father had instructed her on what to do if she found herself in a precarious situation such as this. He'd told her to escape using the pulleys that transported the prisoners' food from the kitchen on the first level to the cells below ground.

Mabel rushed to the end of the passageway and came to the small, square door. She fumbled with the keys until she found the right one. She unlocked the door then reached for the rope, pulling it until the flat board came level with the bottom of the door. Climbing in the shaft, she sat cross-legged on the board. Clutching the rope, she pulled, raising the board upward. Her shoulders and hands burned, but she ignored the pain, slowly lifting herself up ten levels. The thought of the guards finding her was enough to fuel her on. If they caught her, she'd be locked back up with no chance of escaping before the assassin came for her again. She was certain he wouldn't fail a second time.

At the top level, Mabel pushed the door open an inch,

peering inside the kitchen. The room remained empty since Partik, the cook, was out sick. If he'd been there, he would have let her in, pretending not to see her, since he'd been good friends with her father. Having him not witness her escape was probably better. Mabel climbed out of the shaft, her arms shaking from overuse, her hands bloody from the rope. Sweat trickled down the side of her face.

The delivery entrance wouldn't be guarded at this hour. After finding the right key, she unlocked the door and slid outside into the night. Thick, warm air filled her lungs. Mabel closed the door and leaned against it, cautious of her surroundings. She needed to escape. Since only the dungeon and a small town for those who worked there took up the island, her only hope was to make it to the harbor, steal a boat, and sail to Valdis.

The dungeon sat on the southwest side of Karlis. The main harbor was to the east. She had no choice but to make her way through the jungle and to the harbor in the dead of night. She cursed. This day couldn't possibly get any worse.

The guards who patrolled the compound were stationed every fifty feet. They'd been trained to always scan the surrounding land. A hundred-foot perimeter had been cleared around the dungeon. The first floor sat at ground level; the rest—including all the cells—were below ground. Which meant there wasn't much in the way of shadows to conceal Mabel. Regardless, she had to cross the clearing.

Straight ahead, the dirt path used to deliver food and supplies to the dungeon stretched out, leading to the jungle. The moon remained hidden by clouds, the stars concealed as well. Since Mabel wore a navy-blue dress, she wouldn't stand out against the night. She took a tentative step forward. No shouts rang out. She bent her head down, allowing her long, black hair to shield her face. She took another step. And then another. To keep herself calm as she walked out in the open, she counted her steps, trying not to think about an arrow being shot into her back. Even though security remained tight, the dungeon saw little action. She couldn't even remember the last time someone had tried breaking into or out of the facility.

Remaining on the path, Mabel never wavered or ran though her legs begged to. Most guards expected an escapee to run, weave, or act erratically. A firm determination settled over her, giving her strength. She stayed calm, putting one foot in front of the other, as she neared the jungle.

By the time Mabel reached the trees, her shoulders had relaxed. The sweet smell of plumerias hung thick in the air. She stuck to the trail since it led straight to the island's only town and then to the harbor. Knowing she didn't have much time, she couldn't risk going home for supplies. It would be one of the first places they'd look for her. Unfortunately, Karlis offered no hiding places. The only reason the prison guards hadn't decimated the jungle was because several plants of importance grew in the area, plants the kingdom used to make medicines.

Walking at a brisk pace, Mabel estimated she'd reach the harbor in about an hour. The dark night would make stealing a boat easy. However, the real challenge would be sailing it to Valdis. She'd only been sailing a few times with her father. While she understood the basic concept, doing so alone and in the middle of the night would be difficult.

Not only that, she'd never been anywhere other than the small island of Karlis. As a child, she'd learned that the Long Barrier—a sandbank halfway between Valdis and Karlis—was due east of the harbor. Many ships crashed into it, not realizing it was there until it was too late. Which meant she'd have to sail slightly northeast to go around the sandbank, and then straight east, hopefully running right into Valdis. A dull throbbing started in her head just thinking about the obstacles ahead.

"Who are you?" a deep voice demanded.

Mabel jumped, clutching her bloodied hands together. She'd been so distracted with her own thoughts, she'd failed to notice the man looming on the trail ahead of her.

"I...I..." She struggled to find a lie. "You scared me," she admitted, hoping it bought her time to figure out what to say.

"Who are you, and why are you coming from the direction of the dungeon?" The man turned to face her, widening his stance, as if to fight. In the darkness, she couldn't see his face under the hood of his cape.

Most guards would have grabbed her, then asked questions later. Fear coursed through her. She'd just caught up to the assassin who'd murdered the young woman less than an hour ago thinking it was her. She forced herself to remain calm while silently cursing herself for taking the same path as the assassin. She needed to convince him she was a poor damsel who needed help. That way he wouldn't discover he'd killed the wrong person. "I find myself in a bind." She lowered her chin and tried to sound small and helpless. "I'm running away. My father beats me." She didn't say anything else, not wanting her lies to be too detailed. The less she said, the better. "Please don't take me back."

"Your father lives in the dungeon?"

"He works there." She quickly considered her options. "I'm headed to the harbor. I'm going to steal a boat and sail away from here."

"Stealing is illegal, and you can be arrested for it." The sound of crisp metal sliced through the air as the man sheathed a small knife. "I have a boat nearby. I can give you passage."

"I'm trying to get to Monta." A town in Miervades; the island just off the coast of Valdis.

"Do you have family there?"

"No." She swallowed, trying to rein in her rising panic.

"Fine. I'll take you there. I have to sail past it on my way to Sunder."

"I have no money and won't trade one abuse for another. I'll not pay with my body." She balled her hands into fists, prepared to run into the jungle if necessary.

"It'll be an even trade. I'll provide you passage for your help guiding me around the Long Barrier."

Mabel considered his offer. "Deal." She hoped she hadn't made a huge mistake.

———

Mabel and the man had just reached the Long Barrier when the storm hit. Unable to see more than a few feet in front of them, they struck land.

"We can't sail in this," he yelled over the roar of the rain. "Let's wait it out on the barrier." He jumped out of the boat, trying to pull it up onto the shore so they wouldn't be sucked out to sea.

Mabel climbed out to help.

"When I say," the assassin hollered, handing her a rope attached to the front of the boat. The water rushed toward shore again, the boat with it. "Now!"

Mabel pulled the rope with all her might.

The boat flew forward, now half on land and half in the water.

"We need to get it out more," the man said. "You stay in front. I'll push from the back. Wait for the swell."

Mabel nodded though the assassin probably couldn't see in the torrential downpour.

She gripped the rope, ready. The water rushed toward her again, so she pulled. The boat moved faster than before, knocking into her, smacking her head.

Her world went black.

Mabel awoke in a soft bed. "Where am I?" she moaned. Everything hurt.

"Shh," a woman said. "Don't try and talk. You've had a

nasty accident. Your husband brought you here to this inn. I've been taking care of you all week."

Week? Mabel had been here a week? *Husband?* She wasn't married. "Where am I?"

"You're in Zeca. I'm a healer. Your husband is in the harbor repairing your boat. He comes and checks on you daily."

Mabel tried to sit up. She needed to get moving before the assassin came back for her.

"Drink this. It'll help with the pain. I had to put a few stitches in your head to close the gash." The healer held a cup to Mabel's lips.

She drank the pungent liquid. Warmth spread throughout her. Her eyes became heavy.

***

Mabel opened her eyes. She found herself on a pile of blankets, a cloudy sky above her. She sat up. Her head no longer throbbed, and her vision was clear.

"You're awake," the assassin said.

Mabel peered over and found him steering the boat. "I am."

"I was starting to get worried."

She tried not to laugh at the thought of an assassin worrying. "What happened?"

"After you hit your head, I took you to the nearest port. A healer tended to you."

She'd figured out that much. What she wanted to know

was how she got back on the boat. She'd intended to make a run for it to get away from the assassin.

"The healer insisted on giving you a potent medicine that knocked you out. She said it'd help you heal faster. After about a week, I didn't like that anymore, so I snuck in at night and stole you away. Of course, I told everyone I was your husband, so I guess I didn't actually steal you." He winked.

The sea air felt refreshing on her skin and in her lungs. "Where are we headed to now?"

"We're back on course to Miervades. That's where you wanted to go, right?"

She nodded. "To Monta." Where her birth mother was from.

"Being your husband and all, I should probably know your name."

She just stared at him.

"I'm Matsen if that helps," he offered.

The last thing she would do was tell him her name. He'd been sent to kill Mabel Bakken—which he thought he'd done already in the dungeon. He couldn't discover he'd killed the wrong person. "How much longer until we reach Monta?" she asked, changing the subject.

"It'll take us about a week to get there. This tiny boat doesn't go that fast. The mast cracked in the storm. I repaired it as best I could, but I don't want to push it too hard." He glanced up at one of the sails fully outstretched in the wind.

Mabel's hair thrashed around, and she smiled. She loved it out here on the water.

"So, wife, what's your name?" Matsen asked again.

"Gina," she lied.

Matsen's eyes narrowed as he watched her for a minute. When she didn't say anything else, he glanced away. "Well then, *Gina*," he said her name as if he'd eaten a sour lemon, "I'm glad you're doing better."

"How'd you pay for the healer?" she asked.

"I didn't," he replied. "That's one of the reasons I snuck you out of there in the middle of the night. I guess that makes us partners in crime now."

CHAPTER 2

DECLAN

eclan Forberg took a sip of wine from his goblet, wishing for the tenth time that the dinner would end already. He wanted to meet Sasha since he hadn't seen her in over a week. A night alone with her was far overdue. His brothers, Brooks and Orson, sat across from him while his parents sat on either end of the table. He didn't know why they bothered to have this weekly tradition where they had supper alone, without anyone from court. No nobles attended, not even his mother's father, the general. It was just the five of them spending quality time together. They rarely spoke about anything important.

Queen Briar Forberg leaned back in her chair; her sharp gaze focused on something outside the open window while her right finger gently tapped against the side of her plate. She'd barely touched her food.

Someone knocked on the door to the royal wing. A servant admitted a guard who rushed to the entrance of the dining room. "Your Majesties," the guard said, glancing from the king to the queen.

King Rhett Forberg waved him in.

"This just arrived for you." The guard handed an envelope to the king, then took a step back.

The king broke the seal and pulled out the letter, quickly reading both pages, his nostrils flaring as he did so. "That will be all."

The guard bowed before leaving the room.

"Everything okay?" Declan asked, not really caring. It seemed there was always some problem to be dealt with.

King Rhett tucked the papers into his jacket. "About two weeks ago, a woman by the name of Sanda showed up seeking an audience with me. She said it was important."

Everyone wishing to speak to the king said the same thing. "Any idea what about?" Declan asked, hoping to fill the silence so the meal would pass more quickly.

"No," the king replied. "As always, I had one of my men check her identity before I meet with her."

Declan shrugged. If his father met with everyone who wanted a private audience with him, he'd never have a moment to himself. "Is there anything I can do to help?" Since he'd turned twenty-one, his father had been including him in on more meetings and dealings with the dukes. Declan didn't think he'd become king until he was much older since his father was only in his forties and healthy. But it didn't hurt to learn the position now.

"I just received word from Karlis. Sanda is who she says she is. A dungeon guard's wife."

"Someone from Karlis is here?" Orson asked, speaking for the first time since dinner had started.

Of course, that would pique his interest.

The queen looked over at her husband, her eyes narrowing. "You have no idea what this woman wants?"

"Since I haven't spoken to her yet, I do not," he replied. "Do you, perhaps, know something I don't? After all, you seem to be in a foul mood this evening."

Both of Declan's brothers resumed eating, studiously ignoring their bickering parents. However, he knew Brooks well enough to know he'd be filing every word away to dissect later. And Orson, being the youngest at seventeen, only cared when the topic suited him. He'd much rather think about whatever it was he did last night. Rumor was he'd been at the pub on the upper west side. He'd apparently got into a fight before leaving with two women.

"When I heard there was a woman here seeking your audience, I went to see her," Briar admitted. "But Sanda refused to say anything to me, a mere queen. She said she could only address the matter with you."

That explained why his mother was so irritated. She hated to have her authority challenged.

"I'll see her first thing tomorrow morning. And, if you'd like, you may come with me." The king took a drink from his goblet, seemingly unconcerned with the appearance of a woman from Karlis.

On the rare occasion, a guard from the dungeon had come to report some uprising or murder. Often, a letter was sent if there were any problems. Never had a woman, let alone a dungeon guard's wife, come before. Declan thought her presence warranted an immediate visit. But he wasn't the king. At least, not yet.

"It's not necessary for me to accompany you tomorrow," Briar said as she stood. "I was simply trying to help you. However, you seem to have the matter under control, and clearly, I'm not needed. Now, if you'll excuse me, I'm not feeling well and wish to retire for the night." She glided to the door, about to exit the dining room.

"There were two letters from Karlis," the king revealed, causing the queen to pause, her back to them. "The second one mentioned a murder. Do you think it's a coincidence?"

"I haven't the faintest idea," the queen said before exiting the dining room and going to the right.

"Mother seemed perfectly fine to me," Orson commented. "Not ill at all." He glanced at the king and smiled. "She didn't even head to her bedchamber. She left the royal wing all together."

"Perhaps she went to see a healer?" Brooks offered.

Orson snorted. "Only someone extremely skilled could pull off a murder in the dungeons. I wonder if Mother sent her personal assassin there to off someone." Amusement colored his voice.

The king took a bite of his food, diligently ignoring his sons.

"Perhaps," Brooks said, "but we don't know all the particulars. Maybe you should gather information before jumping to conclusions."

"If it looks like a duck...smells like a duck..."

"Why duck?" Brooks mused. "Wouldn't a pig make more sense? Foul creatures."

"If I hinted that mother had anything to do with a pig, I'm sure she'd murder me in my sleep."

The king continued to ignore them all.

Declan didn't want to waste another second. "I need to be going as well." He shoved his chair back and hurried from the royal suite before anyone could stop him.

As he walked along the corridor, he rolled up his sleeves and undid the top two buttons of his shirt. He could finally relax.

Declan turned down the hallway to his right, reaching the guest wing. Whenever he wanted to see Sasha, he'd send a letter with a single word: *tonight*. Then, she'd meet him in the emerald guest suite. He made sure the servants kept the room clean and ready for his own particular use.

Obviously, a handful of servants and some of the palace guards knew about his secret affair with Sasha. Since his parents wouldn't approve of her, he tried not to flaunt his relationship with the woman. Lately, he'd heard talk among the nobles about his dalliances. He'd have to do a better job of hiding it. Sasha's parents owned a winery on the outskirts of the city. And while the nobles may enjoy drinking their wine, they certainly didn't want their crown prince marrying a commoner. No, he'd have to marry someone for political gain. Thankfully that hadn't been pushed on him. It was only a matter of time though.

He opened the door and entered the guest suite.

Sasha lay sprawled on the bed, naked, a single rose next to her. "It's about time. I've been waiting for hours."

Declan smiled and closed the door.

"Your Highness, wake up."

Declan peeled his eyelids open to find his valet, Graham, hovering over him. Declan glanced to his side. Sasha wasn't there. It was one of the things they'd agreed upon early in their relationship—that while they would spend the night together, she would leave prior to sunrise to avoid unnecessary gossip.

"What time is it?" Declan asked. Graham rarely woke him up, which meant there had to be some issue that needed to be dealt with.

"A letter arrived for you," he said, his voice low so that if anyone lurked out in the hallway, they wouldn't overhear. "It's from your contact in Miervades."

Declan rubbed his eyes and sat up, swinging his legs over the side of the bed. His father had put him in charge of overseeing Miervades, the large island just off the northeast coast of Valdis. "Open it."

Graham withdrew the letter and broke the seal. He unfolded the paper. "It says, *It's as you suspected. The duke is shipping coal, wheat, and diamonds to Lima.*"

Declan groaned. The king would be furious. "At least that explains why the deliveries to us have been short." He was going to have to let his father know since this constituted treason. All trade had to go through the island of Oskar.

The thing he hated most about ruling was enforcing the law. Sometimes he understood why a law was broken, bent, or altered. However, the king had instilled it in him from a young age that the law had to be enforced no matter what. They didn't deserve to rule if they couldn't uphold the laws formed so many years ago by their ancestors. It wasn't until recently that Declan had learned the truth.

Centuries ago, a blood oath had been forged between Valdis and the four surrounding kingdoms, sealed in magic by three witches. The rulers of each kingdom were required to enforce all laws as written or they'd die. Since Declan had never seen a drop of magic, he had trouble understanding it. However, his father clearly believed in the blood oath, so Declan had no choice but to do so as well.

After Declan dismissed his valet, he quickly dressed. Donning his usual black pants, black button up vest, and long-sleeved shirt underneath, he pulled his arms through his black trench coat. He laced up his boots then grabbed his small sword from under the bed, sliding it into the sheath around his waist now hidden by his coat. He stretched his neck, rolled his shoulders, then ran his hands through his shaggy dark hair. It was time to be the prince his father needed him to be.

He exited the guest suite and headed toward the center of the palace. Even at this early hour, servants were already scampering about, cleaning, and running errands. A few nobles lingered on the balconies overlooking the courtyard, the open doors allowing the fresh ocean air to waft inside. As Declan made his way from one side of the palace to the other, he felt everyone watching him, judging him. Some nobles curtsied and bowed, but he didn't acknowledge them. He never did.

When he caught sight of his father's esquire, he waved him over. "Where's the king?"

"Your Highness." The man bowed. "King Rhett is in the throne room. A woman from Karlis is being brought before him."

After hearing the news about Miervades, the dungeon guard's wife had slipped Declan's mind. He hurried to the throne room, hoping to arrive before the woman did. He found his father already seated on the throne, the queen nowhere in sight. He was just about to greet his father when the side door opened, and two guards escorted a woman into the room. Instead of saying anything, Declan climbed the steps, standing to his father's right.

"Your Majesty," the woman said, curtsying. "I must speak with you about a private matter." The woman wore a plain blue dress, her mousy brown hair pulled back into a tight bun. Declan put her age around forty.

The woman glanced at the guards. "Pardon me, Your Majesty, but I don't think you want anyone to hear what I'm about to say."

"I'm the king," Rhett said. "I am never alone." He looked at the guard to his left. "Has she been checked?"

"She has, Your Majesty."

"Then leave us."

Both guards exited the room.

Declan had a feeling his father wouldn't have dismissed them if he hadn't been there.

"Now," the king said, "tell me why you're here."

"My husband is—was—a guard in the dungeon. He died three weeks ago." The woman cleared her throat, shifting her weight from foot to foot, seemingly nervous. "You see, when my husband died, he told me something—something I didn't know until then."

Declan folded his arms, watching her carefully. She kept fidgeting with her hands.

"Continue," the king said, urging her on.

The woman took a deep breath, slowly releasing the air. "I want you to know that as soon as I heard the information, I came straight here to tell you. If I had known sooner, I would have said something." She glanced around. "I didn't know you'd keep me locked in a room for the past two weeks."

The king raised a single eyebrow. "I suggest you get to the point. What's your name? Sanda?"

"Sanda Bakken. My husband, Peerson, made a confession on his deathbed." She shifted her weight again. "He said that the child I raised was not of my own flesh and blood."

A sick feeling overcame Declan. He had a notion of where this was going. Someone was trying to lay some claim to the throne. It never worked.

"I delivered a child twenty-one years ago. The child was ill, and I was certain she was going to die. The child got better. Or so I believed. Peerson confessed my own child had indeed died. You see, there was a woman in the prison, and she gave birth to a baby girl the same day mine died. He said they were going to kill her baby, and he couldn't stand the thought of another baby dying for no reason. So my husband switched the babies."

The king went unnaturally still. "Did your husband by chance give you the name of this woman in the dungeon?"

"Yes, Your Majesty. He said her name was Willa Laris."

"And do you know what became of Willa after she delivered the baby?"

"The woman was executed for her crimes against the crown."

"And everyone assumed your dead baby was hers?"

Tears filled Sanda's eyes. "Yes." Tears streamed down the woman's face.

"You're here for a reason," the king said. "I assume Peerson knew why Willa was in the dungeon?"

She nodded, biting her bottom lip. "Willa told my husband the baby's father is you." She motioned to the king.

Declan rubbed his chin. This woman clearly believed the story her husband had told her.

"What's the child's name?"

"Mabel Bakken."

"And where is she now?" Rhett asked, his voice unnervingly calm.

"I had her placed in the dungeon."

The king stiffened.

"Let me explain," Sanda said. "My husband confessed to switching my dead baby with Willa's newborn to both myself and Mabel on his deathbed. Mabel was furious she'd been lied to her entire life. I didn't know what she was going to do. I knew I had to come here to tell you, and I didn't want to leave her there all alone. I put her in the noble wing of the dungeon and gave specific instructions for her to be cared for until I returned. I didn't expect to be gone this long. I wanted to keep her safe."

The king pursed his lips and nodded. "And if something happens to her in the dungeon?"

"No one else is aware of her true identity," Sanda said. "And the guards there knew Peerson. I asked them to watch over her. Most consider her like a daughter. No harm will come to her there."

"Very well. I will send someone to fetch her. You will remain here." He turned to Declan. "Get my guards. Have Sanda escorted back to her private guest room. She is to be kept there until Mabel arrives and I decide what to do."

Declan stood there staring at his father. He couldn't possibly believe this woman's story, so why was he bringing Mabel to the palace?

"Is something the matter?" the king asked.

Declan shook his head, not wanting to say anything in front of Sanda.

"Speak of this to no one," Rhett ordered.

After the woman had been escorted out of the room, Declan turned to his father.

Rhett leaned back in the throne, rubbing his face. "You

have to understand, it was before your mother and I married."

If felt as if Declan had been punched in the stomach. "It's true?"

The king nodded.

Declan had a half-sister...and she was the heir to the throne. He couldn't comprehend what this meant or how he felt.

"No one is to know until I decide how to proceed," the king said.

"You'd put her on the throne over me?" Declan couldn't tell if he felt jealous or relieved. Maybe both.

"The law is clear on this matter."

Of course his father would look to the law on how to handle this mess.

"But that's not what I'm referring to." The king stood and turned to face Declan. "You forget—last night I received *two* letters from Karlis."

It had totally slipped his mind. The first letter verified Sanda's identity, and the second had said something about a murder. "Did the letter say who had been killed?"

"It did."

He recalled his father asking his mother if it was a coincidence. "Mabel?"

"I can't be certain. The letter only stated that someone in cell F32 had been killed. However, it also stated that a woman had escaped from a cell a few doors down. An investigation is underway. Especially since no one is registered to be in cell F32."

The question slipped out before he thought better of it. "Do you think Mother sent her personal assassin after Mabel?" After all, his mother had gone to see Sanda and had been acting strangely.

"I don't know what to think right now."

"So Mabel is either dead or she switched cells with someone and escaped?" The royal line either remained intact and Declan was still the heir, or Mabel would be coming to claim her birthright.

"It would appear so."

A guard entered from the side door. "Your Majesty." He bowed. "The general is in your office. He wishes to speak with you."

"Tell him I'll be right there."

The guard bowed and left.

"Want to join me?" the king asked.

Declan had a dozen letters sitting on his desk that needed to be answered. "No, I have work to do."

"Very well, I'll see you this afternoon."

"Before you go," Declan said, "there is one thing I need to mention. The Duke of Miervades is illegally trading with Lima."

"Miervades you say?"

Declan nodded.

"It's time we pay them a visit."

CHAPTER 3

BRIELLE

Brielle Tranum shivered from the light mist. Thick, gray clouds covered the sky, blocking any trace of the sun. She made her way from the main portion of the town, up the steep hill, and toward her family's castle. The stone pathway turned slick, so she tucked the book she'd just purchased under her cape to ensure its safety. The last thing she wanted was to slip and fall, destroying the book before she even had a chance to read it.

"Good afternoon, Lady Brielle," a man from up ahead said as he made his way down the path.

When he got closer, Brielle recognized him as Barek, one of the men who worked in her father's stables. "Good afternoon," she replied.

"Any idea what all the fuss is about?" He pointed behind her.

Glancing over her shoulder, she observed the bustling town. Nothing appeared amiss.

"The harbor," Barek said, nodding his chin to the north.

Brielle stopped walking and turned around, looking out over the green rolling hills toward the harbor in the distance. Three massive ships were pulling into port.

"They look too fine for merchant vessels," he stated. "And far too large."

His comments mirrored Brielle's own thoughts. "They almost look like the king's warships," she murmured, more to herself than to Barek.

"That they do," he replied. "You best get yourself home now in case there's any trouble."

Brielle couldn't imagine what trouble there would be; however, she nodded and continued up the path, this time a bit faster. The king rarely came to the island of Miervades. If this had been a planned visit, she would have heard about it from her father or sister. She shivered, and it had nothing to do with the chilly air.

When she reached the castle, she removed her cape and ran up the steps to the third floor where the family's sitting room was located. The north wall contained large archways leading to an open balcony overlooking their land, and in the distance, the ocean. Brielle loved that their castle had been built on one of the taller mountains on the island. Being up this high afforded them an amazing view of the surrounding land, including the mines to the east.

Brielle's father stood on the balcony, gazing at the sea.

"What's going on?" she asked. The ships appeared even larger from this vantage point.

"I'm not certain," Duke Jaxon Tranum replied. "Stay inside." He waved her off the balcony.

Hovering in the sitting room near the archways, Brielle inquired after her sister, Kenna.

"I haven't seen her all morning," the duke muttered.

Knowing Kenna, she had to be visiting one of the local villages or out riding her horse. Even at the mature age of twenty-one, she preferred to gallivant all over the island instead of learning her duties as the duke's heir. Their father had been trying to marry Kenna off to a suitable man, but she was proving to be too obstinate. Brielle secretly thought Kenna hoped to marry the crown prince of Valdis so she could live in the capital, Sunder, and be the next queen. Kenna probably saw no problem in Brielle becoming the duke's heir.

But Brielle could never work with her father. Not only did she not care for politics, but she knew nothing about the machinations of the kingdom of Valdis. She much preferred the small life that she'd carved out for herself. Collecting taxes, managing the people who lived in Miervades...none of that sounded remotely appealing to her. She had no designs on title, wealth, or fame. No, she much preferred reading to any of that.

Brielle sighed as she headed over to the corner of the room where she curled up on the chair, trying to remain out of the way. She set her book on her lap, stroking the beautiful leather-bound cover. Peeling it open, she eagerly read the first page, excited to start this new story.

"They're disembarking," the duke mumbled as he made

his way back inside. "If it's the king, it'll take him some time to get here." He started pacing. "I need to close the mines and find Kenna." He hurried from the room.

Brielle turned the page, trying not to worry about the king's presence or the fact that he'd arrived on what appeared to be a warship. Surely when he traveled, he'd be accompanied by soldiers who protected him. Nothing was amiss. If she kept reading, she'd soon be lost in another adventure, and the problems of today would disappear. They always did.

A few minutes later, a bell tolled, echoing across the land, indicating that the mines were closing for the day. The mist turned to a gentle and steady rain. Brielle grabbed the blanket from under the chair and laid it across her lap, trying to stay warm.

Duke Jaxon and Lady Kenna entered the sitting room, arguing. Brielle knew better than to ask what they were bickering about or to try and intervene. Since Kenna was the older sister by a whole three years, she was always right. Even when she was wrong. Brielle remained on her chair tucked into the corner of the room.

"The king and prince are going to be here within the hour," Duke Jaxon said. "I suggest you go and change so you at least look presentable." He mumbled something about her wearing pants and having a flushed face.

Kenna removed the bow and quiver from her shoulder.

"And I suggest you start coming up with a plausible excuse as to why we haven't paid taxes in two seasons."

Brielle turned the page of her book, trying to process all her sister had just revealed. It made no sense for her father not to pay their taxes. Surely, he had the money. Perhaps it had just slipped his mind.

"I assumed the king would send a letter before he'd sail all the way here," the duke said.

"On a warship, accompanied by two additional warships," Kenna pointed out.

The duke sighed. "You know King Rhett has always been a stickler about enforcing the law. It was a calculated risk on our part."

"Yes, but we had no choice." Kenna turned to leave when she caught sight of Brielle. "I didn't realize you were in the room."

Brielle smiled at her.

"Do you ever do anything besides read?" Without waiting for Brielle to answer, Kenna shook her head and exited the room.

The duke pursed his lips. "Her words were far too harsh," he said, turning to face Brielle. "Please understand she's just stressed, and she took it out on you."

"I know," Brielle answered.

"Before I forget, when I was looking for Kenna, I ran into Lukas."

Brielle placed a bookmark between the pages and closed her book. "Oh?" She didn't know what else to say. She'd known Lukas most of her life, and they were good friends.

Recently, he'd been hinting that he wanted more, and she got the feeling he wished to marry her. Now that she was eighteen, it seemed a logical step in their relationship. And the best part about Lukas, he'd never forbid her from reading or treat her illy.

"He asked to talk," the duke said. "I told him now wasn't a good time, but we could meet next week."

She nodded. Faced with the real possibility of marriage, panic started to take root. The idea of tending to a house and raising children scared her. The room suddenly became hot and stifling.

The duke patted Brielle's shoulder. "When Lukas asks for your hand in marriage, I see no reason to refuse."

Her father was giving her an opportunity to object. Somehow, she was at a loss for words. She could read hundreds of pages in a day but expressing herself with her own words eluded her. If only she could be like one of the characters in her books—assertive, well versed, and able to speak her mind.

The duke smiled and headed over to one of the archways, gazing outside. Brielle opened her book and began reading again. Only this time, her mind kept wandering, and she couldn't focus on the story.

A few minutes later, Kenna breezed into the room. She'd managed to tame her hair into a braid woven with flowers, and she'd put on a pale pink dress. "What's the plan?" she asked, coming to stand alongside the duke.

"When the king and prince arrive, I want you to be as cordial as possible." The duke folded his hands behind his back. "You will let me do the talking." He looked pointedly at Kenna.

"Then make sure when you speak, it's something worth saying." Kenna folded her arms. "Explain the situation clearly. If the king is reasonable, he'll side with us."

"I hope you're right," the duke replied with an exasperated sigh.

"And we could be wrong," Kenna pointed out. "Maybe the prince is coming here to form an alliance? Perhaps he wishes to ask for my hand in marriage."

Brielle couldn't help but roll her eyes. "I doubt he'd come with three warships to ask for your hand."

Kenna smiled. "Maybe he's simply showing me his power, so I'll agree to marry him."

"If you married the prince, what would happen to Miervades?" Brielle asked.

Kenna shrugged. "I guess you could be Father's heir."

Brielle shook her head. She could never be the heir to the dukedom. Never. Running her hand over the page of her book, a thought occurred to her. Maybe Lukas wanted to marry Brielle because he knew Kenna would marry the prince. Perhaps Lukas had designs on the dukedom. If that were the case, she'd gladly let him take control of things and handle the day-to-day responsibilities. She wondered if her father had already considered this.

A servant rushed into the room. "Your Grace," she said before a quick curtsy. "The king is here."

Brielle tried to glance outside, but she couldn't see the

road leading up to the castle from her vantage point on the chair.

Kenna rushed out onto the balcony. "There are at least fifty soldiers accompanying him," she said. "A bit excessive if you ask me."

The duke gave the servant instructions about letting the soldiers inside the castle, but Brielle didn't pay any attention. The fact of the matter was the king was here because her father hadn't paid his taxes. She hoped the matter could be easily rectified. However, she doubted it would be that simple. If it were, there wouldn't be so many soldiers at their front door.

Rowdy voices and metal clanking resounded downstairs making it difficult for Brielle to read. Regardless, she kept her book open on her lap.

"There's no need to worry," the duke said. "The soldiers are being offered food and drink. They won't come up here."

Kenna snorted. "I hope you're giving them strong wine so if the king tells them to arrest you, they'll be too drunk to follow orders."

"Really, Kenna. Such talk is unbecoming of a lady." The duke shook his head.

Not for the first time, Brielle wondered why Miervades didn't have a standing army. Granted, they had men who could fight if needed, and they had a handful of sentries on duty at the castle; however, if the king decided to arrest the duke, he could. She supposed if her father did have an army and they stood against the crown, the king would strip the duke of his land and title and then he'd have nothing.

"Father, should I leave the room?" There was no reason for Brielle to be there when the king entered. If there were issues to discuss, such as unpaid taxes, then it really wasn't a conversation that involved her.

"No," the duke replied. "Remain in that chair. We will not run from the king or prince. We've done nothing wrong."

Except fail to pay taxes, Brielle thought sardonically. However, she kept her mouth shut and remained in the chair with her book still sitting on her lap. She'd never had the honor of meeting the king or anyone in the royal family before. Whenever there had been a royal function, her father had always attended alone.

"The prince looks rather tall," Kenna said as she came back into the room. "I like tall men."

While a mild curiosity nagged at Brielle as to what the king and prince looked like, she didn't care enough to leave the chair she'd been told to sit in. She'd always been that way—a rule follower. If her father told her to sit, sit she would. It was Kenna who questioned and challenged authority.

Kenna had once accused Brielle of not having the capacity to think for herself. That had really bothered Brielle because it wasn't true. She was a thoughtful person—she just didn't have to argue with everyone around her to prove it. Not only that, but when her father gave her an order, she usually had enough common sense to understand why he'd given it and the value in listening. She respected her father enough to trust his judgment.

The door to the sitting room burst open. A man—the

king, Brielle assumed—glided through the doorway. He was younger than she'd expected and had to be around her father's age. She had no idea why she thought he'd be older. After all, his eldest son was twenty-one, the same age as Kenna. King Rhett had a striking square face with thick dark hair, eyebrows, and a neatly trimmed beard. Standing tall, his mere presence commanded attention from everyone in the room. He wore black pants, black boots, and a black shirt. He also had on a black leather jacket with red accents. Brielle noticed him clenching his hands into fists.

The prince entered, standing slightly off to the side, behind the king. Brielle couldn't get a good look at him without moving.

She didn't know if she should stand or remain seated. Normally someone would announce the king, giving everyone time to stand before he entered a room. But this man had walked right in without an introduction. Brielle had never been to court, so her etiquette wasn't up to date. Especially since her father wasn't overly formal around the castle.

"Your Majesty, Your Highness," the duke said with a bow.

Kenna curtsied.

No one seemed to notice Brielle sitting in the chair, so she didn't move, not wanting to draw attention to herself.

"Duke Jaxon Tranum," the king said, his voice smooth and rich.

"It is an honor to have you and Prince Declan here," the duke said. "To what do we own this privilege?"

"We are here on business and won't be staying long," the king replied.

"Shall we go to my office?" the duke inquired. "It will afford us privacy to speak."

"That won't be necessary." The king strode farther into the room. "Declan." He waved his son over to him.

Declan came and stood beside his father, affording Brielle a chance to see him for the first time. His dark hair and eyes were like his father's; however, his hair was longer and shaggier, giving him a more youthful look. While he didn't have a beard, his chin did have a couple days' worth of stubble. He, too, wore black pants and boots. Instead of a black shirt, his was white, covered by a black button up vest, revealing only a bit of the white fabric around his thick neck. His jacket was solid black and much longer than his father's, reaching his ankles.

Brielle had heard rumors of the queen's stunning looks. After seeing the king and his son, she supposed Queen Briar would have to be beautiful. She'd always considered Kenna to be pretty. But next to the king and prince, she thought her sister rather plain.

"Since my son is my heir, he has been overseeing some of the dukedoms, yours being one of them," the king said, gesturing toward his son.

"We have proof you've been illegally trading with Lima," Declan said, his voice much deeper than his father's.

Brielle sat up straighter—this was the first she'd heard of such a thing. Neither her father nor her sister seemed surprised by the accusation.

"The law states that all trade is to go through Oskar," Declan added, folding his hands behind his back.

"Lima is directly north of us," the duke said. "A day's journey from here. It doesn't make sense to ship goods to Oskar only to have it sent all the way back up to Lima." Sweat broke out over his forehead. "The cost of doing that is tenfold."

"Speaking of money," the king said, "you haven't paid taxes for the past two seasons. Explain to me how you can be so bold as to sell goods—illegally—to Lima and not pay the crown what the law dictates."

Brielle swore she could hear her own heart pounding. How could her father have gotten himself in to such a mess? Illegally trading with another kingdom and not paying taxes —this wouldn't end well. She gripped her book.

The duke swallowed, his throat bobbing from the motion. "The money Miervades owes the crown is coming."

"When?" King Rhett demanded, folding his arms across his chest.

"You must understand that the people of Miervades aren't wealthy," the duke explained. "After the last tax increase, well, most couldn't afford the additional amount. I didn't collect what was owed. I thought that by trading with Lima, I could make up the difference." He wiped the sweat from his forehead.

King Rhett meandered over to the archways, gazing outside, his back to the room. "I find it interesting that none of the other dukes had a problem paying the increase." He turned to face the duke. "And no one has the resources you do. If anything, you should be the richest dukedom, not the poorest. So, I must ask myself if you're mismanaging funds?"

"We are not mismanaging funds," Kenna interrupted. "We are doing the best we can with our limited resources."

The duke's face turned bright red. "I told you to be quiet," he mumbled.

"You are the kingdom's sole supplier of wheat," Declan said. "If you're trading that commodity away to another kingdom, and not supplying Valdis with what you agreed to, we could find our kingdom in a precarious situation."

"We're doing the best we can, but we need more money," the duke replied.

The king and prince had to see that. Brielle thought her home modest; they didn't employ many servants, and they didn't throw lavish parties or eat in excess as she'd heard the royal family did. Their towns were simple, their people barely getting by.

"Why don't you produce more coal?" Declan asked. "If you sell it through Oskar as you're supposed to, other kingdoms can bid on it. You have the potential to make more money than blindly trading with Lima."

Brielle snorted.

Declan's sharp gaze focused on her, his eyes narrowing.

She wanted to melt into the chair and disappear. She hadn't meant to make a sound. But his comment had shown how little he knew about coal mining.

The duke glanced at Brielle, his brow furrowing with worry. Then, to the king, "My people work long days. Mining coal is tough work. We're doing the best we can."

"Perhaps if you weren't illegally selling it to Lima, you could make your quota to the crown," the king said, his voice turning lower.

"Maybe we need to renegotiate our contracts," Kenna snapped. "Make sure the terms are fair for all parties involved."

"Quiet," the duke said, his voice harsh.

"But Father," Kenna pleaded, "these contracts have been in place for centuries. They no longer make sense. It's only fair to renegotiate."

"It's not that simple," the king mused. "Tell me, Lady Kenna, are you your father's heir?"

"I am, Your Majesty." She held her chin high, pride radiating from her.

"She still has a lot to learn," the duke added.

"She appears to be of marriageable age."

The duke wiped his forehead again. "She is."

The king looked to his son.

"We need to clear up the matter of nonpayment of taxes and wheat owed to the kingdom of Valdis," Declan said.

Brielle noticed he didn't mention anything about the punishment for illegally trading.

"Yes, Your Highness," the duke replied. "Of course."

"When can we expect to get the wheat and money owed?"

The king shook his head. "The law is clear, son."

Declan gave a curt nod. "The taxes and wheat must be given to the crown by Walpurgis night."

Brielle's eyes widened. That didn't give her family much time. Walpurgis night would be here in two full moon cycles.

"I understand," the duke said.

"As you are well aware," the king said, "the law is the law."

"If I fail to pay the money owed and provide the wheat promised, I'll be stripped of my title and land," the duke said.

"Yes," the king replied. "And you're required to give me an insurance payment until what you owe is properly delivered to me."

A sinking feeling filled Brielle. This wouldn't end well.

"What do you want?" the duke asked.

"How about your daughter, Lady Kenna?"

CHAPTER 4

DECLAN

"How, exactly, is my daughter an insurance policy?" Duke Jaxon asked, his voice rising an octave as he spoke.

Declan had been wondering the same thing. However, it made sense. The duke owed a substantial amount of money and a decent amount of wheat. Holding Kenna hostage until payment was received seemed a reasonable thing to do.

The king smirked, and Declan knew he wasn't going to like how his father answered. The king only ever had that look when he'd trapped an opponent into a corner. "Your daughter is an insurance policy because if you fail to pay, I'll kill her."

Kenna cursed.

"And once I pay, she'll return home?"

"No. Once you pay, Prince Declan will marry Lady Kenna. By joining our families, I'm certain we won't have any issues in the future about missed payments or illegal trading."

Declan felt as if he'd been punched in the stomach. However, he remained upright and showed no reaction. He peered over at Kenna. A slight smile spread across her face. It took every ounce of self-control not to pinch his eyes shut or say something to his father. While pretty, Kenna had too much spunk and fight in her. Taming her at court would be difficult. Not that he wasn't up to the challenge, but she wasn't who he pictured marrying. Maybe it was the pale pink dress she wore or the flowers in her hair, but she screamed country peasant. His mother would never tolerate her.

"Lady Kenna is my heir," the duke said. "Isn't Prince Declan yours?"

"He is. I see the issue." The king folded his hands together behind his back and started pacing.

As the duke's heir, Lady Kenna had to live in Miervades to run it, and Declan needed to remain in Sunder to rule over Valdis. Of course, the king knew this before he'd made the suggestion. Which meant he had a plan. Instead of questioning his father, Declan remained quiet, knowing the king would reveal his plan when he was well and ready.

King Rhett came to an abrupt halt. "Who's that?" He pointed to a plain looking young woman curled up on a chair in the corner of the room with a book on her lap.

Declan had noticed her earlier when she'd made an odd noise, as if laughing at him. There certainly was nothing exceptional about her curly brown hair or freckles. There weren't any servants in the room, so he assumed the young woman had to be the duke's other daughter. However, she didn't look like a proper lady. She just seemed too...plain. Simple. He honestly couldn't remember if the duke had even introduced her.

Duke Jaxon cleared his throat, glancing over at the young woman. "This is my daughter, Lady Brielle. Since she is not my heir, you may have her."

The young woman's eyes widened in shock, but she didn't say anything. She simply clutched her book as if she were about to fall off the chair or become ill. Maybe there was something wrong with her.

"Father," Lady Kenna said. "You can't be serious. Come up with something else for insurance. My sister isn't a bargaining chip to be used this way. I won't allow it."

Declan had to refrain from rolling his eyes. It had been okay when Kenna was to marry him, but now that it was the sister, she pretended to be upset. When Lady Kenna inherited, she would be difficult to work with. She spoke before thinking and revealed far too much with her hasty words.

"Hmm," the king said before shrugging. "Lady Brielle will do. She is demur and far more well-behaved than your eldest child."

Kenna's face went fire red. "Father."

Duke Jaxon placed his arm around Kenna's shoulders. "The law is clear in this regard," he said. "And the law must be followed."

Declan pinched the bridge of his nose and headed toward the exit. He'd come there hoping to collect what the duke owed, not a wife. Especially not one so simple and plain. When he reached the doorway he paused, waiting for his father to join him.

"You have until sunset to deliver your daughter to my ship," the king said.

"You're taking my sister now?" Kenna squealed. "Why can't she remain here to prepare for her...wedding?" When she said the word *wedding*, her nose scrunched as if smelling something foul.

Ignoring her, the king said, "You have until Walpurgis night to produce the missing wheat and taxes. If you don't, I'll send Lady Brielle's head to you in a box. Understood?"

"Yes, Your Majesty," the duke replied, his voice trembling.

Declan peered over at Brielle who still sat frozen in the chair, her focus on the king, her eyes wide and her skin pasty. At least she'd be easily managed since she didn't have Kenna's spunk. A tinge of disappointment flared in him. He shoved it away. Picking his wife was something he knew he'd never have the luxury of doing. Who he married was irrelevant. Marrying someone who helped their kingdom and secured his crown was all that mattered. Brielle came from the largest and wealthiest dukedom; they needed to make sure the duke paid his taxes and sold his wheat to Valdis. If marrying Brielle helped his kingdom, so be it.

He turned and strode from the room.

Prince Declan entered the run-down tavern along with King Rhett and six guards. The dim lighting made it hard to see the faces of the dozen or so men scattered throughout the place. "Tell me again why we're here?" Declan mumbled.

The king patted Declan's back. "I need a drink."

If anyone needed a drink, it was Declan. Not to celebrate his engagement, but to toast the end to single life. They made their way to the bar at the front of the room while their guards spread out, remaining near the perimeter. All the patrons were sitting at the round tables, their hands covered with black soot. From the looks of it, they were all miners who must have gotten off work and come straight there.

Declan and his father sat on the stools at the counter.

The bartender slid two mugs of ale toward them. "It's not every day we have royalty in here," the bartender said. "If you need anything else, let me know. We're not a fancy place."

"We're just here for drinks," the king replied.

The bartender nodded and left, tending to the other patrons.

Declan grabbed the closest mug, taking a long swig.

"You might want to drink that a little slower," the king said, looking sideways at his son.

"Was it necessary to throw in the marriage?" Declan really wanted to know why the king had chosen Lady Brielle. She appeared so simple and plain. Perfectly suitable for a commoner, but for the crown prince, it seemed an odd pairing. However, his father rarely did anything on impulse and Declan knew there had to be a plan in place. He just wished he knew what that plan was.

The king shrugged. "It makes sense. We should be more closely aligned with Miervades. It'll solve all our problems with them. Now they won't illegally sell coal or wheat to Lima, and we'll get the amount in taxes they owe. Plus, it'll ensure they pay their future taxes on time."

"Do you think Brielle is up for the challenge of marrying into the royal family?" It was the nicest way he could phrase the thoughts running amuck in his head. He took another drink.

The king pulled his mug closer to him. "She's a better option than Lady Kenna."

"You know as well as I do that Kenna was never a viable option."

The king twisted the mug between his hands, staring at the contents. "With the possibility of another heir, marriage is the best course of action for you."

"Meaning?" He had no idea what Mabel had to do with him marrying. If she was alive, she was the heir. If she was dead, he was the heir. Simple.

"Your mother reminded me of an old law I'd forgotten about. If the heir isn't married with a child by the age of twenty-four, the second in line becomes the heir."

This was the first Declan had heard of that law. "Speaking of Mother, I can't imagine her taking to Brielle. They seem to be...opposites in every way." Nor could he envision Brielle being able to handle his mother. Queen Briar was a force of nature in her own right.

"How your mother feels about Brielle isn't of concern. What is important is ensuring the royal line and making sure we're doing what's best for Valdis. Queen Briar will cooperate and be happy that her eldest son is marrying. There won't be any problems."

While he was glad his father didn't think the queen would throw a fit with the selection of Brielle, he wasn't so certain about their court. For Brielle to survive, she'd have to get a new wardrobe. And do something with her hair. And somehow guard her innocence. Otherwise, they'd eat her alive and she'd be begging to go home before Walpurgis.

Declan heard the door open and shut.

A moment later, a soldier approached. "Your Majesty, Liam Laris has been located."

"What do you want with Liam?" one of the patrons asked.

The bartender stiffened. "Drake, this gentleman is your king. You will address him as such."

Declan finished his drink.

"Excuse me, Your Majesty. Liam is my father," the man, Drake, explained.

The king regarded Drake for a full minute before responding. "I wish to speak with him. Will you escort me to his residence?"

"Yeah," Drake said.

The bartender glared at him.

"Eh, Your Majesty." He stood and put his jacket on.

Declan and his father followed Drake out of the tavern, their soldiers trailing them.

They headed along the street, a light rain still falling.

"Is my father going to be arrested or punished for anything?" Drake asked.

"No, I just want to talk to him," King Rhett answered. "However, if your father breaks the law, he is subject to punishment, as we all are. The law is the law."

"But you're not here to execute him like you did my brother and niece, are you?"

"I have no intention of harming anyone today," the king said.

"Is your niece's name Willa?" Declan asked, wondering if the niece was Mabel's mother.

"Yes."

Then this meeting with Liam had to do with Mabel. Declan clenched his hands together so he wouldn't reach out and strangle his father. The king had been too eager to come to Miervades. Now he knew why.

After it was determined a carriage wouldn't be able to traverse the steep hills to Liam's house, Drake led them through the village and to the outskirts where several wooden houses had been built. They passed them and climbed a hill, the rain starting to fall harder. At the top, a stone house had been constructed, much nicer than the wooden ones below.

Drake opened the door, granting the king and prince entrance.

One of their soldiers entered first, doing a quick sweep of the place. Once he deemed it secure, he let them enter, the soldiers all waiting outside.

A low fire burned in the hearth. An elderly man in his late seventies or early eighties sat on the sofa. His long, white hair hung in thin strands around his face. His skin looked like leather, and his eyes had a hazy film to them. Declan assumed this was Liam.

"It has been a long time, King Rhett," the man said, his voice gravelly from old age. "What do you want?" No warmth came from him. He didn't rise to greet the royals, nor did he offer them something to drink.

"I need to discuss a delicate matter with you." The king glanced around the room. "Is anyone else here besides you and Drake?"

Drake took a step closer to his father, making it clear he wouldn't leave the old man alone with the king.

Declan folded his arms and leaned against the wall. Liam would be Mabel's great-grandfather. The king said he'd had an affair with Willa before he married Briar. Obviously, Willa had been executed for not declaring who fathered her child. Since Liam was Willa's grandfather, Declan understood the hatred radiating from the old man. There was a long history here that Declan didn't know the details of, a part of his father he'd never been privy to.

The king stood before Liam. "I'm surprised you still manage the mines despite your family's crimes against the crown."

"That was years ago, and I've paid dearly for it."

Bold, speaking to the king in such a way. Liam rose a notch in Declan's estimation.

"Since I had no part in the revolution, I kept my position.

The duke is a reasonable and just man." Tears filled the old man's eyes. "Unlike other people in positions of power."

Declan desperately wanted to know what transpired here twenty-two years ago. But his father excelled at hiding the facts or only revealing what he wanted other people to know. Things like truth and honesty were all smoke and mirrors in the royal family.

The king folded his hands behind his back. "Your son and granddaughter broke the law and were punished accordingly."

"My great-grandchild didn't deserve to be slaughtered like an animal minutes after being born," Liam spat.

The law stated that a pregnant mother couldn't be executed. However, once she'd given birth, she could. The only reason the baby would have been killed was if the baby had a claim to the throne, and the mother didn't verify the father, keeping the baby's legitimacy in question.

The king went over to the fireplace, resting his hands on the mantle, his back to the room. "It seems there have been a few new developments." He tapped the mantle twice before turning to face Liam. "When Willa was taken to Karlis, she was sentenced to be executed after she delivered the baby."

"Which she was," Liam said. "We got the body and buried it. Along with the baby."

The king nodded. "I have recently learned it wasn't the right baby."

The fire crackled in the hearth. "I don't understand," Liam whispered. "What are you saying?"

"After Willa's baby was born, her baby was switched with another one, one that died of natural causes."

"The baby we received wasn't Willa's?"

"No."

"Is Willa's child alive?" Liam reached up, clutching his shirt near his chest.

"I have reason to believe she is," the king revealed. "The child grew up on Karlis, living with a family there. They raised her as their own. She only recently learned of her identity. I...believe she has fled the island."

"Do you know where she is now?"

"She knows she's my daughter and that her birth mother came from Monta in Miervades. I thought she might come here to seek answers." The king shifted his weight, as if uncertain or nervous. It was an emotion Declan so rarely saw his father exhibit.

"Why here and not to Sunder to see you?" Liam asked, his eyebrows drawing together in confusion.

"I don't know; it's just a guess. I thought maybe she needed more clarification before she came to see me. I honestly don't know."

"How long ago did she flee the island?"

"I believe it has been about two weeks now. Information is slow to come from Karlis."

Liam rubbed his face.

"Has a young woman by the name of Mabel Bakken presented herself to you? Or has anyone in the village met someone with that name?" the king inquired.

Liam shook his head. "Not that I'm aware of. Is that her name?"

"It is."

"Do you think she's here in Monta?" Liam asked.

Declan pushed away from the wall. "She could be here," he answered. "Or she could be on her way. We really don't know."

"If Mabel shows up here, I want you to bring her to me," the king said.

Liam's head snapped up, his eyes clearing. "Why? Do you plan to execute her?"

"Now that I know she is my daughter, I want to meet her. Since I am your king, you will bring Mabel to me."

Declan knew the man would never agree to bring her to Sunder without an assurance she wouldn't be harmed. While he didn't know what his father intended to do with Mabel, he knew it was imperative she be found. They needed to learn if she would stake a claim to the throne. "My father wishes to meet his only daughter, and I would like to meet my half-sister. We have no other motives than to be acquainted with our family member. I assume you wish to meet her?"

The old man nodded.

"Then you know how we feel."

"Yes," the king added. "The baby did no wrong, and Mabel will not be punished for her mother's misdeeds."

"But what of the law?" Liam asked. "Willa never claimed you as the father."

"I have reason to believe Willa did when she confessed to

the dungeon guard. But I will consult the book of statutes to be sure."

That seemed to satisfy Liam. "Once you meet her, will you keep her at court?"

The king shrugged. "That depends on her and what she wants."

Liam nodded. "I'm old and can't travel. How about if she shows up, I'll send word to you that she's here? Then either one of my sons can accompany her to Sunder, or you can send someone here to escort her."

"Very well, I agree to your terms. But don't delay. I'm eager to meet her."

"You have my word," Liam said.

"If you break our agreement, I'll have your entire family executed."

Liam's face went white.

Declan shook his head. He wouldn't have declared that so bluntly. But his father had always been this way. The law was the law. Period. There was no room for negotiating when it came to the law and punishments.

"I'm leaving behind a unit of my men," the king said. "If you need to get word to me, do it through them."

In other words, they'd be watching Liam and the village to make sure the king's wishes were abided by.

On board the ship, Declan went to his cabin. He needed a minute alone to process everything that had happened today. He plopped on the bed, pinched his eyes shut, and took a deep breath, letting it out slowly. When he opened his eyes, he focused on the ceiling above him. There were many things in his life he couldn't control. Several of the people at court assumed that because he was a prince, and heir to the throne, he could do whatever he wanted. How wrong they were. He did whatever his parents asked of him, what his title required of him, and what the law demanded of him.

The law.

Growing up, he'd had no idea why his father took his job so seriously. Then the day Declan turned twenty-one, his father had explained it to him—the blood oath. His younger two brothers weren't supposed to know about it. Only the one who sat on the throne knew. And since Declan was the first in line...only now he might not be. He rubbed his eyes wondering how Brielle fit into all of this.

Declan always knew he'd have to marry. He'd believed it would be one of the women who attended court. He chuckled. Most of the people at court probably thought the same thing. When he showed up with Brielle, they'd be furious. A smile spread across his face.

Looking at the positives, Brielle appeared to be quiet, plain, and obedient. All amiable traits in a wife. She wouldn't present any problems with her attitude. She seemed to be one of those women who did as she was told and never spoke back. Perhaps the best reason for marrying her, and the one his father had considered the most, was that she came from Miervades. Which meant the correct amounts of wheat and coal would be delivered for the kingdom. Also, the duke should have more incentive to pay his taxes. And if he didn't, Brielle could go directly to the duke to rectify the situation.

Even though Declan had known this day would come, he still felt a pang of sadness and regret. For some reason he'd hoped to marry someone he could have some sort of relationship with, even if only friendship. Though he didn't know Brielle, the impression he'd gotten from her made it clear she would be neither friend nor lover. She just seemed so...bland. But at least bland wouldn't cause him problems. His mother was the opposite of bland and instigated constant drama. Bland seemed preferable to that.

Getting up off the bed, he stretched and meandered over to the small window in his room, gazing out at the turbulent ocean. He hated sailing during a storm on rough waters. But his father would never take that into consideration. It didn't matter what he did or didn't like. All that mattered was duty. Now that they'd accomplished what the king came to Miervades to do, it was time to go home.

With Brielle.

Once her father paid his taxes and delivered the wheat owed, Declan would marry her with little fuss since it was expected of him. At least he wasn't the one leaving his family and home. Unless she was so shallow that court life appealed to her—the parties, dresses, and social gossip. For some reason, he didn't think she'd care for those things. The image of her sitting on that chair, clutching her book, looking like a scared cat, was seared into his mind. It would be difficult for someone so sheltered to adjust to life at court.

She'd probably be homesick, lonely, and depressed. Hopefully someone could help her. He sure as hell wouldn't be able to. His time was so limited that he didn't even have the opportunity to do what he wanted, let alone help someone like Brielle adjust to her new life.

Someone pounded on the door.

"Enter," he called out.

A soldier pushed the door open. "A couple of the men are asking if you'd like to go a round or two before we set sail."

"Where's the king?" Declan couldn't fight unless his father was occupied. Otherwise, the king would insist on being included. And right now, Declan needed some time without the old man hovering around him. He'd had enough scheming and manipulation for one day, and his father only knew one way to fight—he went all out and held nothing back. Often when Declan sparred with him, Declan ended up injured.

"He's occupied with the captain from the other ship. He's leaving it here along with its soldiers to keep an eye on things."

Declan smiled. "In that case, I'm in." He grabbed his practice sword from the corner of the room and followed the soldier to the stern.

When they arrived, a half dozen men stood in a loose circle around two men dueling with lightweight practice swords.

Declan removed his jacket and vest. He undid the top four buttons on his shirt, then swung his arms, stretching his muscles. The duel ended, and Declan entered the ring.

"Who's it going to be?" he asked, a smile on his face. This was just what he needed.

"Me," Ricke said. "Last time we fought, you won. I need to prove that was just luck." He leaned his neck to the side, cracking it. "Ready, Prince?"

Declan swung his sword, aiming high to try and throw Ricke off. Since Ricke weighed a hundred pounds more than Declan, Declan had the ability to move his body quicker to avoid hits. Ricke easily parried the blow and countered with one of his own, sending a jolt through Declan's arms.

"That all you got?" Ricke asked. "You seem kinda soft to me."

Anger coursed through Declan. He didn't want to be thought of as a soft prince. He wanted people to see him like they saw his father—a fierce warrior who excelled with the sword.

Declan stepped in closer to his opponent, twisted, and struck him across the back. Ricke's sword hit Declan's legs, knocking him flat on his back. Ricke jumped on top of him, his sword at Declan's throat.

"I concede," Declan said, furious he'd lost so quickly.

"You're off today," Ricke said as he stood, reaching down to pull Declan up. "Now that you're engaged, your mind must be elsewhere."

The surrounding soldiers all hooted and yelled, clapping their hands.

"I didn't think anyone knew about that." Declan stood, rolling his sleeves up.

"We all figured it out when a lady's things were brought

on board," Ricke said. "That's why we thought you might need to go a round or two."

"Good thinking." Declan scanned the men's faces. "Who's next? This time, I won't lose."

Gilder entered the ring, a vicious smile across his face. "Come on, pretty prince," he taunted. "Hit me if you can."

Adjusting his hand on the hilt of his sword, Declan focused on Gilder's eyes, determined to win this round. He cleared his jumbled head, not thinking about his father, his future bride, or anything other than the man standing before him.

The two men circled one another.

Everything faded away. Declan felt Gilder shift before he saw it. Instinctively, he moved, sidestepping the sword as is slid right past him. He rammed his elbow into Gilder's side before turning away from him. They circled one another again; this time Gilder's eyes narrowed. With both hands on his sword, he lifted it. Declan kicked Gilder's chest and then parried the blow. Gilder stumbled backward.

"Looks like the pretty prince came to play," Gilder said. "You're not doing your usual moves."

Declan ignored him, knowing he was just trying to get a rise out of him.

"Unless it's that new wifey of yours." Gilder chuckled.

Declan attacked with a series of strikes, quick and efficient. Gilder immediately went on the defensive, having to take several steps back. After Declan did the same move three times, he knew Gilder had caught on and would anticipate him doing it again, so he shifted his weight, and brought his sword down, resting it against Gilder's neck.

A death blow if they'd been really fighting.

Breathing heavily, Gilder conceded the match. "You have more of your father in you than you realize."

That was the last thing Declan wanted to hear today.

CHAPTER 5
BRIELLE

rielle stood in her bedchamber, staring outside at the beautiful green rolling hills. This couldn't be the last time she'd be in her room, seeing this view. She still couldn't comprehend everything that had just happened.

Someone knocked on her door. She didn't even bother saying anything. Her sister and one of the servants had been in and out of her bedchamber all afternoon packing for her. Brielle had been too numb with fear and disbelief to do any of it herself.

"Brielle?" Kenna said, opening the door. She came into the room. "The last of your things have been taken to the ship."

Nausea rolled through Brielle. She was going to be ill. Tears slid down her cheeks. As she turned to face her sister, she couldn't help but notice the items still in her room. Spread across her bed, the quilt her mother had made for her while pregnant. It was the only thing she had from her mother since her mother had died in childbirth. So many of Brielle's books were still on the bookshelves. Half her clothes were still in her closet. The silver mirror her sister had given her on her thirteenth birthday rested on her dressing table next to a silver comb.

"You'll get new things at the palace," Kenna said. "We only packed enough clothing for the journey on the ship. Also, some of the things I didn't think you'd want to part from." Kenna went over to the bed, running her hand over the quilt. "Some things should stay here." She came over and stood beside Brielle. "I can't believe you're leaving me."

"I'm not ready to marry."

Kenna rolled her eyes. "Wasn't Lukas going to propose?"

"This is different." She wrapped her arms around herself, trying to hold herself together.

"You're right. This is infinitely better." Kenna grabbed hold of Brielle's shoulders, turning her so they faced one another. "You're lucky enough to be marrying the crown prince."

Brielle knew she should feel honored to be marrying into the royal family.

"This is important for Miervades, too," Kenna continued. "We need this alliance." Her eyes shone with determination.

Brielle wasn't daft; she knew how much her family needed this. "I'll write you when I arrive."

Kenna nodded. "Let us know if you hear anything of concern."

"I will." She wiped the tears from her face. "I'm sorry I'm

acting ungrateful. My day started with me going to the market and getting a new book. I didn't think it would end with me sailing away on a ship, engaged to be married."

Kenna smiled sardonically. "Life rarely goes the way we think it ought to." She released her sister and headed over to the door. "The carriage is downstairs waiting for you. It's time."

Brielle took one last look around her room, trying to memorize every little detail. This was the only home she'd ever known. And now it would no longer be hers. She kissed her fingers then touched the quilt, a silent goodbye to her mother. Maybe one day she'd want the quilt with her. But for now, it needed to stay here where her father and sister lived. In their home.

Brielle exited the carriage and glanced up at the massive ship before her. It appeared larger than her castle. As to how it sailed without sinking, she had no idea. She sighed. If only she were going on some grand adventure and could be happy for what the future held. But that couldn't be farther from the truth. Her father had offered her up for marriage to a man she didn't know or love. All so he could save his title and land. She'd never felt so used. Guilt overwhelmed her for these thoughts and feelings. She knew her father loved her. But she couldn't help the way she felt—logical or not.

The duke and Kenna both climbed out of the carriage.

"Be strong," Kenna said before wrapping Brielle in a hug.

"Don't let them make you feel like you're anything less than you are. You're a beautiful, smart, capable woman. Don't forget it."

Warmth spread through her. "Thank you for your kind words, but I don't have your tenacity." Brielle pulled away from her sister. She much preferred reading about royalty than attending any sort of social gathering.

"You're from Miervades. We're survivors. You've got this." Kenna's face radiated determination, as if she could will it into Brielle.

Brielle turned to her father, having no idea what to say to him.

"Take care of yourself," he said, gathering her in for a hug. "And when you're there, I want you to always keep your eyes and ears open. If you hear anything about Miervades or our family, report back to me immediately." He released her.

"I will."

"Never take your bracelet off," he mumbled close to her ear.

Confusion swam within. The silver bracelet she wore on her right wrist couldn't be removed. It had been on for as long as she could remember. Somehow, someway, it seemed to grow with her.

"Enjoy your time in Sunder," the duke said, taking a step away from her. "There's sure to be a lot going on in the capital of Valdis."

Brielle nodded, wishing she'd paid better attention to her governess's lessons on politics and the royal family. She felt-ill prepared for the journey she was about to embark on.

On the bright side, the king had to have a library, and she would make sure to put it to good use. If the need arose, she could teach herself about the politics of the kingdom.

"I guess this means I'll have to deny Lukas when he asks for your hand." The duke smiled.

Brielle had completely forgotten about him. "Please bid him farewell for me."

"I can't believe you'd even consider Lukas for Brielle," Kenna said, scrunching her nose. "He's not even titled."

A soldier approached. "Lady Brielle." He bowed. "All of your things are on board. The king and prince have requested your presence on the top deck." He motioned to the massive ship.

Craning her neck, she peered up at the beast before her. The top deck stood so high above her she couldn't even see anyone on board. At least the rain had stopped, though thick, dark clouds still covered the sky and cold air whipped around her body.

She turned and faced her father and sister. "Please write to me. I'll miss the both of you dearly." Tears filled her eyes.

"You best be going," her father said, his words almost a whisper. "Kenna and I have work to do."

"Try and enjoy yourself," Kenna said. "Go out. See the city. Buy some pretty dresses. Don't spend all day in your room reading."

Brielle tried not to roll her eyes at that. "I'll agree to that so long as you promise to take care of Father." Kenna had never been overly warm or affectionate. Brielle worried about who'd look after him now that she'd be gone.

"I will."

"I'm so sorry to be leaving you." She kissed her father's cheek.

"I always knew this day would come." His eyes turned glassy.

Taking a deep breath, she turned and faced the ship.

"Lady Brielle." The soldier offered her his arm.

She clutched onto it as he led her up a steep gangplank and into the belly of the ship. The smells, sounds, and darkness overwhelmed her. She gripped the soldier's arm harder, fearful she'd get lost amongst the chaos.

"Right this way," he said close to her ear. He quickly led her to a steep set of stairs. "Up you go."

She reluctantly released his arm and climbed up, thankful to be heading toward the gray sky at the top. When she reached the deck, a gust of wind almost knocked her over. She widened her stance. Her hair flew every which way, making it difficult to see.

"Lady Brielle," the solider said, once again at her side. "The king and prince." He motioned to her right before turning and heading back down the staircase.

Brielle gathered her hair and yanked it behind her neck, tying it in a knot so she could see. The king and prince stood at the bow of the ship about thirty feet away. Summoning her strength, she headed toward them.

Several of the soldiers were yelling things she didn't understand. And then the ship lurched. At that precise moment, Declan glanced over his shoulder, looking right at her. She tumbled to the deck, smacking her elbow. The ship rocked up and down. The wind roared around her. On her hands and knees, she tried to get her balance so she could stand.

Wind filled the sails, men hollered to one another, and then one of the sails swung to the other side. The ship tilted.

Declan knelt beside her. "Do you need help?"

She felt the ship righten, and then it seemed as if it were falling straight down. "I didn't expect it to move so much." Embarrassment coursed through her, and she couldn't even look Declan in the eyes. "I lost my footing." And she was going to lose her dinner soon as well.

He chuckled, the sound low and throaty. "It happens to the best of us." He pulled her to her feet. "The ship is a little worse than usual because of the storm. I'm hoping it'll calm down soon."

Her stomach twisted with nausea. "I don't feel well."

"Come and stand at the front of the ship." He led her toward his father, wrapping his arm around her waist to steady her. "The first time I sailed, I stayed below deck and became violently ill. I've learned the trick is to remain on the top deck for the first hour or two. It'll help your body acclimate."

It was getting worse, not better.

"Is everything all right?" the king asked.

"She's getting seasick," Declan answered. He grabbed her hands and placed them on the railing.

She clutched onto it, hoping to remain upright. The boat picked up speed as it sailed parallel to Miervades. She could still see her green rolling hills; however, the town of Monta became smaller and smaller until it vanished from sight completely. All she'd known and loved her entire life was gone. The boat continued to rise and fall, up and down.

"Lady Brielle," the king said. "It is my understanding that your father will be paying and supplying what he owes. That means we will be moving forward with your wedding to my son the day after Walpurgis."

She nodded, unable to utter a single word for fear she'd vomit on the king's boots.

"We'll work out the details when you're not green in the face." The king turned and walked away.

Clutching the railing, Brielle breathed in and out, watching the land as it flew by, trying not to think about the constant motion of the boat.

She felt, rather than saw, Declan standing a few feet behind her, also focused on the land. They remained that way for quite some time. The sky darkened, and the moon managed to appear between some of the thick clouds.

Declan came and stood beside her, his brow furrowed. "Do you feel that?" he asked.

She assumed he was speaking to her. "Can you be more specific?" Since the entire ship continued to move, she couldn't tell what he was referring to.

"There's...something out there." He gripped the railing, staring out at the land.

Brielle could just make out the hills in the moonlight. "We're near Witch's Cove."

"I've never heard of it. Have you been there?"

"No." No one had. It was forbidden.

"Why is it called that?"

"I have no idea." There were rumors and tales whispered over fires at night, but nothing in books.

"Look," he said. "There's someone out there." He pointed toward one of the hills.

Brielle squinted, unable to see anyone.

"You don't feel a pulling sensation? A feeling of belonging and need?" He finally looked at her.

"No, I don't." She was too ill to feel anything other than her own motion sickness.

They sailed in silence a few more minutes.

"It's gone," he mumbled. "I don't feel anything now. Strange."

Sweat beaded along her forehead. She slid to the deck, breathing shallow breaths.

"You should turn in for the night," Declan said. "I'll find someone to escort you to your room." He turned and left her there, curled into herself on the deck of the ship, tears streaming down her cheeks.

Brielle woke up to someone knocking on the door to her room. Nausea rolled through her, and she couldn't even get out of bed to answer it.

"Who's there?" she said in the loudest voice she could manage. Her head felt like it was being pounded by a hammer.

"Lady Brielle, I've come to escort you to breakfast," an unfamiliar voice said.

She sat up; then wished she hadn't. "I'm not well." Tears filled her eyes. Any hope of making a good impression vanished.

"May I come in?" the man asked.

"Yes." She noticed her door wasn't even locked. After the soldier had escorted her there last night, she'd climbed into bed, not even bothering to put on her nightclothes.

A soldier entered.

She didn't recognize him.

"Prince Declan sent me to check on you," he said. "Are you still unwell?"

She nodded, a sob escaping her lips. Tears flowed down her cheeks. She wanted to go home. She craved her own bed, and she needed her family.

The soldier remained standing next to the door. "I can give you something to make you feel better, but it'll knock you out."

"What do you mean?" she asked, wiping the tears from her cheeks. She couldn't believe anyone was seeing her in this state.

"It's a powerful medicine. It puts you in a deep sleep for days."

That sounded wonderful. She'd love it if she could fall asleep and wake up when they were there. "Yes, please."

He hesitated. "It's not that simple." He shifted his weight from foot to foot. "When we get to Sunder, if you're awake, you'll be disoriented. And, well, kind of a mess."

She frowned. "A mess? How?"

The soldier rubbed the back of his neck. "Well, ah, you'll be...in your own filth."

It took a moment for his words to register. If she took this medicine, she would be unconscious. Which meant she could quite possibly soil herself. She curled up on the bed, considering her options. The last thing she wanted to do was arrive in Sunder, engaged to the crown prince, sitting in her own bodily waste. The other option was to remain sick through the entire journey. She had to consider which was the lesser of the two evils. The ship continued to rock up and down. She'd never felt so awful in all her life. "I don't care." She squeezed her eyes shut. "Just make it stop."

He came farther into the room. "Are you certain?"

She nodded. She couldn't live like this for the next five to seven days.

"I need you to sit up."

She did as he said.

He pulled a vial out of his back pocket. "Drink this." He handed it to her.

For a moment, she considered that he could have ill intentions and want her dead. At this point, she didn't care. She just needed the queasy feeling to go away. She took the vial from him and downed it in one gulp. The liquid burned her throat and had an odd taste.

"Lie down," he said. "I'll let Prince Declan know you've decided to take it." A moment later, he said, "You'll probably need another dose. I'll check on you and give it to you if necessary."

Brielle nodded and laid down, warmth filling her. Briefly, she wondered if Declan had been the one to suggest she take the medicine. Before she could consider the matter further, she fell into a deep slumber.

Dreams, nightmares, delusions...they came and went. Awake, liquid being forced down Brielle's throat. Asleep, running from a cloaked figure. Nothing made sense. Up became down; left became right. Time had no meaning.

And then solid arms wrapped around her. She felt her body moving but not the incessant swaying of the ship. She peeled her eyelids open. The dark night sky greeted her. She blinked. Someone held her though she didn't recognize the man's face. He wore a soldier's uniform.

"Where am I?" she croaked, her voice hoarse and grating to her own ears.

"Lady Brielle," the soldier said. "We are in Sunder."

She tilted her head to the side, trying to see her surroundings. In the moonlight, she could make out a narrow street stretched out before her, a tall building to the one side, glassy water to the other.

"It looks like the middle of the night," she said.

"That's because it is."

"And we're not on the ship anymore." Relief filled her.

"Correct."

"Why are you carrying me?" She blinked, noticing some

of the building seemed blurry. And something smelled foul —she hoped it wasn't her.

"The medicine you were given is still wearing off and you're weak."

That made sense. Her mind did seem a bit fuzzy. "Where are you taking me?"

"I've been instructed to take you to your room at the royal palace," he said.

"Turn here," a female voice said from behind them. "First we're going to the public baths."

"Are you sure?" the man carrying Brielle responded. "Can't she bathe at the palace?"

"Why do you think they docked the ship in the middle of the night and tasked us with her? Why are we walking and not using a carriage?" The woman huffed. "Now follow me and do as I say."

The man grunted.

"In here."

Brielle heard the distinct jingle of keys and then the click as a door opened. The soldier carrying her turned sideways to make it through the doorway with her in his arms. The air turned warm and humid. The man continued walking. Low torches had been spaced every ten feet throughout the long corridor.

"Here," the woman said, her soft voice echoing.

They entered a small, square room.

"Put her down."

The man set Brielle on her feet. In the middle of the

room, a round pool was sunk into the floor, steam rising from it.

"Now leave and stand guard outside the room," the woman ordered.

Brielle looked at the woman for the first time. She had wrinkled skin and gray hair slicked back into a low bun. A simple black dress adorned her body.

After the soldier left, the old woman started unlacing the back of Brielle's dress. "We need to get you bathed."

Realizing the source of the offensive odor was herself, Brielle helped take her dress off. Still a little dizzy, she let the woman remove her socks and boots for her.

"Now get in," the old woman ordered, pointing at the pool. "There're steps on this side."

In the dim lighting, the steaming water appeared green. Brielle stepped into the pool, shocked at how hot it was. She went all the way in, the water coming up to her neck. It had an odd smell, like rotten eggs. Steam curled around her face, making her sweat.

"Can you wash yourself?" the elderly woman asked. "Or are you too weak?"

Brielle felt as if her body moved in slow motion and her muscles remained limp; however, her mind was beginning to clear as the medicine wore off. "I can do it." She glanced around for soap.

"Here." The woman handed Brielle a bar.

"Thank you. May I ask your name?"

"It's Jenice. Now go ahead and clean yourself while I find

you something decent to wear." She went over to a trunk in the corner of the room and began rummaging around in it.

Brielle turned away from the woman and quickly scrubbed her body. Her hair was a tangled mess and she had to work through several knots using the soap. Once she finished, she rinsed off and climbed out of the pool.

Jenice handed her a plush towel.

After drying off, she went over to the trunk to see what the woman had found for her to wear.

"It's simple, but it'll do." Jenice pointed at the plain tan dress she'd laid out.

Brielle pulled it on, thankful to have something clean and soft on.

"Now this." Jenice handed her a long black cape with a hood.

Brielle took it, tying it around her neck and pulling the hood up.

"Good." Jenice looked her up and down. "Now follow me and don't say a word."

Brielle nodded.

They exited the bathing room and spotted the soldier waiting for them. He motioned for the two of them to follow him. Brielle's legs started to shake as she walked behind the soldier, Jenice at her side. However, she forced herself to move, not wanting to be carried again. The longer she walked, the more alert she became and the better she felt.

The three of them exited the building and headed along a cobblestoned street sandwiched between two tall buildings on either side. At an intersection, the soldier led them to the left. They walked block after block, seemingly going in a zig-zag pattern. Brielle wondered if he was trying to confuse her or make sure no one followed them. So far, she hadn't seen another person.

She wanted to ask about the city and inquire if there were any hills or greenery nearby; however, she'd been instructed to remain quiet, so she withheld her questions.

After another ten minutes or so, she heard waves crashing nearby. She didn't think they'd board another ship. At least, she hoped they wouldn't. Even if it didn't sail out to sea and remained docked for the night, she never wanted to step foot on a ship again. Right here, on solid ground, was where she preferred to be.

The soldier turned yet again, leading them away from the sound of the crashing waves and to a stone wall at least twice her height. The three of them walked along the wall until they came to an iron door built into the side of it. A single soldier stood guard on top of the wall. Jenice pulled out a key and unlocked the door. The soldier on top of the wall whistled. Jenice gave the thumbs up, pushing the door open and ushering Brielle through it. The guard who'd been accompanying them waved goodbye, remaining on the other side of the wall. The door closed and Jenice locked it.

Brielle turned in a slow circle, taking in the new scenery. Hedges lined several gravel pathways. Fragrant flower bushes were scattered throughout. A few trees grew well away from the wall, their branches dipping so low they almost brushed the ground. Ahead stood a vertical stone cliff at least fifty feet tall. She craned her neck back to see it, and found the palace carved into the top of it. Several turrets looked as if they were born from the stone themselves.

"Stop staring and get moving," Jenice mumbled as she grabbed Brielle's elbow, guiding her along the garden pathway toward the base of the cliff.

They came to a door guarded by two soldiers. Upon seeing Jenice, they opened the door, letting them pass into the side of the cliff.

"The east side of the city is level with the ocean," Jenice whispered. "That's where we just were. The west side of the city is level with the palace."

Brielle tried to envision it. Maybe once it was daylight, she'd understand better.

"Up you go." Jenice released Brielle at the bottom of a spiral staircase that had been carved into the stone. Torches hung on the walls every fifteen feet providing just enough light to see.

Brielle started climbing. Up and up she went, Jenice right behind her. Brielle supposed the exertion would bother most people. However, she was used to climbing hillsides and steep staircases at her castle back home. Placing her hand on the wall, she let her fingers trail over the stone as she continued her ascent.

The stairs ended at a short landing where they came to another door. Jenice opened the door and Brielle stepped into what had to be the palace proper.

Jenice led the way along a hallway, up another flight of stairs—this one much wider and covered with rugs, and then along a corridor. She stopped at the last door. "You're in here."

Brielle stepped into an enormous bedchamber with a four-poster bed directly ahead, two dressers on either side, a tall armoire to the left, and a vanity table in the corner. The wall to the right contained a single glass door, propped open, leading to a balcony overlooking the ocean. On each side of that glass door were three floor to ceiling windows, all of them open and the curtains between them softly floating with the ocean breeze.

"I'm sure you're hungry after your trip, and I'll have food brought to you first thing in the morning," Jenice said. "But for now, go to sleep. You'll want a clear mind about you if you're to survive around here." She left the room, closing and locking the door behind her.

Not wanting to think about why she'd been locked in the room, Brielle removed her cloak before going over to the bed and climbing on top of it. The gentle breeze, the smell of the sea, and the sound of crashing waves lulled her into peaceful sleep.

Brielle peeled her eyelids open, taking in her surroundings. In the morning light, the walls were paler than she'd thought last night in the darkness. She sat up in the enormous bed and stretched. The curtains floated in the warm, gentle breeze from the open windows, the sound of waves crashing outside the balcony.

"It's about time you're up," Jenice said as she exited a door on the far wall that Brielle hadn't noticed last night. "There's food there for you." She pointed to a tray sitting next to the bed. "All of your things have been brought in. I unpacked your clothes in there." She pointed to the doorway she'd just come through. "Do you need help dressing?"

Brielle shook her head. "I can take care of myself. I didn't have a lady's maid back home." As soon as she said the words, she hoped she hadn't offended the elderly woman. Although she'd introduced herself as Jenice and seemed to be helping, Brielle had no idea what the woman's official title or position was here at court.

"Then I'll be off. I'll return tonight to help you prepare for bed." Without waiting for a response, she left the room. This time she didn't lock the door.

Brielle slid out of bed and went out onto the balcony. She leaned her arms on the stone railing, taking it all in. The palace had indeed been built right into the side of the cliff, the ocean crashing against it about fifty feet below. To the right, the city of Sunder extended as far as she could see, level with the castle. To the left, a steep drop to the ocean, and then the flat land curved outward, lending view to a large harbor in the distance. The buildings to the left of the palace were closer together than those on the other, posher side.

Back home, the air had a crisp, clean feeling to it. Here, it almost felt thick and wet, making it hard to breathe.

Her stomach growled so she went back inside. Sitting on her bed, she slid the tray toward her and ate. The plate was laden with eggs, bacon, and cinnamon bread. The cup of tea was cold. Regardless, she ate and drank everything that had been given to her.

After she finished, she went over to the door Jenice had pointed out before. She opened it and found a large dressing closet. Her trunks were all there, her clothes hung, shoes laid out, and her books stacked neatly in piles.

After removing the dress she'd been given last night, she put on one of her thinner dresses since it was so warm here. Looking at herself in the mirror, she thought the dark green dress complemented her skin tone. She wondered if it was always this warm here in Sunder, or if it was just this time of year. She needed to read some books about the land and politics rather than her usual romance or adventure novels.

Eager to explore the palace, she went over to the door and peered out into the hallway. No one stood guard outside. She hesitated. Jenice didn't say Brielle had to stay in her room. And one might consider it rude if she hid in her bedchamber all day and didn't venture out. The trick would be remembering where her room was located so she could make her way back to it later today.

Steeling her resolve, she exited her bedchamber and headed along the hallway. When she came to an intersection, she turned left, assuming it led to the interior of the castle since her room seemed to be at the corner. At a wide staircase, she headed down, coming to a hallway that was open on one side to the middle of the palace below. On the bottom level, people meandered about, some arm in arm, others hurrying from one side to another. Rugs and sofas were spread throughout allowing people to gather and talk.

"Can I help you?" someone asked.

Brielle turned to face a young woman wearing a plain black dress indicating she was a servant of some sort. "I'm looking for the library." She hoped there was one open to the people here at court.

"Follow me." The woman headed to the right.

Brielle followed her down four flights of stairs, stopping before two large wooden doors.

"It's in there." The woman curtsied and then hurried away.

Brielle reached for the handle, feeling a sense of calm wash over her. She opened the door and entered a three-story room. Three of the walls were covered floor to ceiling with books. The fourth wall, straight ahead, held a combination of both plain and stained-glass windows, allowing light to filter into the library. In the middle of the room, several sofas had been arranged facing each other and a few tables were scattered throughout.

Turning in a slow circle, Brielle took it all in. In the corner of the room, a narrow set of stairs led to the second and third levels. She had no idea how the books were arranged, so she went to the wall closest to her, examining the titles, her hand trailing over the spines.

When she reached the stairwell, she took it to the second floor. She walked along the narrow aisle, books to her right, a thin metal railing to her left. At the corner, she was about to turn when a gentleman blocked her path.

She sucked in a breath, hoping she wouldn't get in trouble for being there, and looked up into the deep brown eyes of a young man, not much older than her.

"Lost?" he asked.

She bit her lip, not sure how to respond. Declan hadn't mentioned if he or his father would be telling anyone at court about her. She decided to shake her head instead of answering him.

The handsome gentleman looked her up and down. "You're not from around here, are you?" He winked. "If you tell me what you're looking for," he waved his hand toward the books on the adjacent wall, "I'm certain I can help."

He had strong cheekbones with dark, thick brows and full lips. His brown hair was neatly trimmed, giving him a clean and put together look. The black pants he wore appeared to be made from fine material and his silky gray shirt seemed like something a noble person would wear, not a servant. However, a noble person wouldn't have addressed her, so she figured he had to work there. "Are you the librarian?"

He chuckled. "You could say that."

"I'd like something on..." Suddenly embarrassed to admit she wanted a book on the history of Sunder, she clasped her hands together, trying to figure out how to ask for what she wanted without sounding like an uneducated peasant.

"What's that look for?" he asked.

"What look?"

"You scrunched your nose in disgust."

She hadn't realized she'd done that.

"If I'm boring you, I can leave." He smiled, clearly teasing her.

Lifting her chin, she replied, "I'd like to read something about this city." There, that didn't sound too bad.

"Right this way." He turned and headed to the left, using a cane she hadn't noticed before as he walked. He appeared to favor his left leg, and he moved with a slight limp.

"What's your name?" she asked.

"Brooks."

"I'm Brielle." She wondered if he had some sort of injury or illness that required him to use the cane.

He stopped and reached for a book, a sardonic smile on his lips. "Brielle," he mused. "So you did just arrive here." He went to the adjacent shelf and pulled down another book. "Before you delve into Sunder's illustrious history, there's a book I recommend you read first. It's a bit more practical." He handed her both books, tapping the one on top.

She reached for them, scanning the title of the first one: *The Royal Line.* She looked up at him, her eyebrows scrunched together in confusion.

He leaned toward her and whispered, "I'm *Prince* Brooks Forberg. Second in line behind my *brother*, Prince Declan."

Heat creeped up her neck and over her face. She wanted to crawl behind the bookshelf and hide. He wasn't a servant. He wasn't even some important noble. He was Declan's brother, and he was a prince. When he'd said his name was Brooks, she should have known who he was.

Apparently, he thought so too since he'd given her the book.

"My error."

Lifting his cane, he tapped the side of her leg. "If you're going to survive here, you can't afford to make such mistakes." He winked and headed for the staircase. "Hurry up," he called over his shoulder. "We have much to discuss."

CHAPTER 6

MABEL

Sitting on the deck of the small boat, Mabel gazed at the stars above. Out here, on the water, they appeared so close. Almost as if she dared reach out, she'd touch them. She peered over at Matsen steering the boat. He never seemed to sleep. After monitoring him for the past week, she had no doubt he was the assassin sent to kill her. His movements were soundless, his hands calloused from sword work, he sniffed his food before eating, and his eyes held a calculating look to them. At times she noticed his brow furrow with concern. As if he'd seen too much, done too much. He'd probably experienced more death than everyone locked in the dungeon she'd just escaped from.

"We're almost there," Matsen said. The water lapped against the side of the boat as he switched the sail, angling toward land.

"After you drop me off, will you continue straight to Sunder?" She still couldn't believe he'd offered to sail her to

Lima. She shivered just thinking about the amount of time she'd spent at the side of an assassin. But when they'd arrived in the town of Monta in Miervades, not only had there been a very large warship docked in port—the king's warship, but a man had been waiting there for her. He handed her a letter that explained people were looking for her and she couldn't enter the town without great risk to herself. The letter urged her to go to Phom in Lima where someone from her family would meet her.

After she'd read the letter, she tore it apart and threw it in the ocean. Then she'd asked the man where she could acquire a boat. Matsen immediately offered to sail her wherever she needed to go, insisting it wasn't a problem for him. She'd accepted his help only because she saw no other option.

Keeping her identity a secret from him became increasingly difficult with each passing day. Spending so much time in such proximity lent itself to slip-ups even if they didn't speak to one another much. Though she had a lot of questions for him, she couldn't voice any because then he'd do the same. The less they knew about one another, the better. However, sometimes she wondered if he suspected who she really was, and he was just waiting for her to admit it. Why else would he help her? It couldn't possibly be out of the goodness of his heart. He was an assassin; he had no heart.

He probably planned to kill her the second he had confirmation.

"I've decided not to go to Sunder," Matsen revealed.

She'd assumed he was going to Sunder to tell the king his mission was a success. However, if he wasn't going there anymore, then he had to know he didn't get his intended target. "Where will you go?" It felt as if the night sky got darker, the air colder.

"I thought I'd help you out."

Her breathing sped up. "You've already done more than necessary. I'm grateful, but I don't need your help any longer."

"What do you plan on doing once you're in Lima? Where will you live? How will you get money for food?"

She rubbed her face, exhaustion heavy like a blanket over her shoulders. "I have a friend there," she lied. Ditching the assassin was proving to be more difficult than she'd imagined.

"And how do you plan on finding your friend?"

He wasn't making this easy for her. "I'll ask around." She didn't need him watching over her. Traveling alone, she could blend in. Adapt. She preferred it that way since she knew she wouldn't stab herself in the back.

"You're a young, unmarried woman. I'm not dropping you off in a foreign kingdom without making sure you're taken care of."

"I'll be fine on my own." The boat neared the shore. Flat land with dense, tall palm trees greeted them. "I don't see any lights," she murmured. If they didn't land near the city, she had no idea how she'd find the family member who was supposed to meet her there.

"I saw a cluster of lights, so I'm headed this way to avoid

them." He expertly steered the boat toward the shore. "We'll dock just over there."

She had to get away from him. She stood and went to the bow, pretending to look at the shore where he planned on docking. The second he turned to pull in the sail, Mabel climbed on the railing and dove overboard. She'd intended on a graceful entrance into the water but instead, smacked it, stinging her stomach in the process. Kicking ferociously, she aimed for shore. Swimming in a dress proved to be more difficult than she expected. However, she swam as fast as she could, trying to make it to land as quickly as possible. It wouldn't take much to ditch the assassin once she reached the tree line.

"What are you doing?" Matsen shouted as he leaned over the railing.

Ignoring him, she kept swimming. The strong current pulled both Mabel and the boat parallel to the island.

A large splash resounded next to her, making her lose her bearings for a moment. She stopped swimming, treading water to see what had happened. Matsen's head popped above the surface, mere feet from her.

She took a deep breath, about to go under again.

"If I planned on killing you, I'd have done it by now."

Ignoring him, she resumed swimming, heading straight for the shore. Turning Matsen's words over in her head, she tried to understand what he meant by them.

When she reached shallow water, she stood, heaving in breaths as she trudged out of the sea and onto the beach. She started shaking from the cool air. Wrapping her arms around herself, she ran for the trees, searching for a place to hide.

Matsen's footsteps sounded behind her. Mabel ran faster, weaving between the trees. Something slammed into her back, knocking her to the ground. She struggled to get up, but Matsen remained on top of her.

"Stop struggling and let me talk," he ground out. "I'm not going to hurt you." He released her and stood.

She rolled over, spitting sand out of her mouth. Now she was cold, covered in sand, and beyond irritated.

Matsen removed his shirt, wringing it out. Water dripped to the ground.

"Who are you and what do you want with me?" she demanded. If the king had sent him to assassinate her, she wanted to know why he hadn't done so already.

A slow smile slid across his face. "Matsen." He put his shirt back on.

She rolled her eyes.

"You already know who I am," he said, resting his hands on his hips. "And I know who you are, *Mabel*."

She stood, assessing him, trying to figure out what he intended to do with her and why.

"I wasn't a hundred percent sure at first," he continued. "I had a hunch. Then after a few days together it became apparent."

"I don't understand." She hadn't said anything to him that would have hinted at her being Mabel. "If you were sent to kill me, why haven't you done so?" She could think of only one plausible reason he wouldn't have completed his mission—if he'd figured out her real identity, the secret her father had whispered on his deathbed.

"Now that's the funny thing." He took a step closer to her. "Do you know anything about the blood oath?"

She had no idea what he was talking about. She took a step back, away from him.

"Tell me who you really are," he said, his voice low and throaty.

She shook her head.

"Do you even know who you are?" He took another step closer to her, tilting his head to the side, observing her.

"What's the blood oath?" she asked, trying to move the conversation away from her true identity. She suspected he'd know if she lied.

The corners of his lips rose. "I swore a blood oath to the royal family. I can't kill a single member." He raised his eyebrows, as if waiting for her to confirm something.

She shrugged. "I can't be sure of who I am." All she had were her father's words on his deathbed. He'd been delirious when he'd revealed she was the king's firstborn child and heir to the throne.

"Let me see your arm."

Curious, she lifted her arm out to him. He pushed her soggy, wet sleeve up, revealing her forearm. He turned it over, running a finger over the veins near her wrist. Then he moved so quickly she almost jumped from fright. He pulled out a dagger, as if to slide it across her wrist.

"See," he said. "I can't kill you." The dagger hovered an

inch from her skin even though he was pressing it as hard as he could.

Shaking, she yanked her arm back, pulling her sleeve down.

He put the dagger away. "The oath I swore is sealed in magic. It prevents me from killing you. Which means you're royalty."

"If I'm royalty, why would the king send you after me knowing there's this blood oath in place?" It made no sense.

"The king didn't send me. Someone else did. And I'm not sure if this person knows I'm bound by magic."

Before tonight, she would have insisted magic didn't exist. But after seeing the dagger, she wasn't so sure now. "Who sent you?"

"I'd rather not say just yet. I'm still trying to work a few things out."

Her eyes narrowed. She didn't like him having the upper hand.

"We need to get you dry, and you need to sleep. Then in the morning, we'll head toward the town of Phom."

Even though she didn't need anyone watching over her, she decided to remain with the assassin. For now. Once she got to the town, she'd reevaluate the situation.

The sun shone directly overhead when Mabel and Matsen reached the first cluster of buildings. She hadn't expected there to be an actual civilized city. Everything she'd read about Lima had said it was a land of wild people who ruled themselves, so chaos ensued.

"I assume the note you received in Miervades directed you to come here?" Matsen asked.

"It did."

"And were you given a name of who you need to find?"

"No." Not only did she not know who to meet here, but she didn't even know her birth mother's last name. Her father had revealed that her real mother's first name had been Willa, but that was all.

"Let's go to the local market and see if there's any gossip. If we don't discover anything there, we'll hit up a tavern." He slowed his pace so as to not garner unnecessary attention. "Keep your eyes open to your surroundings but try not to stare or have direct eye contact with anyone. And if they speak with an accent, don't talk, just smile, and nod."

"Anything else?" She didn't like him barking out instructions to her, even if it was good advice.

His eyes scanned her from head to toe. "Try to blend in." He reached out and plucked a piece of seaweed from her hair.

There wasn't much she could do about her clothing or appearance. Instead of saying anything, she ignored him and continued along.

The city had been built right into the side of a cliff. Most of the structures were several stories tall, made from a smooth stone-like material of muted colors such as white, tan, and brown. However, the doors had all been painted bright colors like teal, orange, purple, or pink.

They took one of the narrow streets and headed up, making their way toward the center of the town. The cobbled streets became more crowded as they traveled. People hurried to and fro shopping in the stores or eating at various establishments. The entire time, Mabel kept thinking of what she'd learned as a child. Lima had always been described as a savage land with wild people. So far, everything she'd seen indicated the exact opposite. Perhaps not all of Lima was like this. Or, more likely, she'd been misinformed. The question became why.

Matsen bumped into a man and quickly apologized. "At least everyone is speaking the same language as us," he mumbled.

She agreed as they turned onto another street, this one blessedly flat. Mabel's legs burned from the steep ascent. After a little bit, she spotted several brightly colored awnings up ahead. They headed toward them.

"Do you think that's the market?" she asked, being sure to keep her voice low.

"I hope so. I don't want to walk up or down these blasted hills anymore."

When they neared the awnings, Mabel saw that several vendors had set up shop on this street. The vendors were jam-packed together, the edge of one touching the edge of the next. Some sold fruits, others hand-carved wooden knick-knacks. There were so many people crowded together, that moving from vendor to vendor became difficult.

Mabel wondered if she could lose Matsen in the crowd. Even though he'd swore he couldn't kill her, it didn't mean he wouldn't find someone else to do the job for him. She had no idea where his loyalties lay—if he even had any.

Stopping at one of the tables, Mabel examined the beaded jewelry. Everything was so brightly colored and beautiful. She'd never worn a bracelet or necklace before. She wondered if the towns in Valdis sold similar items.

She meandered to the next table, not bothering to see if Matsen hovered nearby.

"A beautiful shawl for a beautiful woman?" an elderly lady asked. She smiled, her front teeth missing.

"I'm just admiring everything," Mabel said, running her hand over the soft material of a blanket.

"I think the pretty lady needs that shawl," Matsen said as he approached from behind Mabel.

The elderly woman's smile grew even wider. "The blue one suits her lovely hair."

"I agree." Matsen handed over a few coins in exchange for the blue shawl. "Did you make this?"

"I did," the elderly woman beamed.

"It's truly lovely, just like you." He nodded at the woman before wrapping the fabric around Mabel, leading her to the next vendor.

"Where'd you get the money?" she asked, pulling the soft material tightly around her. Even though the sun shone overhead, the air had a crisp bite to it.

"I have my ways." He winked. "Let's visit a few more shops. Keep your ears open."

They made their way along the street, perusing several of the tables along the way.

Mabel came to a flower vendor and stopped, inhaling the fragrant scent the bouquets gave off. Each arrangement had a variety of colors, each more stunning than the last.

"Are you Mabel?" a young sounding voice asked.

She turned around and found a boy, no more than nine or ten, standing there. Her brows pulled together in question.

"Here." He held out a piece of paper. The second she took it, he darted away, disappearing into the crowd.

Mabel unfolded the paper. An address had been scribbled on it along with a map.

Matsen leaned over her shoulder. "I assume that's the address of your friend?"

She folded the paper and shrugged. She had no idea if this would lead her to her family member. For all she knew, it could be a trap—an assassin waiting to finish the job Matsen couldn't do because of some magic.

"Mabel?" he asked. "What's wrong?"

She eyed him. "Nothing." If this did lead to a family member, then she could part ways with Matsen. Tell him she no longer needed his protection, and he could leave. Surely this family member of hers would agree and support her.

Without saying a word, she made her way out of the market. At the corner, she opened the paper, examining the map. Once she had her bearings, she turned, heading one block over. After a few more turns, she came to an aqua colored door with a marking on it. The mark matched the map.

She hesitated and glanced over her shoulder.

Matsen stood a few feet behind her, his attention on the building, looking at the windows and rooftop. "It appears safe," he mumbled.

She hadn't been waiting for his permission to knock. She'd been considering if she even should knock. Once she did, who would open the door? A family member or an assassin?

Mabel raised her hand, it hovered a moment, and then she dropped it to her side. She saw no reason to bother meeting someone from her family right now. She took a step back. The people who'd raised her were her family. Not some stranger she'd never met.

The door flew open. "It's about time," a man said, smiling from the doorway. "You look just like your mother."

CHAPTER 7

DECLAN

Declan strolled out of the royal sitting room and onto the balcony overlooking the turbulent ocean below. The sound of the waves crashing against the cliff instantly calmed his jumbled mind. He had so many things to do after being gone for a few days. However, exhaustion consumed him since he'd barely slept last night. After they'd docked in the harbor, he'd needed to make sure Brielle was taken care of before disembarking.

He peered at one of the balconies below and to his left, knowing she was in that room. His future wife. Clutching the railing, he shook his head, still unable to comprehend why his father had picked Brielle for him to marry.

"Brother," Orson said from behind him.

He forced his grip to loosen, and he casually leaned his forearms against the railing. "What do you want?" His brother had probably heard about Brielle and had come to gloat.

Orson chuckled as he came and stood next to Declan, turning his back to the ocean so he faced the sitting room. "Mother is in the throne room asking for you."

"And she sent you to fetch me?"

Orson folded his arms. "Not quite."

"Then get to the point." Declan needed to meet with his father to go over some land contracts in dispute with the duke to the north, though he'd much rather be training with the soldiers at Jurgis. However, that was not his destiny in life. That duty fell to Orson since Brooks couldn't effectively wield a sword—at least a physical one. Brooks's talents lay elsewhere.

"I don't know what's going on." Orson looked sidelong at Declan, giving him a chance to explain if he wanted to.

He didn't want to. He had no explanation for the fiancée he'd returned with.

"General Risberg is with the queen." Orson leaned his back against the railing, crossing his feet at the ankles, appearing relaxed and casual to anyone who might pass by.

He didn't fool Declan. General Sullivan Risberg, the man in charge of the Valdis army, was also their grandfather. If Sullivan was with the queen, his daughter, then there was a problem. He rarely came to the palace and instead, remained on the small military island of Jurgis. Orson would be Sullivan's successor when the general finally chose to retire. Or rather *if* he ever chose to relinquish control of the army.

"Ever since you and Father left with three warships, Grandfather has been in quite the mood. It really isn't becoming of someone his age to act like a child who had his sword stolen."

Declan heard the unspoken question in there. Orson wanted to know why they'd taken the warships without telling Sullivan first. Not that they had to run it by him—the king could do whatever he wanted. However, it was unusual for the king to do so without organizing it through the general. Even Declan had questioned it at the time. His father had simply said the less who knew of their excursion, the better. Declan had a feeling the king didn't want Sullivan to know about Mabel's existence yet. But if the queen knew, then the general knew. And Declan had an inkling his mother was fully aware.

He might as well get this encounter over with. Pushing away from the railing, Declan headed back inside. "Are they in the throne room?"

"They are."

"Are you coming with me?"

Orson chuckled. "No one voluntarily walks into a viper's den."

Shaking his head at his brother, Declan left the royal wing, making his way toward the throne room. After the trip with his father, he needed to unwind. As soon as he was done with his mother and grandfather, he'd send word to Sasha telling her to meet him tonight after he finished working. Just the thought of being with her eased some of the tension building in the back of his neck and along his shoulders.

As he passed the library, he peered inside, expecting to

see Brooks hunched over a book at one of the tables. It wouldn't surprise him if his brother had managed to read nearly every single book in there by now. He didn't know how Brooks could stand to spend so much time in one room.

The tables were all empty. Even the sofas were bare. The sight was so foreign to Declan that he came to an abrupt halt, blinking to make sure his eyes didn't deceive him. The only explanation he could think of was that his brother had become ill while Declan was gone, and he was in bed recovering.

A soft laugh echoed through the library, and Declan stepped inside to see the source of the distinctively feminine laugh. No one ever laughed in a library. Nothing exciting or important happened in there. And as far as Declan knew, no one other than Brooks ever stepped foot in there.

As he made his way farther into the room, he spotted movement at the back wall. In front of one of the tall windows overlooking the ocean, Brielle sat curled up on the high-backed chair, a closed book resting on her lap, her hand gently holding it in place as she listened astutely to Brooks who sat on the chair next to her talking and gesturing animatedly.

Declan quietly hurried from the library, not wanting either Brielle or his brother to see him. For starters, he didn't have time to talk to either of them right now since he needed to get to the throne room. Also, he wasn't sure how he felt about the situation. Not much could pull his brother away from his books, especially at this time of day. Yet, there he was, speaking to Brielle. Perhaps his brother was simply trying to get to know her. However, he didn't think Brooks knew about the engagement yet. Ironically, those two were better suited for one another than Declan and Brielle were. They both seemed to enjoy reading books though neither was reading at the moment.

He slid his hands in his pockets and headed toward the throne room, lost in thought. He'd never seen his brother interested enough in a woman before to bother having a conversation with her. Brooks always complained that most women were vampent idiots. After Declan spoke to his mother, he'd have to go back to the library and see what, exactly, was going on between Brooks and Brielle. Most likely he had nothing to worry about. Brooks was probably just being nice to Brielle to figure out why she was here and if she posed any threat to the royal family. Maybe the two of them had simply hit it off as friends. Though Declan wasn't sure that was a good idea. Not that he knew Brielle well enough to have an opinion on the matter, but he got the impression that the two of them together could be lethal. Regardless, since Declan was going to marry her, he couldn't have her caught up in Brooks's scheming.

Declan entered the throne room, not finding his mother or grandfather anywhere. He went over to the door just off the dais, knocking.

"Enter," the queen called out.

Declan stepped into the private antechamber and found his mother lounging on one of the plush white sofas while his grandfather paced along the perimeter of the room.

Closing the door behind him, he waited for them to address him.

"Sit," the queen commanded, pointing at the sofa across from hers.

Often, Declan found his mother in this room conducting business. Not only did it afford a level of privacy, but the opulence suited her well. The room had three walls of solid glass offering an unobstructed view of the ocean and surrounding land.

He strolled over to the empty sofa and plopped down, trying to look relaxed even if his nerves were on edge. All he had to do was make sure he appeared calm and in control.

"Tell us about your trip," the queen ordered. She wore an overtly snug, shimmering gray dress that stood out against the white sofa and highlighted her blonde hair which had been braided and wrapped around her head. A silver crown adorned with diamonds rested on top of the intricate hairdo.

"I assume Father already told you about our journey." He tried sounding bored. If his mother insisted on playing these games, he would too.

"He neglected to mention anything about your trip." Her words were short and clipped, her agitation clear.

Declan shrugged.

General Sullivan Risberg stopped pacing and faced Declan. "Do you understand that I'm in charge of the Valdis army?"

Declan hoped that wasn't a serious question, and he didn't appreciate the condescending tone. "If you wish for me to acknowledge your position as the general of our army, you should extend me the same courtesy and acknowledge mine." He smiled, knowing his grandfather hated when he pulled rank. But Declan had learned from the best. As he sat there in the den of vipers, he knew he had to use whatever means necessary to prove he couldn't be trifled with.

Queen Briar smiled, her eyes alight with pleasure.

Sullivan pursed his lips, his face darkening. "Of course, forgive me, Your Highness." He steepled his fingers. "May I speak freely?"

"You may." Declan waved his hand, indicating the general could say whatever he wanted to without following formalities. Not that it mattered. His mother and grandfather chose to meet with him here, away from watching eyes, because they were up to something. Speaking from the heart or invoking their relations to Declan wouldn't work in luring him into a false sense of security.

Sullivan came and sat next to his daughter on the sofa, both watching Declan closely. After a minute of silence, the general finally said, "I need to know why your father took off with three of my warships. Is there something going on that I should know about?"

Declan forced himself to ignore the jab about the warships being Sullivan's. His grandfather had phrased it that way to test Declan's loyalties. He had to tread carefully. Especially since Sullivan considered the warships to be his and not the crown's. Slouching on the sofa, Declan glanced outside, trying to seem uninterested. He sighed and said, "The king put me in charge of collecting taxes from the dukes. I thought you knew this?" He returned his focus to the room, now looking directly at his grandfather.

"I do," Sullivan answered.

He shrugged. "Duke Jaxon Tranum owes the crown money, and I went to collect it. Father knew you'd be upset if I didn't take a sizeable number of men with me, thus the three warships. Since it was my first trip on official business, Father went along to make sure I didn't screw it up."

The queen's face remained like a statue, never moving, so Declan had no idea what she was thinking or feeling.

"Was your trip successful?" Sullivan asked.

Declan shrugged. "I think so."

"Think?" Queen Briar said. "Either it was, or it wasn't." Her delicate fingers picked up the wine goblet on the side table, bringing it to her lips.

"The duke will send the money by Walpurgis."

The general leaned forward, his elbows resting on his thighs. "You didn't return with the money?"

Briar set her wine goblet down. "Your father wouldn't return without the money unless he had some sort of guarantee in place." Her eyes narrowed slightly, the first indication her face wasn't chiseled from stone.

Declan wanted this conversation to be over. He knew one way to stun his mother. "You're correct. It seems I'm now engaged to the duke's daughter. If the taxes aren't delivered on time, she dies. If the duke pays, we wed."

The queen raised a single eyebrow. "Was the union your idea?"

"No. It was Father's."

Briar turned her head to look at Sullivan.

"Maybe he's not as aloof to the situation as you'd feared," the general mumbled. "This could solve the problem."

"I'd still prefer not to have the problem in the first place," Briar replied.

"Regardless, it was a smart move on his part." Sullivan stood and went over to the glass wall, staring outside toward Jurgis. "I'm assuming you are not engaged to the eldest daughter?"

"No, it's the younger one." The quieter one, the plainer one.

"In the future, please make sure I'm aware of your travel plans. I can't protect you or the king if I don't know what you're doing. And you're my eldest grandchild."

"I didn't realize it'd be an issue." Declan wouldn't apologize. His father was the king and he the crown prince. The two highest ranking people in the kingdom. He answered to no one other than his father.

"Where is this woman who is to be your wife?" Briar asked.

"Here. We brought her with us."

"I want to meet her."

Of course, she did. The queen wanted to know if she'd have an ally or rival at court. "Very well. I'll arrange for Lady Brielle to have supper with our family this evening." He stood. When neither his mother nor grandfather said anything else, he exited the room, thankful to be out of there.

As Declan hurried through the castle, he replayed his grandfather's words over in his head. He wondered what it meant when Sullivan had said that the king wasn't as aloof as the queen feared and that perhaps Declan's marriage to Brielle would solve the problem. He hated questioning his father's motives. But clearly, he had them and hadn't shared them with Declan. Which hurt. But he understood. The first lesson his father had taught him was to never trust anyone —not even his own family. Sometimes those closest to us could be the most dangerous. To lead this kingdom, to be its king, he'd have to make sure to keep everyone at arm's length.

When Declan arrived at the king's office, he found his father sitting at his desk with a quill in hand. Declan went over to the bookshelf, scanning the spines, looking for something that might offer some insight as to the laws concerning illegitimate children who were suddenly discovered to be alive and heir to the throne. There had to be a law for this situation. Especially when that child was supposed to be dead. Because whatever the law stated was what the king would do. He never faltered or failed to uphold the law.

"Why didn't you tell Mother we were going to Miervades?" Declan asked.

The king shuffled some of his papers together. "Is that a serious question?"

"After all these years, you still don't trust her?" Declan kept his back to his father, not bothering to face him as he spoke since he already knew the answer.

"I don't trust anyone. Not even you. So don't ask me questions you already know the answer to."

"What about love?" He turned so he could see his father's face. "Was there ever a time you loved her?" Would Declan be stuck in a loveless marriage as well? And based upon how close in age Declan and Mabel were, he couldn't help but wonder why his father had married his mother. Rhett had claimed to love Willa, but then he'd married Briar. Maybe it was because Willa was a commoner whereas Briar was a distinguished noble woman. After Rhett had wed and learned of Willa's pregnancy, he had to have been devastated. Declan could only imagine Briar's reaction to all of it.

"Your mother and I respect one another and get along just fine."

Declan sat in the chair on the other side of the desk, across from his father. "But you loved Willa." And his father would have married her if he could.

Rhett's eyes darkened. "How is this relevant?" He set his quill down and leaned back in his chair, observing his son.

"Now that I'm engaged, I'm curious."

"Marriage is a contract between two families. Love is something else entirely."

To royalty, maybe. But Declan suspected to commoners, people married for love. At least, that was what Sasha had insisted.

"Is there anything else you'd like to discuss before we get to work?" the king asked.

"Mother wants to meet Brielle. I told her we could all

have supper together this evening. Like one big happy family."

"Fine." The king rubbed his face. "I need to tell you that I'm going with a dozen men to speak to each of the dukes. I need to inform them of the situation and that I am searching for Mabel."

Which meant there had to be some law that required him to tell the dukes about Mabel. "Do you want me to go with you?"

"No. I need you to remain here to watch over things. You will be the acting king while I'm gone. See that there aren't any other complications."

"Of course." Declan could easily handle the kingdom's mundane tasks in his father's absence.

"There's one more thing," the king said, lowering his voice. "I don't want anyone here in Sunder to know where I've gone or what I'm doing."

Declan groaned. Everyone—especially the queen and the general—would want to know where the king had run off to and why. He'd have to come up with something to throw people off and to keep them from talking.

"I'd like to leave in two days' time. We'll need to introduce Brielle to the court before I leave. At the very least, she'll provide a useful distraction in my absence."

"I'm not sure Brielle is ready." Not only did she not look the part of the kingdom's future queen, but the people here at court would be furious one of them wasn't selected to marry the crown prince. They'd take their jealousy out on

Brielle. It'd be like throwing a bunny to wolves. There was only one possible outcome.

"Your mother can help her navigate the complexities of court."

Declan couldn't imagine his mother helping anyone do anything, but he kept that to himself.

The king reached for a stack of papers, sliding them over to Declan. "While I'm gone, make sure you spend some time with Brielle both publicly and privately. We have a lot riding on this marriage."

"Anything else?" Declan stood and gathered the papers.

"Don't trust anyone."

"I never do."

CHAPTER 8

BRIELLE

Jenice yanked Brielle's hair back, deftly braiding it with quick efficiency. Brielle pursed her lips, watching in the mirror as the braid wrapped around her head like a crown before being pinned in place.

"What's the problem?" Jenice asked as she took a step back, inspecting her work.

"I never wear my hair up." It made her uncomfortable to have her neck exposed. And no one back home ever did their hair like this.

Jenice muttered something under her breath before opening a wooden box on the vanity table. "Now turn on the chair so you face me."

Brielle did as instructed. "What's in the box?"

"Face powder. Close your eyes and hold still."

Brielle did as she was told, though she wanted to argue. She supposed if she'd had a mother growing up, she'd be used to such things. But neither she nor Kenna wore fancy clothes or put face powder on, especially for supper. "Is this really necessary?" The letter she'd received from Declan stated it would just be the immediate royal family and no one else. She could understand looking presentable, but this seemed to be a bit extravagant.

"Yes. And you'll wear what I tell you to as well."

Brielle had been informed that there would be a celebration tomorrow evening where she would be officially presented to the members of court as Prince Declan's fiancée. That she expected to be dressed up for, but not this.

"All done." Jenice snapped the box closed. "Before you look at yourself in the mirror, put your dress on. Then maybe you'll be less inclined to argue with me."

Brielle went over to the bed where the dress had been laid out. "Where'd you even find a dress to fit me?" Nothing she owned was half this elegant. She stepped into it, the dress sliding over her body like a glove. While thankful that the sleeves were long and the neckline high, she was concerned that the entire dress was made from sheer fabric, the color of her skin, with an emerald green flame-like pattern strategically placed throughout.

"The royal seamstress made it," Jenice said as she exited the dressing closet holding a green swath of fabric matching the dress.

"I can't wear this," Brielle said, standing before the mirror. Although the dress didn't show anything, it offered hints at what was beneath.

Jenice chuckled and then wrapped the thin piece of silk

around Brielle's waist, tying it so that the front remained open to showcase the dress while the fabric draped behind her, dusting the floor. "That better?"

"I suppose so," Brielle said, observing herself in the mirror. "At least my rear end is covered now."

"Rear end?" Jenice laughed. "You can say ass."

She could, but she chose not to.

"Remove that silver bracelet," Jenice said. "It's too plain and doesn't match your dress."

Brielle fingered the simple bracelet. "I can't." She had no idea how to explain that the piece of jewelry had been molded around her wrist. The only way to get it off would be to cut it off with special equipment.

Jenice reached for her wrist, taking hold of the bracelet, and tugged. "There's no latch?"

Brielle shook her head.

Jenice looked at it closer. "The silver almost shimmers. Strange." She released her arm. "Well, I suppose you'll have to wear it then." She tapped her chin with her pointer finger. "I wonder if I can have another bracelet or two made to complement it."

Brielle had worn it for so many years that she usually forgot it was even there.

"I think you're ready then." Jenice stood back, examining Brielle.

"Why is it so important that I have a specific look for tonight if it's just the royal family?" The green shadow on her eyes matched the dress, making her look unrecognizable.

"You're meeting the queen," Jenice replied, as if that explained it all.

"I'm not comfortable right now." Brielle didn't feel like herself. "I don't want to pretend to be someone I'm not."

Jenice folded her arms and scanned Brielle from head to toe. "Are you not going to be the next queen of Valdis?"

"Eventually." But that could be decades from now.

"You must look the part," Jenice said. "Otherwise, these people will chew you up and spit you out. You won't even make it to the wedding."

Brielle read between the lines, understanding that Jenice was referring to the queen. It was important that the queen believe Brielle a suitable match for her son, and someone who would be worthy of being the next queen. If she didn't succeed in convincing the queen of these things, the queen would make life difficult.

In addition, she realized the queen would be her mother-in-law. This would be the first mother figure she'd ever had in her life. Suddenly, she wanted to please this woman whom she hadn't yet met. The idea of having someone to confide in, discuss books with, and have a cup of afternoon tea with overwhelmed her.

A knock resounded on the door to her bedchamber. Jenice rushed over and opened it.

In the mirror, Brielle watched Jenice say something to whomever was there, then she curtsied and left.

"Lady Brielle," Brooks said as he came into the room. "I've come to escort you to dinner."

She turned to face Brooks, standing in the doorway, cane in hand, looking every bit the prince he was. He wore navy blue pants along with a matching vest over a white fitted shirt. The color brought out his eyes, giving him a handsome, regal appearance.

"Do I have the wrong room?" He chuckled. "You don't look like the young woman I met in the library."

"I'm afraid I don't recognize myself either." Kenna would have loved it here, being fussed over and wearing such a fancy gown. Brielle felt guilty for not enjoying it, for being sad about having to be dressed up for a supper with the royal family. If she needed to appear to be someone other than herself, it meant being herself wasn't good enough.

Brooks shifted his cane in front of his body, both hands on its handle, bearing the brunt of his weight. "Let me tell you a secret." His eyes focused on hers, as if he could see straight inside of her. "Everyone here at the palace is playing a part. They keep their true selves hidden away. To survive, you will need to do the same. Otherwise, I fear you'll be taken advantage of."

"What part do you suggest I play?" she asked while wondering what part he was playing and if she'd met the real Brooks or not.

"Hide your sweet nature. Believe that you are beautiful and deserve to marry the crown prince. Never show fear or intimidation. Everyone here, except the royal family, is beneath you."

She remembered her sister's parting words not to let

anyone at the palace intimidate her, including the royal family. While Kenna may very well have been better suited to being here and marrying the prince, Brielle was the one chosen. She needed to rise to the occasion and make her father and sister proud. "Don't you mean that the crown prince deserves to marry me?" She smiled, suddenly feeling bold in the dress and makeup.

Brooks chuckled, the sound deep and throaty, making her toes curl. "That's my girl. Now let's go do this." Shifting his cane to his left hand, he held out his right arm for her to take.

Her fingers curled around his arm, and they exited her room. He walked with a slight limp; however, she'd didn't mind the slower pace. The tight dress proved to be more difficult to walk in than she'd thought it would be, especially with the cape dragging on the floor behind her. The last thing she wished to do was trip on the material and fall on her face.

"Shouldn't Prince Declan be escorting me to supper?" Not that she cared Brooks was taking her. Their conversation in the library had been enjoyable. They'd discussed books for hours, and she'd discovered he'd read even more than she had. Of course, he'd read a lot on the laws of the land and politics—neither of which had remotely interested her before coming to the palace.

"That's a difficult question to answer."

"How so?" She thought it relatively simple.

"It depends on what sort of relationship the two of you plan on having."

His answer surprised her. "We're getting married." She thought he knew this.

"Yes," he said, drawling out the word longer than it should be, giving her pause. "But what sort of marriage will it be? Shall the two of you be wed in name only? Will you each take a lover—after you've produced an heir of course? Will you live together, sleep together?"

Her face warmed; she hadn't considered any of this. "I assumed we would be married in the traditional sense of the word." Saying that out loud sounded silly to her own ears. "You must think me a naive simpleton." While she knew it was an arranged marriage, she'd assumed she and Declan would get to know one another and live as husband and wife.

"Is that what you want?" Brooks asked. "A traditional marriage?"

"Yes." Until now, no one had bothered to ask her what she wanted. Since she wasn't her father's heir, she'd always assumed she'd fall in love and marry. Or marry someone like Lukas who she knew and would get along with. Marrying a stranger and for political necessity had never crossed her mind. "Is that not what Prince Declan wishes?"

Brooks shrugged. "I don't know. You'll have to ask him."

"Why are you being kind to me?" she demanded, suddenly realizing he had to have ulterior motives. Whether it was attempting to make his brother jealous or gain an ally, she didn't know. What she did know was that she would not be a pawn in these political games. If she played, it would be as a knowing and willing participant and on her terms.

He looked sidelong at her. "Honestly, I'm trying to determine the sort of person you are and if you're trustworthy." He stopped and faced her. "You're marrying the crown prince. You will be intimately connected to the royal family. *My* family. I know nothing about you. I don't even know why my father chose you for Declan. The easiest way to figure out the sort of person you are is to spend time with you. If you have ill intentions toward my family, I will discover them. And I will end you."

Shock like a lightning bolt jolted through her, and she had no idea how to respond.

Brooks smiled. "Like I said, everyone here at the palace has a role to play. It's time you played yours." He resumed walking, pulling Brielle along with him. "You need to anticipate people asking these bold, intimate questions. You can't flinch or show any emotion. In fact, you need to have an answer ready to go."

Her head was reeling with all Brooks had told her. Tonight, when she was alone in her bed, she would have to rehash this conversation, turn it over, stew on it. Brooks could have lied and said he'd simply wanted her as a friend since they were about to be in-laws. But he'd chosen to be honest with her for a reason. That little hard glimpse of his real persona scared her. It made her wonder what else he was hiding. As he'd told her to play a role, she now understood he played one as well. She couldn't ever forget that.

"Are you nervous to meet the royal family?" Brooks asked, his voice friendly once again.

"No." She'd already met Rhett, Declan, and Brooks. The only two she hadn't met were Prince Orson and Queen Briar, whose names she now knew thanks to the book Brooks had given her. The book had also revealed that Brooks had a twin brother, Gareth, who'd died at the age of eight from the same illness that left Brooks with an injured leg. She wanted to ask him about it, but they didn't know one another well enough for that sort of conversation. At least not yet.

"Be forewarned," he said. "My mother can be very critical. She'll attempt to find a hundred things wrong with you. Just ignore her—we usually do."

The more Brooks talked, the more nervous she became. She needed to change the subject to calm herself before they reached their destination. "I want to thank you for your help earlier today finding those books and for sharing your library with me. My library at home isn't nearly as extensive as yours."

"The library is my second home, and you are welcome to it any time."

"Why do you spend so much time there? Being a prince, I thought you'd have a lot of duties to attend to." Especially since he was second in line behind Declan.

They walked in silence for a minute. "Since I'm... crippled, I'm unable to manage the army—which is what the second son is supposed to do. Therefore, I'm the one who maintains my father's books. I'm good at it, so it gives me a lot of free time to read. Plus, I advise my father since I know so much about the history of our kingdom and its laws."

When he spoke, he kept his eyes focused up ahead and didn't look at Brielle.

She wondered if he was withholding something from her. "Are you upset you can't lead the army?" she asked. "I don't see you as an army man."

He chuckled. "I would have hated it."

"It's funny how things work out, isn't it?" She smiled up at him.

They turned down a corridor leading to two large doors, guards standing on either side. This had to be the royal wing. Brooks released her arm and opened one of the doors, ushering her inside a large sitting room.

The bright and airy room consisted of over a dozen windows along the right wall, including two opened glass doors leading to a large balcony outside. Four sofas and a low table were arranged in the middle of the room though no one sat there. Declan and a man a few years younger than him stood off to the side arguing. Brielle assumed that had to be Orson, the youngest prince. The king and queen walked into the room at the same time Brooks closed the door. The room went silent, and everyone turned to stare at Brielle.

The king came forward. "Lady Brielle, it's good to see you." He took her arm, leading her farther into the room. "I'd like to introduce you to my wife, Queen Briar Forberg." They stopped a few feet in front of the queen.

"Your Majesty," Brielle said with a curtsy. When she righted herself, she looked straight at the queen, momentarily stunned by her beauty. Briar seemed like a painting because she had flawless skin, perfect makeup, her dress—a shimmering silver—accentuated every curve, and her blonde hair had been pulled back into braids wrapped around her head and topped off with an ornate crown.

"So, you are to be Declan's wife," the queen said by way of greeting, her eyes scanning Brielle from head to toe.

Before Brielle could answer, the king turned to his youngest son. "And this is Prince Orson Forberg."

"Lady Brielle," Orson said with a bow. "It's a pleasure to meet you." He stood and winked.

Brielle had no idea what to make of that.

Brooks went over to Declan, whispering something to him.

"Lady Brielle," the king said, "why don't you have a seat and tell us about yourself." He released her arm.

"Yes," Orson said with a wicked smile on his face. "We'd love to hear all about you." He plopped on one of the sofas, spreading his arms across the back of it while propping his right foot on his left leg. "Don't be shy. We're all family now."

Declan whacked the back of Orson's head. "Behave yourself and don't scare her off." He sat next to his brother, exhaustion lining his handsome face.

Brooks went over to the windows, staring outside, his back to them.

The king and queen sat on one of the sofas, so Brielle sat on the one across from Declan. She pulled the fabric of her cape around her waist in front of her, making sure she was fully covered. Orson chuckled.

She had no idea what to say.

"Why don't you tell us about your family," the king prompted.

"My mother died in childbirth," she said. "My father and older sister raised me. It's just the three of us. Our castle isn't half as grand as your palace here."

"Did you attend one of the schools in Valdis?" the queen asked.

"No." She clasped her sweaty hands together. "My father hired a governess to handle my schooling." Truth be told, she learned most everything from books.

Just then, a servant entered the room announcing it was time for supper. The family moved to the adjacent room, and Brielle followed them. Inside, a long table extended from one end of the room to the other. Six place settings had been arranged around the table. This room, like the previous one, had one wall filled with windows all open to the outside, allowing the ocean breeze to blow through.

The king and queen each sat at the heads of the table. Orson and Brooks sat on one side, leaving the last two chairs across from them for Declan and Brielle.

Servants brought in plates, setting one before each person. Brielle glanced down and saw some sort of white meat, squared potatoes, and green beans.

"Shark," Declan said under his breath.

"Excuse me?" She glanced at him.

He jerked his chin toward her plate. "It's shark. One of my mother's favorites."

She'd never had shark before.

The queen lifted her fork and began eating. Once she took her first bite, everyone else did the same.

Brielle took a piece of the shark, trying it. It was tougher than she'd thought it would be, but she enjoyed the taste.

As she ate, she felt everyone watching her.

"I thought you said she was homely," Orson said to Declan. "She looks like every other woman here at court."

Brielle felt her face warm. She remembered what Kenna had said to her about not letting the royal family intimidate her. If she let them walk on her, they would. Pretending to be a heroine from one of her books, she forced herself to look directly at Orson and said, "I know. It's shocking what a dress and a little makeup can do. Imagine if Jenice had her way with you."

Declan choked on the wine he was drinking.

Orson burst out laughing. "I didn't think you had a backbone since I hear all you do is read."

She glanced at Brooks, wondering if he'd told Orson that. The corners of his lips pulled down slightly, and she didn't think Brooks had said anything to Orson.

Brielle felt two paths extend before her. She could either run away crying or let her fury fill her enough to fight. She chose the latter. "And I didn't think you capable of stringing two sentences together since all you do is play soldier." Her entire body started shaking. Not only did she hate confrontations and avoided them at all costs, but she hoped she didn't upset the king enough for him to order her execution on the spot. She lifted her chin, forcing herself to at least pretend to be confident.

"You'll fit in here just fine," Orson responded. "Welcome to the family."

She kept her hands in her lap so no one would see them shaking.

"Tell me, Lady Brielle, why your mother died in childbirth," the queen asked, shifting the conversation.

Taking a calming breath, she answered, "She was a small woman, and I was upside down. They could only save one of us." She picked up her fork and resumed eating.

"And your father chose to save you," the queen said. "I would have done the same. That way if something happens to his heir, he still has a backup."

"Actually, my mother made the choice." Brielle focused on her plate, willing herself not to cry in front of these people. "She told my father that she'd lived a full life, experienced joy and love. She wanted the same for me, so she made him save me." She still remembered the first time her father had explained it to her, telling her of her mother's love for her.

"I think any mother would have done the same," Briar said, her voice cold.

"I forgot to mention that the festivities for Walpurgis are underway," Declan said, changing the subject. "I met with some of the city council members today."

The conversation moved to the festivities being planned for the celebration. Brielle tuned them out and instead, focused on her plate and eating. Even though she didn't know the queen, she got the feeling the woman wouldn't be the mother figure Brielle had hoped for. But maybe the persona she showed was only a shield, and the real woman beneath was kind and caring.

"And let's not forget," Orson continued, "if the duke fails to pay his back taxes, you won't be getting married. The Walpurgis celebration could be Lady Brielle's last event."

At hearing her name, Brielle glanced up.

"I'm certain he'll pay," the king responded. "He won't risk his daughter's life."

"Let's hope so. Otherwise, I'll have to escort Lady Brielle to her execution." Orson shoved his chair back and stood. "Now, if you'll excuse me, I'm needed down on Jurgis. We're running an exercise tonight." He sauntered from the room, winking at Brielle on his way out.

A sick feeling filled Brielle. She wanted to be away from this royal family and their constant barbs at one another.

"And I need to be going as well. I have some reading to do." Brooks stood and left the room.

Brielle set her fork down, unable to eat another thing on her plate.

"Declan, dear," the queen said, reaching for her wine goblet, "why don't you escort your fiancée back to her room. I think we're finished here."

"Of course, Mother." Declan stood.

Brielle thanked the king and queen for supper before following Declan from the dining room. He led her through the sitting room and out into the corridor where the two guards remained posted.

"Does the entire royal family live in this wing of the palace?" she asked.

"In theory." Declan glanced over his shoulder at the guards behind them. "Once we marry, I'm not sure if we'll live with my family or elsewhere." He stopped at the end of the corridor. "I hope we'll be given our own wing to reside in."

She hoped so, too. The idea of living with his family did not appeal to her. For the first time tonight, she allowed herself to look at Declan's face. They'd barely spoken, and she did not feel like she knew him any better than before. He seemed withdrawn and closed off. Like his father. She felt as if she knew Brooks and Orson better than Declan. Standing there before him, she had no idea what to say to engage him in conversation. She didn't know what his interests or hobbies were, what he enjoyed doing, what his favorite foods were. She knew nothing about him.

"Can you find your way back to your room from here?" he asked.

She blinked, trying to hide her shock. He didn't even plan on walking her to her room, which meant he didn't care to get to know her. That fact stung more than it should have. "I know the way," she lied. If he didn't want to spend time with her, then she didn't want to spend time with him.

"Goodnight." He bowed and headed down the hallway to the left.

She watched him walk away, wondering where he was

hurrying off to. When she could no longer see him, she turned and went the other way. When she rounded the corner, she came face-to-face with Brooks.

A smile slid across his face. "Care to join me on the rooftop to stargaze?"

She felt tears threaten, and she wished Brooks were the one she was marrying, not Declan. "I'm tired and wish to retire for the night." She moved to pass him.

He stuck out his hand, stopping her. "We need to talk," he whispered. "No one is on the rooftop, making it the safest place."

She nodded, afraid that if she spoke, her voice would crack. She just needed to hold it together for a little while longer. Then, when she was alone in her bedchamber, she could let it all out.

They stopped before a door at the end of a hallway. Brooks opened it, revealing a narrow spiral staircase leading up. He motioned for her to go first. She started climbing, going around and around for what felt like at least ten stories. When she came to an end, she pushed open the door, stepping out onto the top of one of the palace's turrets. This one was only fifteen feet or so in diameter, surrounded by a low wall that came up to her waist. Resting her elbows on the wall, she gazed out at the view. To one side, the dark ocean below extended out before her. On the other side, the city basked in lights. If she could choose only one word to describe it, it would be mesmerizing.

Brooks joined her a few moments later. She'd forgotten he walked at a slower pace due to his injured leg.

"You handled dinner well," he said as he leaned against the wall next to her.

"Why did you bring me here?" She shivered from the wind coming up off the ocean.

"Two reasons."

She turned to face him.

"What can you tell me about Witch's Cove?"

The question caught her off-guard. "Why do you ask?"

"Declan mentioned something to me about it, and I'm curious."

She shrugged. "Not much. It's just a cove east of Monta. It's rocky and the currents are dangerous. A lot of ships have crashed there over the years, so hardly anyone goes there anymore."

"You haven't heard stories about a group of reclusive women living there?"

"Are you referring to the story *Witches Night*?" she asked. It was a bedtime tale told to scare children into behaving.

"I've never heard of it."

"It's about a young boy who runs away from home. He claims to feel something luring him, so he follows it. He ends up going to the cove, thinking he sees someone there. When he arrives at the top of it, he discovers a large fire and a group of witches singing and dancing. He secretly watches but manages to slip and fall off the cliff. He almost drowns. Thankfully, the witches save him but there is a price to pay. Every year the boy must return and give them five drops of his blood. If he fails to do so, he'll die. My father used to tell me that if I ran away from home, the same fate would befall me." She chuckled, remembering being terrified to leave the house at night as a child. "It's a story everyone tells their children to keep them from exploring the dangerous cliffs at night."

"Does *Witches Night* take place on a specific day of the year?" he asked.

She shook her head. "It's just a made-up story." She didn't even think it had ever been written down in a children's storybook. "And the second reason you brought me here?"

"I like you."

It warmed her that one person in this palace cared for her.

"I hope we can be friends."

She was immediately on guard, wondering what he wanted from her.

"And as your friend, I need to warn you to be careful. Don't trust anyone here, and you must guard your heart."

"I can't even trust you?" she asked, curious to hear his answer.

He smiled. "Everyone here is bound by something. Never forget that."

An answer that wasn't an answer.

"Why are you warning me to guard my heart?" She didn't think she was in danger of loving anyone here at the palace.

"Declan is the crown prince. He is also my brother."

She didn't understand what Brooks was getting at.

"I love my brother. I am bound by duty to the crown prince."

Brielle didn't respond because she didn't know what Brooks was trying to say. She didn't think he had any romantic inclinations toward her and was stating why they couldn't be together. Even if she did feel something for Brooks, she wasn't stupid enough to act on those feelings. She was going to marry Declan, and she would honor that marriage. If she didn't, and there was ever any question about the royal line, she would be executed.

"You should know that my brother is with his lover tonight." Brooks pointed at the turret to the right.

She froze, unable to move. She couldn't even look at the window he was pointing to. "Why are you telling me this?" What could he gain from revealing his brother's secrets?

"We are all here to serve my father. Each of us has a purpose. Yours is to marry Declan and produce an heir. That is all. There is no great love story or happy ending. We are all trying to survive."

"You don't think I know that?" Did he think so little of her that he had to treat her like a naive child?

"I tell you this so that tomorrow, when you are presented to the court, you're prepared to deal with everyone. I saw how you reacted to Orson tonight. You said exactly what you needed to put him in his place. He was testing you. But doing so took its toll on you. I could tell you didn't like being confrontational and that it was hard for you. Tomorrow will be a thousand times worse. I'd like to see you survive. The royal family needs you and this marriage."

"Because you need Miervades's wheat and money?" With Brooks's behavior, she suspected there had to be more to it than that.

"Declan needs an heir." He pushed away from the wall, clutching his cane. "There will be many that want to see you fail. I'm betting on you. Don't disappoint me." He turned and left.

Brielle remained on top of the turret, more confused than ever.

CHAPTER 9

DECLAN

Declan sat up in bed, running his hands through his hair. Sasha remained asleep, her breathing steady. The candle burned low, casting a soft glow over the room. A gentle breeze came in through the open window, caressing his bare skin.

For some reason, an overwhelming desire to leave inundated him. He stood and dressed, not used to feeling guilty about spending time with Sasha. Over the past few months, Sasha had been available to him whenever he wanted her. He rubbed his face. It wasn't until tonight that she said something about turning down the proposal of another man so she could continue to be with Declan. He'd been so wrapped up in his own enjoyment of her, that he never stopped to consider what their relationship meant to her.

To be honest, a small part of him kept thinking about Brielle. Not because he found her attractive or cared for her in the slightest, but because he was engaged to her. A natural feeling of honor and commitment had taken root.

While his father didn't have mistresses, the king had still managed to have a child with another woman. The child had been conceived before he married. Declan didn't want to find himself in the same situation. If Sasha became pregnant, her child would be his heir. But Sasha could have no part in that child's life since she was a commoner. The similarities between her and Willa were disturbing.

He needed to end it with Sasha.

Leaning down, he kissed her back and then left the room. Since he wasn't tired, he decided to head down to Jurgis and join the military in their midnight exercise Orson was running. That would take his mind off of things.

Passing the library, he noticed a single candle lit in the back corner. He went in and found Brooks hunched over one of the tables, a handful of books spread out, each of them open.

"Doing some light reading?" Declan joked, scanning the books, and seeing most of them had to do with Miervades. "What's all this for?" He grabbed one of the books, pulling it closer so he could see what it was about.

"I'm just doing some research," Brooks answered, not bothering to take his eyes off the page he was currently reading.

"About?" he prompted.

"Witch's Cove."

"Why?" He knew he never should have said anything to Brooks about what had happened when he'd sailed by it.

"Because Brielle is from Miervades."

"So?" He didn't see what her being from Miervades had to do with Witch's Cove other than its location.

"What do you know of the rebellion that happened twenty-two years ago?"

"Grandfather squashed it." He also knew his father had been sent there and that was where he'd met Willa. He sat on the chair across from Brooks.

"Do you know why the people were rebelling?"

"I believe it was over taxes."

"Do you know why Miervades pays so much in taxes?"

"Are you asking me because you think I might know the answer or is this a rhetorical question?"

"I have a feeling we're missing something." Brooks sat back in his chair, looking at his brother. "Brielle being here... there's more going on. I'm certain of it. What if they're planning another rebellion?"

"Brielle doesn't seem like the type of person who'd be involved in treason or espionage." He didn't think the duke was planning anything either.

Brooks chuckled. "The good ones never do."

"What do you think of Brielle?" Declan asked. "Do you trust her?"

"I can't figure out whether I do or not."

"You're usually a good read of character."

"There are times where I see such intelligence in her eyes...I can't tell if she's hiding something from me or if she's just naive. Maybe both." He rubbed his temples.

"Will you do me a favor?" Declan asked.

"Of course."

"If you discover anything important about her, please tell me before you tell Father. I want to know who I'm marrying, and I fear Father might neglect to share some pertinent information with me."

Brooks yawned and then stretched his arms above his head. "Here's a thought. You can also spend some time with her. Get to know her."

He hated wasting time like that. It was one of the reasons he only saw Sasha at night. "We'll see," he said as he stood.

"Just remember, Father chose her for a reason. She's not the duke's heir. She is of little consequence. So why would the King of Valdis pick her, an unknown woman, for the crown prince to marry?"

At the time, it had made perfect sense to Declan. But when Brooks put it that way, it made him question everything.

Declan's valet held up two jackets—one solid black and the other a deep midnight blue with a silver pattern interlaced throughout it.

"Do you know what Lady Brielle is wearing?" Declan asked.

"I do not," Graham answered.

"Since this is our engagement party, I don't want to clash with her." He needed to send a strong message to his court.

He wanted them to start seeing him as their future king, capable of ruling and being strong like his father.

"The queen has made it perfectly clear that she is wearing white, and no one else is to wear that color."

Declan figured his mother would wear something dazzling this evening so as not to be outdone by Brielle. Briar had looked rather perturbed last night when Brielle arrived wearing that stunning dress. He knew Jenice had picked it out for Brielle to show the queen that Brielle would be a worthy princess. While the dress looked attractive on Brielle, it hadn't suited her personality. When the queen wore a dress, she wore it like a piece of armor. Brielle seemed too mild-natured for the seductive dress.

"I'll go with the solid black jacket." That way he'd complement Brielle no matter what she wore.

"A safe choice." Graham helped Declan put the jacket on.

"Have you heard any rumors I should know about?" Declan asked.

Graham took a step back, pursing his lips. "There are always rumors."

"I know." And in every rumor there tended to be a grain of truth. "I'd like to hear what people are saying so I know whether to fuel the rumors or stifle them." He needed to put on a united front with Brielle. He probably should've had a conversation about this with her.

"I've heard Lady Brielle was chosen to tempt your brother so he'd commit a crime and you could officially get rid of him."

Declan lifted his eyebrows at that. "People can be quite creative."

"They were seen speaking intimately in the library."

"What else?" Interestingly enough, the rumor referred to Brooks and not Orson who was closer in age to Brielle.

"The queen is jealous of her youthfulness."

"That one's probably true." He turned and faced the mirror again, fixing his hair.

"And I've heard that she is the king's secret lover brought here under the guise of your fiancée so the king can continue his nightly rendezvous with her."

Declan turned to face Graham. "I've never heard rumors of my father having an affair before." Strange that they should start now. "Interesting that there are rumors tying her to both Brooks and my father." He had no idea how a rumor about her and his father had begun.

"And my mother did hear that the women at court think she's a simpleton with no fashion sense."

"If Jenice hears anything else, let me know."

Graham nodded. "Do you require any further assistance, Your Highness?"

"That will be all. You're dismissed for the evening." His valet left, probably eager to be with his new wife since they were expecting a child any day.

Declan realized his family had never had to deal with another woman competing for attention with his mother. Tonight would be interesting to see how the two women handled one another and how the court responded. He adjusted his sleeves one more time before leaving his room and heading toward the ballroom where the celebration should be well under way.

The royal family planned to arrive about an hour after the party started. They would be introduced to everyone, and then Lady Brielle would enter. Declan didn't think she'd like the attention, but there was nothing to be done about it. She'd have to learn to get used to this sort of thing now that she was going to be his wife.

When he said *wife*, an odd sensation swept through him. He pulled the collar of his shirt away from his neck, trying to breathe. He still couldn't figure out why his father had chosen her for him.

Nearing the ballroom, the sound of music filled the hallways. Declan headed to the adjacent room where his family should be gathered, waiting for him. Too bad he was late. He'd planned it this way to avoid having to talk to them about Brielle. His own thoughts were too jumbled about the situation.

He entered the room.

"It's about bloody time," Orson said, punching him in the arm.

Brooks stood off to the side, leaning on his cane. His face looked slightly whiter than usual, and Declan hoped his brother was okay. The king and queen were sitting on the sofa, their heads bent toward one another in a private conversation.

"Sorry I'm late," Declan said by way of greeting. He adjusted the sleeves of his jacket again. "Is Brielle ready?"

"She's been ready," Orson said. "Now let's go and get this over with."

The queen stood. "I want the three of you on your best behavior this evening. Are we clear?"

Orson snorted. "What do you think we're going to do? It's a royal ball."

Her eyes narrowed. "You will not get into any fights, insult any of the ladies, and you will not consume any alcohol."

"Rich, coming from you, Mother." Orson shook his head.

The king mumbled something to Orson and Orson quickly apologized to the queen. She held out her hand and he kissed it. "Your wish is my command," Orson said. "I will behave perfectly all evening."

She patted his cheek. "That wasn't so hard, was it?"

Brooks lifted his head, looking directly at Declan.

"Come, brother," Declan said. "Let's go and celebrate my engagement."

Brooks joined him.

"Is everything okay?" Declan whispered. "You don't look well."

"I was up all night doing research. Now I suffer from a lack of sleep."

"Did you find anything interesting?" Declan said as they neared the doors leading to the ballroom.

"I did. But it is a conversation for another time."

Declan squeezed his brother's shoulder. "Of course."

A trumpet sounded and then the doors opened, revealing a ballroom packed with people. The herald announced Prince Orson. He entered the room without a backward glance. Declan knew he'd head straight to the table serving drinks since he hated these formal occasions. Brooks was announced next. He entered the room slower than usual, and Declan hoped he was okay. When Declan heard his name called, he entered the ballroom and stood next to Brooks, waiting for his parents to be announced.

When the king and queen entered together, everyone dropped to a low curtsy or bow. The king ordered everyone to rise. Declan caught sight of General Sullivan hovering nearby. The king addressed his subjects, the queen at his side.

Briar barely moved as Rhett spoke, but her eyes scanned the room, looking at those present. As she'd intended, she was the only one wearing white. The queen's backless dress scooped low in the front, revealing the top portion of her bosom. The slit in her dress exposed one leg all the way up to her thigh. The men couldn't take their eyes off her. The queen's beauty gave her a sense of power over everyone in the room that Declan's father couldn't contend with. It unnerved him. He'd always viewed his father as the powerful one. Now, he realized his mother wielded just as much power but in a vastly different way.

The king spoke about tradition and the Forberg family line. Then he mentioned Brielle's name, and the back doors swung open.

Declan's breath caught at the sight of her. While he knew Jenice would dress Brielle in something to rival his mother, he hadn't expected this.

Brielle stepped into the ballroom, the complete opposite of the queen in every way. She donned a midnight black dress with diamonds on the material shining like stars. The long-sleeved dress was form fitting on top and draped down to the floor in soft waves. It had an elegance to it that made Declan smile. Brielle didn't show an ounce of skin other than her face, neck, and hands. However, it made him stare at the simplistic beauty of it, and of her.

Last night at supper, she'd appeared out of place in the seductive dress. Tonight, she seemed confident, poised, and queenly. His mother had to be furious with Brielle for stealing the spotlight.

Brielle stopped a few feet before Declan. It took him a moment to realize everyone was waiting for him to respond. Brielle glanced up at him with an emotion in her eyes he couldn't decipher. He would have to get to know her better to understand her. Strange that he wanted to even bother.

He extended his hand, and she took hold of it. He held on firmly as he led her to the center of the dance floor where he slid one hand to her waist, the other taking her right hand in his. Everyone in the room gathered around to watch them dance.

The music started, a beautiful, slow tune, and Declan took the first step, Brielle following his lead. Her eyes never wavered from his, and he could feel that she trusted him to not only get her through the dance, but this night. And he would. They twirled around the dance floor, moving together seamlessly with the music. For a moment, he forgot the two of them were performing for an audience and on display. His left hand slid up her arm to her neck, pulling her toward him. The song slowed. His feet stopped. And he leaned down, placing his forehead against hers, their lips only inches apart.

The room erupted in applause, bringing reality back into focus.

Brielle's eyes blinked rapidly, so Declan took a step back, breathing a little heavier than usual.

The next song started, and other couples began dancing.

Brooks appeared out of nowhere. "I'd like a dance with my soon-to-be sister-in-law."

Brielle peered up at Declan, as if seeking his permission.

He found that interesting. "Yes, of course." Declan released her.

Brooks lifted his free hand and Brielle took it, smiling at him. She slid her hands to his shoulders so he could rest one hand on her back and the other on his cane. Brielle never moved her feet allowing Brooks to remain in place so he wouldn't lose his balance.

Declan noticed his grandfather getting closer, probably so he could dance with Brielle as soon as the opportunity arose. The general probably had a million questions for her.

"Your Highness," Sasha said from behind Declan. "Will you honor me with a dance?"

Taking a deep breath, he turned to face Sasha, wondering what her motives were for being here tonight. She was not of the noble class and therefore, wasn't officially invited. If she was upset about his engagement, she didn't show it.

"I don't think it's a good idea for us to dance." He slid his hands in his pockets.

"You can't leave me standing here in the middle of the dance floor all alone," she said, tilting her head to the side and smiling coyly at him.

He didn't want to make a scene. "Let's go stand off to the side and talk." He needed to end things with her; he just hadn't planned on doing it tonight in the middle of his engagement ball.

"Why can't we dance? Your fiancée is dancing with another man."

"Not another man. She's dancing with my brother."

"Does she know she's engaged to you and not to him?"

Declan glanced over in time to see Brielle laughing at something Brooks had said. While he knew there was nothing romantic going on between the two of them, a pang of jealousy took root, but he couldn't let it bother him. Brooks had a way with words, and the two of them had formed a friendship of sorts.

"Dance with me," Sasha repeated. "We need to talk, and people are starting to wonder why you're standing there like a tree stump."

CHAPTER 10
BRIELLE

rielle looked up into Brooks's eyes. "Well?" she asked. "How did I do?" She had to remember to dance in one place so she wouldn't throw his balance off since he still held the cane in one hand.

"You were perfect," he whispered. "Just the right amount of class in the way you carried yourself. You also pulled off the love-struck woman while dancing, and, quite honestly, you look simply stunning. When you walked in, my mother's face was priceless." He pulled her a bit closer, their chests touching.

Brielle thought that perhaps they should have more space between them; however, she didn't want Brooks to trip on her dress and fall. Being this close allowed them to remain in one place.

"After we're done dancing," Brooks murmured, "Orson will come over and take a turn. When he's done dancing with you, he and I are getting out of here."

"Why are you leaving so soon?" She liked having a friendly face there. "You're the only member of the royal family who actually talks to me."

He chuckled. "Orson and I hate these things. And since everyone who's anyone is here, it's a great time to spy."

"Don't you have people who spy for you?" It seemed rather risky for the princes to be doing their own dirty work.

"We do. But if we use our spies all the time, then they know all the secrets, too. Some things we must do ourselves."

Brielle couldn't help but admire Brooks's intelligence.

She peered over his shoulder and saw Declan dancing with another woman. She supposed there were a great many women who'd like to dance with the crown prince. The woman slid her hand into Declan's hair then whispered in his ear. "Who's that with your brother?" They looked far too comfortable with one another.

"Sasha." He didn't even turn to look.

"Is she his..." Brielle couldn't bring herself to say the word *lover*.

"He was with her last night if that's what you're asking."

"How long have they been like that?"

"Not long. A couple of months. She's not suitable, so he doesn't take their relationship seriously."

Brielle felt sick to her stomach. "Can I ask you a personal question?"

He nodded.

"Do you take lovers who you aren't serious about? Is this typical behavior of princes?" She glanced over to the side of the room and caught sight of Orson talking with two women. "Or maybe it's just the people in your family who behave in such a manner?"

Brooks patted her back. "Remember all our conversations. We're in a public setting. Appearances are everything. Never forget that."

She hated when he didn't answer her directly. Frustration built. Not with Brooks or Declan, but with herself. He'd warned her this was coming and yet, it still bothered her. She needed to remain calm and in control so she could present a regal image to the court.

Brooks leaned in closer. "And to answer your question," he whispered, his breath caressing her ear. "I would never be with a woman I didn't love. That's not who I am."

She leaned back slightly so she could see his eyes and found herself believing him.

"Are you all right?" he asked.

"Absolutely."

"Orson is on his way over." The music came to an end. Brooks took a step back and bowed slightly. "Thank you for the dance." He released her hand.

Orson slid in front of Brielle, a wicked smile on his face. "I see you saved the best for last." He winked.

"I needed to warm up with your brothers so I could handle you," she teased.

He laughed. "I'm so glad my father chose you. You liven things up around here." The music started. "Shall we?" He held out his hand for her to take.

She slid her hand in his.

He yanked her closer. "Hold on." He took off, dancing across the dance floor, twirling her around as if he'd done this a hundred times.

Brielle couldn't help but laugh, all thoughts of Declan and his lover forgotten as she danced with Orson.

The music abruptly changed course and slowed.

Orson spun Brielle around, pulling her in toward him. "You good?" he asked.

"Yes, thank you."

"There's a man hovering behind me to my left." He reached up, clutching her chin to keep her focus on him. "Don't look now. Wait until we turn. Let me know if you recognize him." Moving to the music, Orson turned them.

She caught sight of someone ducking behind another person. "I didn't get a look at him."

"Be on guard," Orson mumbled. "I don't know who he is or what he's doing here, but I'm going to have one of my men tail him."

"I'm sure him being here has nothing to do with me."

"I have a feeling it has everything to do with you. And I'm rarely wrong. I'll come see you later tonight. If the mysterious man approaches you, I win, and you have to do something for me."

"Like what?"

"That's for me to know and you to find out." He laughed and twirled her around one last time as the music came to an end.

She wanted to hit his arm, but he managed to get away before she could even lift her hand. He disappeared in the throng of people. Smiling, she turned to head over to the refreshment table, needing a drink after that last dance.

A man took a step in front of her, blocking her path. She looked up into the eyes of a familiar face. "What are you doing here?" she asked.

Lukas smiled. "Your father sent me to keep an eye on you."

"I wasn't informed that a representative from Miervades would be here." It was good to see someone she knew.

"I'm not here on official business," he said. "I'm only here for you." He held out his hand.

"I'm on my way to get a drink." She pointed to the refreshment table. The king and queen stood nearby talking with a handful of people.

Lukas took her wrist, pulling her to the other side of the dance floor.

"What are you doing?" she hissed, trying not to make a scene.

"I want to dance with you," he replied. "There's more room over here." He turned and faced her.

Not knowing what else to do, she put her hands on his shoulders, and they began dancing. "When did you arrive?" she asked, trying to make small talk.

"A few hours ago."

"Did you come by land or sea?"

"The same way as you—by boat." His hands held firmly onto her back, caging her in.

"How long are you here for?" She realized this had to be

the man Orson was referring to earlier. Which meant she lost the bet.

"I'm not certain." His brows drew together, and he gazed down at her. "It should be me marrying you, not him."

"Imagine how different things would be if you'd asked me." She'd be home, safely in bed, not dancing at this royal party.

"I asked your father."

Her father had told her that Lukas asked to speak to him, not that he had spoken to him.

"He was supposed to be drawing up a contract." His grip on her tightened.

Brielle had no idea what to say. She knew Lukas had been interested in her, but as far as she knew, her father had signed the contract with the prince first. And, if she was being totally honest, marrying the prince was a smarter move for Miervades.

He nuzzled her neck, making her uncomfortable. She tried pushing him away, but he didn't budge.

"Do you know how to get out of the palace?" he whispered, his lips not visible to anyone who might be watching since he'd angled his face toward her neck.

His hot breath brushed her neck. "You're too close," she said. "I need some space."

"Answer the question."

"Yes. Now give me some room." She had no idea why Lukas was acting so strangely this evening.

"Do you know how to get to Oskar?" He stopped dancing

all together, holding her upper arms and staring at her as if the fate of the kingdom depended on it.

The intensity in his eyes scared her. "What's going on?" she asked.

"We don't have much time. Can you get from the palace to Oskar?"

"No." She didn't know her way around Sunder, let alone how to get to the trading island of Oskar.

"I need you to figure out how to get from here to Oskar. If something happens, you are to go there and wait for me. Do you understand?"

An uneasy feeling took over. "What could possibly happen?" There had to be something going on that she didn't know about.

"Did your father inform you about the terms of your engagement?"

Brielle nodded, suddenly bone cold. If her father didn't intend to pay the taxes he owed or send the required wheat, she needed to know since her life depended on it.

Lukas straightened and looked at something over her shoulder. She glanced back and saw Declan heading straight for her. When she turned toward Lukas, he released her and rushed away, weaving between the dancers until she could no longer see him.

"Is everything all right?" Declan asked.

"I...I don't know," she answered honestly. Her head swam with all Lukas had—and hadn't—said. The music, the smells of the various perfumes, and the people so close together, it became too much, and she needed a break from it all.

Declan slid his hand to the small of her back, guiding her from the dance floor. "It seemed like that man was upsetting you."

She nodded.

"Do you know him?"

"I..." She rubbed her forehead. If her father didn't have the money to pay the taxes, he never should have sent Brielle as the insurance. He could have come up with another option. One that didn't end with her head being chopped off.

"Would you like to dance?"

She realized she'd stopped at the edge of the dance floor. Looking into Declan's eyes, she thought she saw a hint of concern there although she couldn't be sure. "No. I've had enough dancing for one day."

"Me, too." He grabbed hold of her hand, leading her off the dance floor, straight past his parents who were talking to a high-ranking military man, and out of the ballroom.

The second they reached the hallway, Brielle sucked in the fresh air, thankful for the reprieve. As they made their way through the palace, she expected Declan to let go of her hand. However, he held on firmly. For some reason, she didn't mind.

He turned down an empty corridor, stopping before a tapestry. Lifting the fabric, he revealed a secret door. He pushed it open and ushered Brielle inside. "This way," he whispered.

Traversing along the narrow passageway, she felt as if she were a character from one of her books. She would have loved it here as a child, exploring the secrets of this palace. How many people had stepped foot in here through the years? How many even knew of its existence? A hundred questions about Declan's childhood came to mind, but she stifled them all, remaining quiet so they wouldn't be discovered.

After going up several flights of stairs, they exited into the main portion of the palace. After another turn, she recognized where they were.

Stopping at the door to her room, she opened it and stepped inside. All she wanted to do was climb into bed and not think about everything that had just happened with Lukas. When she turned to close the door, she found Declan hovering in the hallway.

"May I come in?" he asked. "I think it's time the two of us had a talk."

She regarded him, trying to discern his motives. There had been plenty of time for him to talk to her these past few days, so she didn't know why he'd waited until now. Unless it had to do with Lukas. Sighing, she opened the door wider and gestured for him to enter.

He meandered into her room, looking around.

She closed the door then came and stood awkwardly beside him. Since she didn't have a sofa in her room, there wasn't anywhere for them to sit that would be appropriate.

Declan strode over to the balcony's doorway, his back to her. "My father is leaving directly after the party tonight."

She had no idea if this was normal behavior for the king. "Where's he going?" she asked, not really caring but feeling it was the polite thing to say. She kicked off her shoes before walking around the perimeter of the room, lighting a couple of candles.

"That is a very good question." He slid his hands in his pockets, his back still to her. The cool ocean breeze cascaded into the room. The curtains flowed softly around him as he stood in the doorway leading to the balcony.

Exhaustion consumed her, so she said the first thought that came to mind. "I'm sorry you're stuck marrying me. I'm sure you'd much rather wed someone you at least know or are friends with." She reached up, pulling the pins out of her hair.

"I haven't considered who I might *want* to marry. It's never been an option. I always knew I'd have an arranged marriage."

She massaged her sore scalp. Every time she had her hair up like that, she got a raging headache. "Hold on a minute." The dress she had on scratched her skin, making her want to tear it off. Going into her dressing closet, she removed the dress, sliding on a red silky nightdress Jenice had set out for her. It covered all the necessary parts and she'd only lit half her candles, so Declan wouldn't be able to see too much.

She exited the closet. Declan still stood in the doorway to her balcony, so she went over to her bed, climbing on top of it. She sat, leaning against the pillows. "Oh bullocks." She moaned.

"What?" Declan said, turning around to face her.

"I forgot Orson is supposed to come and find me later tonight. I just want to go to sleep."

"Why is Orson coming to see you tonight?" He took a few steps toward her. Since she hadn't lit any candles on that side of the room, she couldn't see his face.

"It's about that guy at the party." She'd lost the bet since she knew who he was. Orson better not ask her to do anything ridiculous; but it was Orson, so she expected nothing less.

"The one you were dancing with?"

She nodded. "Orson saw him hovering around and asked if I knew him. I couldn't get a look at the time. He said he was putting one of his men on him."

"That explains his comment as he left." Declan ran his hands through his hair. "Do you know who he is?"

"I do." This was not the conversation she wanted to be having with Declan right now. She needed time to think over everything that had happened before she told him anything.

He folded his arms, waiting.

She didn't have to tell him anything. She could keep Lukas's identity a secret. There was no reason to tell him her suspicions that her father wasn't going to pay. But if she didn't start talking to and trusting Declan, he'd never reciprocate. Although, there may be no point. If the duke didn't pay, she was as good as dead. Which was why Lukas had shown up. If her father didn't come up with the money, then she'd have to sneak away with Lukas to avoid being executed. The king would be furious, and he'd strip the duke of his land and title. Fighting back would spark a war. Her father would be killed. Perhaps the only way to save her family along with herself was to try and get the king to change his mind. Brooks and Orson seemed to like her. It might be just enough to save her head. Literally. But would it be enough to save her father and sister?

"The man's name is Lukas," she said. "He is from Miervades."

Declan moved closer to the bed. "An old friend? Or lover?"

She wrapped her arms around her legs. "A friend. But he was going to propose. He'd talked to my father right before you arrived."

Declan nodded. "Did you know he'd be here?"

"No." Tears filled her eyes.

"Did you want to marry him?"

"No."

Declan sat on the edge of the bed; it dipped under his weight. He twisted to face her. "So, he showed up here claiming his undying love for you? Did he want to steal you away?"

She shook her head. "I don't know what he wants or why he's here exactly. I think I know, but I'm not certain. It's just a guess." She stretched her legs out, trying to figure out what to say that expressed her emotions. Sometimes she wished she could write her thoughts on paper because they sounded better in her head. The moment she spoke them, the words became jumbled and her ideas unclear.

"What is it?" Declan asked.

"You don't know me." She pulled her legs back up,

wrapping her arms around them again. "I want to be honest with you." She clutched her hands together, resting her chin on her knees. "I've never been involved with politics. My sister, Kenna, was aways the one to shadow my father. I never bothered. I never thought I'd be thrust into a position where I needed to navigate through the intricacies of court. I thought I'd lead a quiet life."

He unbuttoned his jacket, sliding it off. Then he undid the top two buttons of his shirt, pulling the material away from his neck. "I figured as much."

"I'm ill-prepared to be your wife. I don't know the first thing about being a princess or a queen. I'm going to mess it all up." She tilted her head back, staring at the ceiling. "If we even marry." Tears filled her eyes. She looked back at Declan. "I could be dead in a couple of weeks if my father doesn't pay and deliver the wheat."

He grunted and then leaned back on the bed. His chest rose and fell. "Are you afraid your father won't hold up his end of the deal?"

"Yes." Her voice sounded pathetic to her own ears. "I can't imagine why he wouldn't. But that's what I'm talking about. I don't know anything. I don't know if he has the money, if he's choosing to withhold it, or why he didn't pay in the first place."

He folded his hands atop his stomach, considering her. "Here's the thing. You can learn all of that. There are books and people here who can teach you what you need to know. You'll be fine."

"I like reading."

He chuckled. "I know."

"Do you?"

"Hmm?"

"Do you like to read? I know nothing about you."

"Not really. I don't have much time to read for fun." He tilted his head toward her. "Does that bother you? That I'm not a reader?"

"I haven't met many people who are."

"Brooks is. He's read more than anyone I know. He's probably better suited for you than me. He can offer you stimulating conversation and talk about books for hours."

"Then he'll make a good friend." Having similar interests didn't make people suited for marriage. At least she didn't think so. "Can I ask you a question?"

"You can ask."

"Who was the woman you were dancing with this evening?" Brooks had said her name was Sasha. She wanted to hear what Declan had to say about the situation.

"No one you need to concern yourself with." He focused on the ceiling again.

It felt as if the air had been sucked out of the room. She'd been so open and honest with him, and he had no intention of doing the same with her. She closed her eyes. She wouldn't make that mistake again.

"I...uh...told Sasha—that woman you asked about—that we can't see each other any more now that I'm engaged to be married."

She looked over at him, shocked that he'd opened up. "I'm sorry. I don't want to come between you and someone you care about." The last thing she wanted was for him to resent her.

"We're just friends. I don't love her. Besides, I don't believe in taking a mistress."

While Brielle liked that he wouldn't be sleeping with other women when they were married, it could simply be that he wanted his heirs to have the same mother and be legitimate. Not that he wanted to be true to her for love's sake. Especially since there was no love between them. They were having a hard enough time just trying to be friends.

He reached into his pocket and pulled something out. "Now that we're engaged," he opened his hand, revealing a thin gold ring with a single emerald stone—the royal family's color, "you should wear this until the wedding."

She took the ring and slid it on her finger.

Someone knocked on her door. Declan stood and went over to answer it. While he spoke to whoever was there, Brielle slid out of bed and walked over to the balcony, stepping out onto it. The sound of the waves crashing below soothed her.

"That was Orson," Declan said from right behind her, startling her. "I told him what you said about Lukas. He wants to talk to you about him tomorrow after breakfast."

She nodded.

"And he said something about winning a bet?"

She rolled her eyes.

"It seems both my brothers are quite taken with you," he whispered.

She froze, not knowing how close Declan stood behind

her, but she could almost feel the heat radiating from his body.

"Why is that?" he asked.

She closed her eyes, sucking in a deep breath. When she opened her eyes, she focused on the ocean. "I have no idea."

When he didn't say anything else, she turned to face him. He was standing right behind her.

Her eyes widened.

"I like your hair down better. It suits you." He reached out, as if to touch one of her curls, but thought better of it and dropped his hand to his side. "It's getting late. I should be going." He turned and left before she even thought of asking him to stay.

CHAPTER 11

MABEL

he man opened the door wider. "Come in," he said.

Mabel hesitated.

Matsen stepped around her, entering the house.

"I'm Jorrg," the man said. "There's no need to stand out in the middle of the street. Get on in here."

"Yes," Matsen called from inside. "Do come in." His voice held a hint of laughter to it.

Not knowing what else to do, Mabel entered. She found herself in a small sitting room, the walls brightly colored as seemed to be the style in Lima. There were two sofas and two chairs situated around a low table. One large open window let in a cool breeze. Matsen stood off to the side, his arms crossed.

Jorrg closed the door before coming to stand at Mabel's side. "I'm your mother's cousin. We played together when we were kids." He smiled. Jorrg looked to be in his late forties, and he had brown hair and brown eyes. "Have a seat."

Mabel sat on one of the chairs. For the first time, she was glad Matsen was with her. He remained standing, observing the room, as if he expected it to be lit on fire at any moment.

Jorrg sat on the other chair. "Since you're here, that must mean you know who you are."

Mabel leaned back in the chair, trying to decide how to proceed. Even though this man claimed to be her family, she didn't know him. She had no idea what his intentions were. "Why don't you tell me who you think I am?" she countered. From the corner of her eye, she saw Matsen's lips rise in a half smile.

Jorrg nodded. "Of course. Your mother, Willa, fell in love with Prince Rhett. He wasn't the king yet. It was during the time of the revolution. When Willa's father was arrested for being one of the leaders, the king sentenced him to execution. Willa never forgave the prince for not stepping in and saving him. He claimed he couldn't. She refused to have anything to do with him after that."

Mabel sat very still, listening. She hadn't expected to hear a story about her birth mother—a woman she couldn't even imagine. When she thought of her mother, she still pictured the woman who had raised her.

"The revolution was squashed. After that, the prince married some noble woman. On his honeymoon tour, he saw Willa. She was pregnant and due soon. He demanded to know if he was the father. She refused to say, so he had her arrested. Willa went on trial and still wouldn't reveal the father's identity. She didn't want the prince to have any claim on her child and was willing to die rather than give him her baby."

Mabel raised her eyebrows. "She was willing to die? Pregnant?" Mabel would have lied and claimed a different man as the father. Or she would have admitted the baby was Rhett's child and then run away after she delivered. There were options. Her mother didn't have to be so stubborn.

"The law is very specific. Pregnant women are not allowed to be executed."

"What's the difference between executing a woman carrying a child in her womb versus holding the baby in her arms?" In the end, they both died.

He shrugged. "We were just so happy when we heard you were alive."

"How did you learn of my existence?" Seeing as how she didn't even know who she was until a couple of weeks ago.

"When the woman who raised you learned your true identity, she went and told the king. He came to Miervades searching for you."

Shock rolled through her. "The king is looking for me?" She glanced over at Matsen whose face gave nothing away.

"You were born before the crown prince," Jorrg explained. "That makes you next in line for the throne."

Matsen had told her that the king didn't send the assassin after her, that it was someone else. Assuming that was true, she wanted to know why the king came to Miervades and what his intentions were toward her. She looked over at Matsen. "Who sent you to assassinate me?"

Jorrg tensed. "I don't believe you've introduced yourself," he said, his voice suddenly laced with a hard edge.

"I'm a friend," Matsen replied, his hands held up in a placating gesture. "As soon as I realized who Mabel is, I aborted my original mission."

Jorrg's eyes narrowed. "And your mission now?"

"To keep Mabel safe."

She noticed he hadn't given his name. "You haven't answered my question," she said. "Who sent you to kill me?"

"I'll answer you privately. Then if you wish to share with anyone else, you may."

Mabel stood.

"I have a room prepared for you upstairs," Jorrg said. "I'll show you the way." He led her up a narrow flight of stairs to a hallway with three doors. "You can stay in here." He opened the door on the left revealing a simply furnished bedchamber. "As the heir to the throne, I hope you plan on claiming your birthright."

She patted him on the shoulder. "I need time to process everything." Mabel entered the room and went over to the window. She glanced outside, seeing the cobbled street below. Out in the distance, the vibrant blue ocean.

The door clicked shut. "The queen sent me," Matsen revealed.

Mabel hadn't expected that. She pinched her eyes closed, thinking through it. When she opened her eyes, she turned to face the assassin. "Explain."

He rubbed the back of his neck as he came farther into the room. "I'm the queen's personal assassin."

A shiver ran down her spine. "And the queen wants me dead because I'm in line to the throne." She leaned against the window ledge.

"Mabel," he said, moving to stand before her. "You're not merely in line for the throne. You're the crown princess. You will be the queen when the king dies. You're first in line for the throne."

She had trouble wrapping her mind around it. Her entire life she'd lived in poverty. The only child to a lowly dungeon guard. The woman who'd raised her had taught her to read and write, she had no friends, and she'd spent a lot of her days either roaming the island barefoot or going to work with her father. And now here she was being told she was not only royalty, but next in line for the throne.

Dozens of questions sprang to mind, so she started with the simplest one. "What does it mean that you're the queen's assassin?"

"My family has been in service to the queen for generations. Hundreds of years ago, my forefather took a blood oath sealed in magic. He promised to be the queen's personal assassin, called upon whenever needed. In exchange, my family was given a title and land. Each generation, one young man from my family is chosen to uphold the oath. That duty is now mine."

His story fascinated her. "You mentioned a blood oath before." When he'd shown her he couldn't harm her. "Who sealed the oath in magic?" And was it something she could learn?

He shrugged. "I was told a witch, but I've never met one."

"I don't believe in magic." She'd never seen anything that hinted at magic existing until Matsen had tried slitting her wrist.

"Neither did I. Then my father died and the duty of being the assassin transferred to me."

Mabel took note that he hadn't revealed his last name, and she couldn't help but wonder who his family was. "How does the oath work?"

"I must assassinate who the queen wants. The magic compels me, and I have no choice but to follow the queen's order."

"But you can't harm me?" Also, apparently, because of another blood oath.

"That's the tricky part," he said, a sly smile spreading across his face. "She ordered your death. It's illegal for a member of the royal family to order the death of anyone in line to the throne."

"She has to know that." The queen wouldn't have made such a grave error.

He shrugged. "She should. But maybe since you haven't been acknowledged, she thought it didn't count. So instead of waiting for you to claim your birthright, thereby making it too late to eliminate you, she decided to do it before you had a chance to lay claim to the throne. Again, this is all speculation." He sat on the edge of the bed. "Regardless, since you are of royal blood, I can't kill you."

She noticed he said *kill* and not *harm*. She'd have to keep that in mind. "By being here with me, don't you feel guilty? I assume you hold some loyalty to her. Shouldn't you go to Sunder and tell her what happened?" Then again, she wondered if an assassin could ever be truly loyal.

"It's obvious you've never met the queen." He smiled ruefully. "She isn't the sort of person who has many loyal followers."

"Why are you helping me?" He didn't have to explain any of this to her. He could have gone home and enjoyed his time not having to do the queen's bidding.

He chuckled. "I have my reasons."

"I want to know what they are." She couldn't trust him unless she knew his motives. But pushing him could be dangerous. He had no reason to be honest with her. Maybe she should seduce him. Sex could be a powerful motivator and compel a man to do a woman's bidding. She looked at him through hooded eyes.

"There's one other thing you should know," he said, his voice slightly hoarse. "I'm forbidden from forming any sort of a romantic attachment to you—or anyone in the royal family for that matter."

That made sense. And definitely eliminated a complication. "Oh darn," she said. "I was hoping that in the middle of grieving for my dead father, who I learned isn't my real father, and trying to figure out if I should claim my royal birthright, that I would fall in love with the assassin originally sent to kill me."

"I was trying to put your mind at ease."

Her mind was a raging volcano. There was so much she needed to think through and process.

"I have a question for you," Matsen said. "Since Queen Briar sent an assassin after you, maybe you should send her a message, so she knows you're not one to push around?"

"What do you have in mind?" She assumed he wasn't being literal and was referring to something more creative.

"You are going to claim your birthright," Matsen said with a nod.

"Probably." There was no reason not to, but she needed to think through everything to make sure it was what she wanted. And having Matsen and Jorrg pushing her toward what they wanted only irritated her. She wanted to be the one in control.

"With the royal family, every move you make has to be strategic and thought out, like a chess or poker game. I think it's time for you to make your first move, for you to play your first card."

Mabel rolled her eyes. "While I appreciate the analogy, I don't particularly like the hand of cards I've been dealt. I need time to study and process."

He smiled. "As you wish. Just don't wait too long to decide. You need to act quickly before the queen has time to regroup and attack again."

Mabel considered him. The queen may very well know by now that Mabel hadn't been killed. Matsen was right; she needed to make a move. "Okay, let's send her a message."

Mabel tossed and turned. Images of someone trying to kill her assaulted her dreams, making them nightmares. She envisioned herself falling in love with a man, only to have that man kill her father. Then she pictured herself pregnant and her lover returning, married to another woman. Then everything shifted to her being locked in the dungeon, about to be executed.

She flew upright, breathing heavily. Her birth mother had dealt with so much. And now, the people who'd killed her wanted Mabel dead as well. All because they valued power. She slid out of bed and went over to the window. The cloudless sky had already started to lighten. She needed some fresh air to clear her head.

After putting on one of the dresses that had been provided for her, she went downstairs where she found Jorrg sitting at the table eating.

"There's plenty of fruit if you'd like some," he said, waving for her to take a seat across from him.

"Do you live here or in Miervades?" she asked, sitting on the chair.

"That's a tricky question." He winked.

"How so?" It was too early in the morning for cryptic answers.

"Your family is in charge of the mines in Miervades," he said, taking a bite of an apple. "They do some illegal trading with Lima. We maintain a house here to facilitate our business transactions."

So far, she knew two key things about her family. One, they were involved with the revolution twenty some years ago. And two, they were illegally trading with Lima. Given these two things, she had to assume her family did not support the king. From what little she knew about the royal family, she understood completely.

"What are we supposed to do now?" she asked, eating some grapes. While she had an idea of what she intended to do, she didn't want to say too much or give anything away. Even though this man claimed to be her family, she owed him nothing and felt nothing for him.

"The best course of action is for you to claim your birthright by writing a letter and sending it to the dukes of Valdis. Once you do that, you should go to the royal palace and officially meet with the king."

She took a sip of tea. It was bland and she didn't care for it. "What's the point of writing the letter? Why not just go to the palace and announce myself?"

"As soon as you deliver the letter to the dukes, it changes things. There are rules that must be followed. The royal family can't kill you then."

"Because it's illegal to kill a member of the royal family?"

"Yes. And the king is required to uphold the laws of the land."

"Doesn't the king make the laws?" she asked.

"The king's ancestors made the laws. He simply upholds them."

"What's to prevent him from changing them?"

"The laws can't be changed."

She found that hard to believe and wondered if the blood oath Matsen had mentioned was more extensive then he'd let on. "So, I write these letters and then go to Valdis?" As far as plans went, it felt weak. Her only focus so far had been on staying alive. Now she realized she needed to think about the future and what she wanted to do with her life.

"Yes, that's the plan."

Mabel rubbed her eyes. The walls felt as if they were closing in on her, and she needed fresh air. "I'm going to take a walk down to the ocean." She stood. "I'll be back in a few hours."

"Would you like me to accompany you?"

"No, I need some time to think." She headed to the door. "Oh," she turned to face Jorrg again, "I assume Matsen left this morning?"

"He was gone before I woke." He lifted his eyebrows, as if waiting for her to explain where the assassin had gone.

Without answering, she turned and exited the house. She didn't need to share with Jorrg what Matsen was doing.

She went down the street, heading straight for the ocean. Back home on Karlis, the island was fairly flat, devoid of these ridiculously steep hills. Her house was only about a half mile from the ocean, affording her a quick walk to the beach. Here, while beautiful and exotic, it was too much. The amount of people everywhere she went, the bright sights, and the loud sounds overwhelmed her. She missed her quiet island.

Last night, she'd decided to claim her birthright. Not necessarily because she wanted to, but because she hated the king for all that he'd done to her family. He'd ordered her mother's execution, and the queen had tried to kill her. They both deserved to be punished for what they'd done. They couldn't be allowed to hurt other people like they'd hurt Mabel. If she stayed here in Lima and didn't claim her birthright, the royal family would continue to ruin lives. She had to set them straight.

"Mabel Bakken?" someone said from behind her.

She glanced over her shoulder and saw an older man. "What can I help you with?' She instantly felt on edge, and she didn't know why.

"My name is Rulf. I'd like you to come with me. There are some people who'd like to speak with you."

For the first time since meeting Matsen, she wished he were at her side. "I'm busy." She turned to walk away, wondering how he knew her name.

"I work for the Lima government," he said from behind her. "Those in charge think they can help you."

Mabel stopped. Nobody ever helped anyone else without gaining something from it. She may be from a small island, but she knew enough about human nature to understand most people desired power and money. If he claimed the Lima government could help her, it meant they wanted to use her for their own benefit. Fury filled her. She was sick and tired of everyone around her telling her what to do. For once, she wanted to be the one in charge of her own life.

She turned to face Rulf. "You must have the wrong person."

Footsteps sounded behind her. She glanced over her shoulder and saw another man standing behind her. These two men had her boxed in. Rage simmered below the surface.

"I think we have the right person."

The fact that they knew her name and what she looked like concerned her. Considering her options, she realized she didn't have many. As Matsen would say, it was time to play another card from her hand. She forced a smile on her face. "In that case, I would love to meet them."

Rulf's shoulders relaxed. "This way." He headed to the east, toward the heart of the city.

Mabel followed him, not bothering to make idle chit-chat. The other man walked behind her, keeping a respectable distance. As she followed Rulf, she took note of the buildings she passed in case she needed to make a run for it. Not only did she have a good sense of direction, but she noted places to hide if the need arose. They passed the market she'd visited yesterday. Finally, the man stopped before a tall building. Mabel craned her neck back, counting six levels. So far, she'd only seen two to three story buildings. This one had been painted bright white with turquoise shutters on each of the windows. The large door—twice as tall as Mabel and at least four times as wide—had also been painted turquoise.

"In here." Rulf held open the door for her.

In Karlis, the dungeon was underground making it dark, damp, and confining. Since this building was above ground, and she could see several ways to exit it, her panic remained at bay as she stepped inside. Cool air greeted her. The man who'd been following her remained outside.

Rulf led her down a long, sterile hallway and to a closed door at the very end. "Please wait here." He went inside, leaving her alone, which she considered a good sign and indicated they considered her more of a guest than a prisoner.

Folding her hands together behind her back, Mabel observed her surroundings, more out of habit than anything else. The man who'd raised her always told her to have an exit strategy in case something went wrong. She counted ten doors on either side of the hallway and didn't see anyone else around. The door she'd entered through was to her left, at the other end of the hallway. Given the number of windows she'd seen from the outside, any of these doors probably led to a room with at least one window. Since she was on the ground level, she could easily exit through a window.

The fact that this building was taller than the others indicated it had some sort of importance. Since Rulf said the Lima government wanted to meet her, she assumed this housed the leaders of the city. It did seem to be a bit extravagant for people who enforced the law and collected taxes. However, since she hadn't been anywhere besides Karlis, she really couldn't compare since she'd seen so little of the world.

Rulf opened the door. "They're ready for you." He motioned for her to enter.

Mabel stepped into a large, rectangular room with approximately fifty chairs arranged in a semi-circle. At the front of the room, there was a table with five people—three men and two women.

Mabel walked down the center aisle, between the chairs, noting that a person occupied every single chair. Scanning the faces of those present, she counted only six were women. She stopped three feet before the front table, looking at the five people seated there, making eye contact with each one.

She'd been taught a thing or two about interrogation tactics. Even though she didn't know what these people wanted with her, she thought it best to be prepared for anything and not appear weak.

"Mabel Bakken?" the woman in the center asked.

"And you are?" Mabel countered.

"Cecel Herke," the woman answered. "Thank you for coming."

Mabel gave a curt nod.

Cecel must have assumed that was answer enough because she continued addressing Mabel. "I am the chief of our governing board." She motioned to the people all around Mabel. "Together, we make the laws for Lima. Each person here has been selected by their city to represent their city."

Mabel had never heard of such a thing. "You have no king or queen?"

The woman smiled. "In theory, we have a royal family, but they are merely a decoration and have no power or authority in Lima." Cecel folded her hands on the table, watching Mabel. "We understand Valdis is ruled by a king. He makes the decisions without input from his people."

"Yes," Mabel said, noticing the hint of malice in Cecel's

voice. "Why am I here?" While she had questions about this governing board and how it ran the kingdom, she couldn't get sucked in and sidetracked. She needed to appear unmoved. These people had brought her here for a reason, told her about the way they govern for a reason, and they clearly wanted something from her. She needed to keep her guard up.

Cecel took a deep breath, releasing it slowly. Lifting her chin, she said, "We have been buying coal and wheat from Miervades for decades. We've always worked directly with Duke Jaxon Tranum. However, he wrote and explained that he is no longer able to provide the amounts we need because King Rhett Forberg is demanding the duke give it all to him. Miervades relied on trading with us as a substantial part of their income. Without a trade agreement, they will become poorer. However, Duke Jaxon has no say and must abide by his king."

An uncomfortable silence followed. Cecel must have expected Mabel to say something, but she refused to respond. She didn't know if Cecel wanted her to side with Miervades since that was where her birth mother had been from. Perhaps Cecel was simply appealing to Mabel's sympathetic side. Too bad she didn't have one.

"Coal and wheat are vital to our economy," Cecel explained. "Here in Lima, we don't have large fields for growing wheat. It rains far too much and our northern regions are very mountainous and cold. Our people rely on the coal to heat their homes."

"I'm sorry," Mabel said, yawning, "why am I here?" Lima

meant nothing to her. She didn't have time to stand there listening to all of this.

"I'm going to get to the point," Cecel said. "It is our understanding that you are the true heir to the Valdis throne?"

They were on dangerous ground. She hadn't even declared herself to Valdis yet.

"Where did you hear that information?" Mabel would not admit anything to these people. This wasn't her kingdom, and these people were not her friends. She didn't even know where Valdis stood in all of this. As of now, she had no friends and would proceed accordingly. The only person who mattered to her was her—and she would put herself first in every decision she made.

"Let me counter that by asking why are you in Lima?" Cecel said.

Mabel chose not to answer.

"Are you aware that King Rhett threatened your great grandfather, Liam?"

"Recently?" Mabel asked, wanting clarification that they were discussing something that had just happened or if she was referring to the revolution which took place decades ago.

"Yes. The king went to Liam demanding that if you showed up, he would turn you over to him. Liam asked Duke Jaxon for his help. The duke came to us wishing to keep you safe from the king. That is why he sent you here."

Mabel thought her family had sent her here, not the duke. Jorrg should have told her. She'd assumed her family was separate from the duke, not intimately connected. It left a sour taste in her mouth. "What agreement was made?" For surely Lima had been given something in exchange for assisting the duke.

"We wish to support you by whatever means necessary as you claim your birthright and make a bid for the throne."

The words rang in the air, sending a chill through Mabel. "In exchange for?"

Cecel folded her arms, leaning back in her chair, studying Mabel. "Very well," she mumbled. Then, louder, "We wish for Miervades to be free to trade of its own accord, not governed by Valdis's strict laws."

"I'm not sure I can help you." Mabel was certain Cecel wasn't telling her everything.

"Do you know anything about the revolution which took place twenty-two years ago?" Cecel asked.

Mabel shook her head. What she knew was rather limited, and she wanted to hear what Cecel had to say about it.

"The revolution happened because Miervades wanted to secede Valdis. Unfortunately, Valdis squashed the revolution, and Miervades is still part of the kingdom. They pay heavy taxes and cannot trade with other kingdoms."

Mabel had to force her face to remain blank, free from all expression. This all sounded rather suspicious to her, and she wanted to know what Lima had to gain from it.

When Mabel didn't respond, Cecel continued, "We believe that if Miervades can trade freely of their own accord, then they'll be able to trade their goods for full market value. As it stands now, they sell it to the king who in turn sells it to other kingdoms. The one earning a profit is the king, not Miervades." Cecel motioned to the man sitting at her right. "I've had a contract drawn up stating amounts of wheat and coal to be shipped to us along with how much we will pay. The duke signed it. All you have to do is change the law and allow Miervades to trade of their own accord."

Mabel did not appreciate the duke already assuming she'd be on his side, working with him simply because her birth mother came from Miervades. It was not only presumptuous of him, but bold and premature. She hadn't even joined the Valdis royal family and already people were using her. Instead of letting that upset or intimidate her, she needed to remember that it worked both ways. "If I declare myself and claim my birthright," she made sure to emphasize the word *if*, "I will only be the crown princess, in line to rule. I will not be the queen until the current king passes." She refused to call King Rhett her father. He was not her father in any way. "I don't see how I can help you. I won't have the power to make or change laws."

A smile slid over Cecel's face. "We have a plan to put you on the throne sooner rather than later. In fact, our plan is already underway. Now, do we have a deal?"

CHAPTER 12

DECLAN

Declan entered his office and took a seat at his desk. His father had only been gone for a few days, and Declan's workload had more than doubled. At least the time went by quickly without the king around. However, he did need to find some time to set aside for Brielle.

He thought back to the conversation they'd had in her room a couple of nights ago. It still surprised him that she'd revealed as much as she had. It wasn't a lot, but the little tidbits she gave had shown him a willingness on her part to trust him if he earned it. As if she'd held a tiny seed in her hand. She hadn't yet given it to him, but at least it was there. Now all he had to do was get her to share a little more, trust a bit, and they'd have the start to a friendship. Which was enough for him.

He tapped his hand on the desk, contemplating. Unless the duke chose not to pay the taxes owed and produce the wheat he needed to. If that happened, Brielle had no future. That bothered Declan more than it should. Someone so young and innocent didn't deserve to die for her father's crimes. Again, the law in this case was wrong. He was certain of it. But if it wasn't enforced, the consequences would be catastrophic for the royal family.

The image of her in that red nightdress with her wild hair flowing around her shoulders was seared into his mind. Had she known red was his favorite color? He rubbed his eyes, needing to focus.

The men he had watching Brielle reported that during the past week, she'd barely left her room. When she did, she went to the library. Declan didn't think she'd been out of the palace since she'd arrived here. Perhaps he should venture out with her. Not only would it be good for the people of Valdis to see them together, but it would give him that time he wanted to get to know her.

At least nobody had spotted Lukas lurking around the palace again. If Lukas thought he could whisk Brielle away, he was sorely mistaken.

A soft knock sounded on the door, and Brooks and Orson entered.

"Better make this quick," Orson said. "Otherwise, Grandfather will wonder where I've run off to." He plopped on the sofa under the window, kicking his legs up on the arm. "I have to lead two drills before supper." He sighed louder than necessary. "I swear I wish that man would just retire and let me do things the way I want."

"Are you done complaining?" Brooks asked as he

lumbered into the room, his cane thumping lightly against the stone floor. He took a seat on the chair in front of the desk, opposite Declan.

"Thank you both for coming," Declan said, keeping his voice low. He'd ordered his valet, Graham, to make sure the hallway remained empty during this meeting so no one could eavesdrop. However, it was best to be overly cautious. "Do either of you have the information I requested?" Since asking them to do some research a few days ago, neither had mentioned finding anything, and he was starting to worry.

Orson rubbed his face. "Yeah," he mumbled. "I found some stuff in the military archives."

Declan started tapping his finger on his desk. He'd suspected there might be something there even though he'd hoped there wouldn't be. "And?" He was almost afraid to ask.

"I'm guessing you already know. It certainly explains why everyone has been so bloody crazy around here lately."

"What am I missing?" Brooks asked.

Orson sighed. "There was an uprising in Miervades twenty-two years ago. Grandfather, the king, sent Father to deal with the rebellion. He managed to put a stop to it with military forces. The leaders were executed, and the citizens punished. End of rebellion." Orson sat up, folding his hands and resting his arms on his legs. "Here's where it gets interesting. The leader was a coal miner's son, Poe. Father had him executed for treason, obviously. But that's not the curious part. Poe had a daughter around Father's age. Her name was Willa, and she was also arrested and taken to Karlis."

"Was she executed as well?" Brooks asked.

Orson raised his eyebrows. "She was. But not for a couple of weeks."

Brooks pinched the bridge of his nose. "Was she with child?"

"Yes. And once the child was born, the child was executed," Orson revealed.

"There would only be one reason to kill a baby," Brooks said, looking at Declan.

Declan nodded. "Father confirmed it. He had a relationship with Willa before he married. When he saw Willa pregnant, he asked who the father was. She refused to answer. That is the reason she was executed."

"And the child was killed to prevent any question about the royal line," Brooks said, nodding.

Orson stood. "But that doesn't explain why Father, Mother, and Grandfather have been acting strange lately, does it? The archives state the child was killed, but everyone is behaving otherwise." He started pacing.

Declan knew his brothers would be able to figure it out. "Father believes the baby was switched at birth. There's a woman here in the palace who claims her husband was the one to do it."

"We have a sibling we don't know about?" Brooks said, disbelief coloring his voice.

"A sister. Mabel. Father is out looking for her as we speak." Declan leaned back in his chair.

"What does this mean for you?" Orson asked.

"I have no idea."

"I'm not sure how I feel about having a sister," Orson said. "One woman in this family is more than enough." He shrugged. "Though I suppose once you marry, there'll be another. Brielle, I don't mind. Anyway, do you need anything else?"

"Not right now," Declan answered.

"If you need me, you know where to find me." Orson gave a curt nod and left.

"What about you?" Declan asked. "Did you find the information I requested?"

"I'm still trying to process the Mabel situation," Brooks muttered as he set his cane aside and stretched out his leg. "But yes, I did find what you asked for. I had to review Father's accounting books and do a little research to be sure."

"And?"

"It's as you feared. Miervades doesn't have enough money to pay their taxes. They do have the wheat though. In order to try and come up with the money they owe, they've been illegally selling wheat and coal to Lima."

Declan drummed his fingers on his desk, thinking. "Why don't they have the money?" When he'd visited Duke Jaxon, he hadn't seen any signs of opulence. In fact, he found the town and the duke's home rather plain. The other dukes in Valdis had homes befitting of their stations. At the time, he'd wondered why Jaxon lived so simply. It had never occurred to him the duke might be having financial difficulties.

However, he couldn't imagine why the duke would be in trouble since Miervades was rich in resources.

"The issue is that their taxes increase by ten percent each year. They've been struggling for quite some time to pay. Which is why they started illegally trading—to try and make more money. Unfortunately, it finally caught up to them."

"Brielle mentioned she was afraid her father couldn't pay." Declan rubbed the back of his neck.

"She'll be executed, and her father stripped of his title," Brooks stated.

"If the duke sends the required wheat, I wonder if it'll buy him some more time to pay his taxes?"

Brooks shook his head. "Father is already on dangerous grounds bending the law as much as he can. The only reason it even worked is because he took Brielle as insurance. Without her, the deadline couldn't have been extended."

"Why such a steep increase in taxes every year?" The other dukes' taxes remained steady.

"Because Miervades has the mines. They should be rich with coal and diamonds. When the laws were originally established, the other dukes were jealous Miervades had so many natural resources. Their island is truly richer than the rest of Valdis. The law was written that way to try and be fair."

"If that's the case, then why aren't they rich?"

"Through the years, they started mining less coal, less diamonds, and thus making less money. That, coupled with their taxes steadily increasing, was a disaster just waiting to happen."

And the law was the law; it couldn't be changed. Contracts and things of that nature could be amended. But the laws written in the book of statutes couldn't be altered.

"We've danced around the subject, you and I, but we've never broached it," Brooks said, his voice barely a whisper. "Do you know about the blood oath?"

Declan could scarcely believe his ears—no one was supposed to know about the blood oath but the one sitting on the throne or the one who'd inherit it. "I do." His father had told him about it when he turned twenty-one. He had no idea how Brooks had come to hear about it. "Since you brought it up, I assume you know about it as well?"

Brooks looked outside, his eyes going to a distant memory. He nodded. "Gareth and I stumbled upon it. Gareth didn't believe in magic, so he put it to a test. The result of us messing with something we didn't understand ended in his death and me injured." Brooks looked back to Declan, a sadness filling his face.

Shock rolled through Declan so fiercely he almost fell over. He'd always been told that Brooks's twin brother, Gareth, had died from an illness, and that same illness had caused Brooks's leg to be deformed. "How?" How had they learned about the blood oath and how did they test it out?

"I can't go into specifics. Father forbade me from telling anyone. But I knew what Gareth was doing and didn't stop him. That is why I was injured."

Declan's shock was replaced with another emotion— anger. These laws that couldn't be broken or changed were too rigid, too unforgiving, and didn't allow for unforeseen circumstances. Sometimes there were perfectly good, reasonable explanations for someone breaking a law. The punishment needed to be adjusted depending on the intent. But there was no human understanding behind these laws. If the king chose not to enforce the law, the king would die. Declan's younger brother, Gareth, had died as a child because of the blood oath. And Declan had had enough.

"I know what you're thinking," Brooks said. "I've been looking for a way to end the blood oath for years. It's one of the reasons I am always in the library researching."

"And you haven't discovered anything?" If the books didn't have the information, someone, somewhere had to know about how the blood oath was created and how it could be ended.

"I've managed to piece together a few things." He reached over and grabbed his cane, preparing to stand. "But not enough to do anything yet." He rose to his feet. "I'm still trying to process the fact that we have a half-sister."

Declan still hadn't come to terms with it.

"Did the woman who told you about Mabel give you any information about her?" Brooks asked.

"No." Declan hadn't thought much about the woman, Sanda, until now. Perhaps he should pay her a visit. Ask her some questions about Mabel to try and learn the type of person his sister was.

"Do you know if Mabel plans to claim her right as the heir to the throne?"

"I have no idea." He rubbed his face.

"If she does, how does that make you feel?"

Declan sighed. "Scared, relieved, mad." He shrugged. At least he was being honest.

Brooks chuckled. "You do realize that if Mabel claims her birthright, Mother will have a fit."

"I don't know if she can claim her birthright since she's legally dead." He hesitated before continuing. "And I'm certain Mother sent her assassin after Mabel. We think he failed though. A woman was found dead in Mabel's assigned cell and another woman went missing."

Brooks laughed. "So, Mabel swapped places with someone else once again. At least she seems smart. A survivor."

"Or someone is helping her." Perhaps a friend or lover. Someone she'd grown up with on the island.

"Regardless, this won't end well," Brooks muttered. "Mother won't tolerate it."

"True." The queen would never allow her husband's bastard child to sit on the throne before one of her own children.

"Do you need me to research anything else for you?" Brooks asked on his way to the door.

"No." Declan wanted to figure out how to handle Mabel, end the blood oath, and help Brielle. "We're going to have to execute her," he whispered. The mere thought made him sick to his stomach though he couldn't explain why.

"Are you referring to Brielle?"

"Yes."

Brooks paused at the door, his free hand on the handle, his back to Declan. "Do you care?"

"I don't know." She shouldn't die over a stupid law. However, he'd executed people before for similar offenses.

"Do you *want* to marry her?"

Declan said the first thing that came to mind. "I have to marry somebody." And he'd never given much thought to who he'd marry. Now that he'd met Brielle, he was warming up to the idea. And there was something about her that intrigued him. While she seemed quiet, shy, and reserved, she was also interesting and there was more to her than she let on. She easily cleaned up to look the part of the future queen even though he somehow preferred when she wore a plain dress and let her hair down all wild and curly around her face.

"If you don't want to marry her, then do nothing. The law is the law, and the situation will take care of itself. However, if you care for her and you want to marry her, there could be a way."

Declan laced his hands behind his neck, considering his brother. Even though Brooks had to use a cane to walk, he was just as dangerous as Orson, if not more so. The real threat in the royal family was not the future general of the Valdis army who could wield a sword better than most men in the kingdom, but with Brooks who spent his days in the library. Brooks was intelligent, cunning, and the mastermind behind all their plans. If anyone could save Brielle, it was going to be Brooks.

Declan went to the library in search of Brielle. When he didn't find her there, he headed to her room. A pang of nervousness swept through him as he knocked on the door. It had to be the fact that he knew her father wouldn't pay the taxes he owed thus forfeiting her life. There was no other logical explanation for this odd feeling inside of him.

"Come in," Brielle called out.

He stepped into her room and spotted her curled up on a chair, reading a book. "It has come to my attention that you've been spending most of your time in the palace, reading," Declan said by way of greeting.

Brielle glanced up from her book, not even bothering to stand. "Is there something you need me to be doing?" she asked, her brows pulled together in confusion.

"Don't you want to go outside and explore the grounds?"

She shrugged and went back to reading. "This is all I ever did back home."

He had the urge to tear that book from her hands and fling it out the window. Life was passing her by, but she didn't even realize it because she was so focused on her made-up stories, living in her fantasy worlds. "I thought perhaps we could spend the afternoon together." His hands became sweaty, and he had to wipe them on his pants.

"Doing what?" she asked, still focused on her book.

"I'd like to take you on a tour of the city." He clasped his hands behind his back. There were countless women who'd love to spend the day with him; meanwhile, Brielle wouldn't even look at him.

Thunder boomed outside.

Brielle glanced out the window. "You want to take me on a tour of the city? It's going to rain."

When Declan had first thought of the plan, it seemed like a good idea. That had been before the dark clouds rolled in, covering the sun, and casting gray shadows over the land. "If we leave now, we can see some of it before it starts raining." He hoped.

"I'm good here." She turned the page.

Unable to help himself, he walked right up to her and plucked the book from her hands.

"Don't lose my place!" She reached for the book, eyes wide.

He spotted a bookmark on the side table and grabbed it, sliding it into the book before closing it with a satisfying thump.

"What did you do that for?" She stood and tried reaching for her book again.

He raised it, just out of her reach. "We are going on a tour of the city. You'll get your book back when we return." He headed for the door, hoping she followed.

"Fine." She hurried after him. "You could have just asked."

He thought he had. She seemed to be in a foul mood today. Out in the hallway, he said, "Did I do something to upset you?"

"No." Her focus remained straight ahead. "Are you aware that your brothers check in on me daily?"

Surprise rolled through him. "No." Neither one of his brothers had mentioned it. "Do you not want them to?" If they were bothering her, he would ask them to leave her alone.

"No, that's not it." They descended a staircase. "It's just that I'm not engaged to either of them."

Realization dawned on him, and he chuckled. "Are you mad that they pay more attention to you than I do?"

"I'm not sure." They exited the palace. "I know you're busy." She folded her arms.

His brothers were busy, too.

Brielle sighed and said, "But it would be nice for us to get to know one another. The only reason I can think of for you to be avoiding me is if you know my father won't pay his taxes and you don't want to waste your time with someone who's going to die soon." Tears filled her eyes.

He grabbed her arm, pulling her to a stop. "I'm here now, wanting to spend time with you." The part about her dying he didn't respond to. He was still considering what Brooks had suggested.

"Oh," she whispered, her cheeks becoming red as she stared up into his eyes.

Declan suddenly realized they were too close, so he let go of her arm and took a step back, putting a respectable distance between them.

Brielle chewed on her lower lip, focusing on her feet.

He hoped he hadn't made her uncomfortable. Just then, the carriage pulled around to the front of the palace, stopping beside them. He'd much prefer riding. However, he wasn't sure if Brielle rode and since it looked like it could begin raining at any moment, the carriage seemed the best option.

He opened the door and held out his hand for her.

"Is this for us?" she asked, waving to the carriage.

"I thought it would be the best way to see the city." His hand remained outstretched.

She hesitated a moment and then slid her hand into his. He gripped it tightly as he helped her step into the carriage. When he let go, he glanced at his hand, surprised it felt warm from the brief contact. He climbed in after her. She'd scooted to the other side, her shoulder touching the window. Trying not to take offense, he sat on the bench beside her, making sure to keep a comfortable space between them. But they were in a carriage, and there was only so much room.

Declan knocked on the roof, and the carriage pulled away from the palace, heading toward the city.

Glancing at Brielle sidelong, he wondered why she'd chosen to wear that ugly dark green dress. It did nothing to improve her coloring and appeared too frumpy for her figure. Quite honestly, it looked like something a commoner would wear. Which meant she had to have brought it with her from home. There was no way that dress would be considered fashionable anywhere, even in Miervades. He'd tasked Jenice with seeing to Brielle's wardrobe. He'd have to ask her to get rid of Brielle's old clothes entirely, so she'd be forced to wear her new dresses. Maybe Jenice could even have a conversation with her about appropriate attire for her to wear here in Sunder. If he said anything to Brielle, she'd take it badly.

"Are we still going to tour the city?" she asked, her focus outside the carriage, seemingly watching the buildings they passed by.

"We can drive around the city and I can point out various things of importance, or we can go to Oskar." The island always provided entertainment since it was crowded with traders from nearby kingdoms and full of unique goods for purchase. It offered a lot more variety than Sunder's stores which tended to cater to the upper class. Perhaps the vibrant trading island might appeal to Brielle.

"I'd like to see Oskar."

Declan knocked three times on the roof so the driver would know where to take them. Now he could relax since they wouldn't be parading around the city. He didn't have to worry about how he looked or carried himself. Plus, the journey to the island would give them more time alone to talk. If he could figure out what to say to this woman.

"The book you were reading earlier, is it any good?" he asked.

"Why do you ask?" She finally looked at him.

"I'm trying to get to know you." Forget it. He'd enjoy the ride in peace. He turned his attention outside the carriage, not really watching anything in particular since frustration filled him.

"My family always teases me for reading. I assumed you were doing the same."

That surprised him. For some reason, he assumed her family had nurtured the habit.

"I'm about half-way through a romance book. So far, it's pretty good."

It seemed like most of the books she read were simply for fun and not to further her education. He'd hoped she would have taken more of an interest in Valdis and read something about the people, culture, or history.

"Is that it?" she asked, pulling him from his thoughts. She pointed to the islands in the distance.

"Yes." He loved Oskar and to reach it, one had to travel across a half dozen smaller islands connected by bridges. He didn't get to go there often but when he did, he always felt at home. "We'll have to go on foot. The carriage can't cross."

"That doesn't make any sense," she muttered, her brows pulling together. "How do you transport goods? By foot?"

"Let me clarify. We can't take the royal carriage there. It'll attract too much attention."

"Oh." She folded her hands in her lap, twirling her thumbs.

"Are you okay?" he asked.

She shrugged. "There's so much I don't know."

Which brought him back to his earlier thought about her reading up on Valdis instead of her romance novels.

"Brooks recommended a few books, but I've been struggling to understand some of the things without having seen them. Like Oskar. Now that I have a visual, it makes sense."

Surprise filled him. She was doing as he wished, but not

because of him. Which was his own fault since he'd barely spoken to her. Another emotion he couldn't pinpoint took root.

"Thankfully Brooks had been in the library my first day here," she continued. "When I first met him, I had no idea who he was. It worked out in my favor though since we started talking and became friends. If I'd known he was a prince, I never would have spoken to him or had the courage to ask him for book recommendations."

Again, she said something he didn't expect. She was reading up on Sunder of her own volition.

The carriage rolled to a stop. The driver opened the door, and the two of them climbed out.

"It's quite humid here," Brielle mumbled, pushing her curly hair away from her face.

The couple of times he'd seen her hair down, it had been wavy and wild. Today, the waves had turned to tight curls.

"The material of your dress doesn't help," he commented. The clothing she'd brought here was made from heavier fabrics instead of the thinner, cooler ones most people in Sunder wore. Yet another reason she should wear what Jenice supplied her with instead of what she'd brought.

"Your Highness, will you be needing any assistance?" the driver asked.

"No," Declan responded. He felt for his knife, making sure he had it on him. "The two of us will travel alone from here." He removed his jacket, tossing it in the carriage before unbuttoning the top two buttons of his shirt, trying to appear more casual. Brielle already looked like a commoner, so she didn't need to do anything. Satisfied, he led the way to the first bridge.

The sky seemed even darker than before. Thunder rumbled. With the storm approaching, nobody from court would be out here today.

At the entrance to the first bridge, a handful of soldiers stood guard, helping to direct traffic. Since Declan and Brielle were heading out toward Oskar, they didn't have to show anything proving citizenship. Those wanting to step foot off that bridge into Valdis had to have papers.

Declan kept to the right, Brielle at his side as they quickly fell in line with the people walking. Since the weather promised rain, there wasn't nearly the amount of people there usually were. Normally, they'd be shoulder to shoulder. Today, however, there was a comfortable gap between each person.

At the first gate, Brielle reached out, grabbing onto his shirt. He didn't say anything, not wanting to bring attention to the two of them. The soldiers let them pass, simply making sure they entered the bridge in orderly lines because the bridges could only handle so much weight.

On the first bridge, Brielle remained at his side, clutching his shirt as she walked. A violent gust of wind caused the bridge to sway. Brielle let out a little squeal and her grip tightened. Declan placed his hand on her back, trying to let her know there was nothing to worry about. They exited the bridge, stepping onto the first island which consisted mostly of rocky terrain void of trees and vegetation. The military kept it that way to easily observe it from afar.

"I didn't expect there to be so many people," Brielle mumbled.

"This is nothing." He reached down, taking her hand, not wanting them to get separated.

She squeezed his fingers, holding on as if her life depended on it. They continued moving forward, remaining in a long line of people. Declan glanced at the faces of those heading the other way toward Valdis. Many were loaded with supplies on their backs. No one bothered to look his way since most people kept their heads down, trying to make it to the mainland before the storm hit.

Declan and Brielle neared the gate for the second bridge just as a bolt of lightning shot across the sky.

CHAPTER 13

BRIELLE

B rielle shivered, an eerie sensation filling her from the impending storm.

Everyone continued to shuffle forward. She held onto Declan's hand, not wanting to lose him in the throng of people. They were shoulder to shoulder, in two lines, passing under another gate. When she stepped onto the second bridge, she felt it sway from the wind, and she feared it would collapse into the ocean. Glancing over the railing, she saw the turbulent water below along with several sharp rocks, and her eyes widened. Anything made of wood would be smashed to pieces in a matter of minutes.

Declan squeezed her hand in reassurance. "The currents right around here are so rough that boats can't make it to shore. That's why we have the bridges. They've been here for years. You have nothing to worry about."

She absently nodded, preferring a swaying bridge over a ship any day.

They reached the second island. The people remained in lines, walking straight for the third bridge. Like the last island, this one also contained mostly rocks, making it ugly and inhospitable. Since Valdis was so plush and green, it surprised her how barren these islands were.

The third bridge felt wider and studier. Brielle crossed it with ease, letting go of Declan's hand. When they stepped onto the third island, she noticed a marked difference. Instead of the rocky terrain, there was grass with a few exotic trees. The two of them remained in line, heading toward the fourth bridge. At the entrance, there were guards on each side, monitoring everyone crossing.

They passed through the gate and then climbed a set of stairs before reaching the bridge.

"Why is this one suspended so high in the air?" she asked, feeling it sway more than the previous ones.

"It allows ships to pass beneath if needed."

She peered over the side, noticing the water wasn't nearly as rough here. "They won't crash into rocks below the surface?"

"No. It's clear here."

They stepped onto the fourth island. It was much like the last one and contained mostly grass and a few random trees. The last two bridges and islands were the same without any noticeable differences.

"I'm glad we didn't have to sail to Oskar," she commented, more to herself than to Declan as she crossed the seventh and final bridge.

"We could have taken a boat," Declan said. "But that

would have required a proficient captain who is familiar with these waters to navigate through them. I prefer to walk, as do most from Valdis."

It suddenly dawned on her that people from other kingdoms traveled to Oskar to sell and buy goods since the island served as the largest trading hub in the world. Strange that she hadn't given it much thought before now. There was so much for her to learn. While she'd shied away from politics thinking the subject rather boring, she now realized some of the knowledge was just general information about her own kingdom which she should know. Whether she was a princess or not, she was a citizen and needed to learn more about Valdis.

They descended the steps of the last bridge and stepped foot onto Oskar. The island looked nothing like the previous six. The other ones had been small, plain, and simple. Oskar was so massive she couldn't see where it ended. People were everywhere meandering along the streets lined with single-story buildings. Shock rolled through her. "I didn't realize there were permanent structures on the island." She'd assumed there'd be tents for those selling goods, not buildings.

"A lot of traders come in for a week or two at a time. There has to be somewhere for them to stay. Most of the buildings are inns, but there are several taverns and food establishments as well."

As if to prove his point, the smell of smoked meat and baking bread filled the air.

"Why are the buildings only one story? Why not make

them taller so they can accommodate more people?"

"They'd never survive the storms," he murmured as he led her to the left. "Stick close by. And try not to say my name."

She nodded, realizing she wasn't sure she'd ever addressed him by Declan.

Just then, lightning shot across the sky. The dark, thick clouds made it feel later in the day than it was.

Declan headed south, walking with confidence as if he knew exactly where he was going. As if he'd been there a hundred times. Maybe he had. Brielle didn't know him at all. She did find it crazy that the crown prince of Valdis was just casually walking around the city without being recognized.

Declan turned down a street lined with vendors selling goods on either side. It was packed with people shopping.

"Here's a pretty necklace for a pretty woman," a man cooed at Brielle.

She paused to examine the jewelry he had laid out on the table, admiring the brightly colored stones strung on chains. Declan didn't stop, so she thanked the man and hurried to catch up.

"A hat for the beautiful lady!" another man called out, shoving two hats toward Brielle's face.

She smiled and shook her head. When she glanced in Declan's direction, she didn't see him. Dread filled her. He would be furious with her for getting sidetracked and losing him.

Someone bumped into her from behind and she lurched forward, knocking into the woman in front of her. The woman turned around and cursed at Brielle before stalking away.

"Please," a child said, tugging on Brielle's hand. "Can I have a coin so I can buy some food? I'm so hungry."

"Oh, you poor thing." Brielle squatted so she could be eye level with the child. "I don't have any money on me, but I'm sure we can find someone who has some food they can share with you."

"No one comes to Oskar without money," the child spat before scurrying away.

Stunned, she stood. "Bri," Declan said, grabbing her arm. "What are you doing?"

It took her a moment to realize he'd addressed her as Bri. She looked up into his concerned eyes. "I was trying to help that child." The kid was already asking another person for money.

Declan rolled his eyes. "Let's go."

"But don't you want to help those in need?" Especially children? She didn't understand his lack of concern.

"That kid has food," he said, speaking close to her ear. "He was just trying to swindle you for money."

"A child?" Who would have taught him such a thing?

"Everyone here is looking to make money. Never forget that."

"Are we headed anywhere in particular?" she asked as a light rain started to fall.

"I'm hungry." He led her inside a tavern.

The small room contained a dozen or so round tables, about half of them full of patrons.

Declan made his way to the bar at the far end of the room, taking a seat toward the middle. He tilted his head to the side, stretching his neck. Brielle had noticed him do that from time to time and wondered if it was a nervous habit. After tucking her hair behind her ears, she sat next to him.

"I'll have the usual, times two," Declan said to the bartender.

Brielle glanced at the people in the tavern. "I'm the only woman in here," she whispered.

He shrugged.

The bartender returned carrying two bowls of soup and two mugs of ale. He slid the items before them.

Brielle grabbed her spoon, taking a bite of the hot stew.

"I haven't seen you in a while," the bartender said.

Declan nodded. "I've been busy."

The man leaned in close, as if to wipe the surface near Declan. "A group of *people* were in here the other day." He glanced at Brielle.

"She's with me," Declan mumbled.

"Word is they're from the Lima army. They're here looking for the king."

"Any idea why?"

"Some are saying they want to assassinate him."

"That would violate a lot of treaties." Declan took a sip of his ale.

"I'm hearing the Lima royal family knows nothing of it. That the wild savages in charge ordered the hit. They're working around something."

Declan set his mug down a little harder than necessary.

He withdrew a velvet pouch from his pocket, pushing the entire thing toward the bartender who deftly took it, sliding it under his apron.

The door opened and closed. Two men entered, sitting at the far end of the bar. The bartender went over to greet them.

"Let's go," Declan mumbled.

Brielle had so many questions but knew now was not the time to voice them. She stood and followed Declan outside the tavern. The light rain had turned harder. Declan grabbed her hand, hurrying her along the now mostly deserted street. He opened a door and ushered her into another tavern. This one had lively music playing and over a dozen people dancing. The tables were all packed and, at the bar, people stood shoulder to shoulder. The noise level made Brielle cringe. Between the music, the laughing and talking, and the sounds of mugs clanking, she was already getting a headache. Not to mention the smell. Body odor, stew, and ale. She wanted to gag.

A group of people stood up from their table and headed toward the door. Declan quickly went over and snatched the table. He pulled out one of the chairs. "Sit," he ordered Brielle. "And don't move from this spot."

She nodded, having no intention of going anywhere in this establishment. If she did, she'd end up getting jostled around and she much preferred right where she was.

Declan left, heading into the throng of people where Brielle quickly lost sight of him. She glanced around, surprised he'd left her alone. At least she was at a table instead of the packed bar or standing around the perimeter of the room.

"Can I buy you a drink?" a man asked, taking a seat next to Brielle.

"No, thank you."

"You look like you could use it."

She smiled, feeling super awkward since nobody was sitting with her and she didn't have any food or drink in front of her.

The man remained sitting there, making her uncomfortable. "I'm here with someone," she said, hoping he'd take the hint and leave.

"So am I." He winked. "Tell me, are you from Miervades?" He lifted his hand, capturing a server's attention, and raised two fingers. The server nodded.

She shifted her weight on the chair. "Why do you ask?"

"You speak with an accent," he said. "And since I'm from there, I can hear it when you talk. Plus, the way you're dressed screams that's where you're from." He chuckled.

Her clothing was a bit plain compared to what other people in Sunder wore. However, on Oskar, there seemed to be a multitude of styles and she didn't stand out as badly as she did at the palace.

The server arrived with two mugs. She set them on the table, ale splashing over the sides.

Brielle rubbed her face. When the server left, she mumbled, "It has been a long day. I'm tired and not in the mood to converse. I'm sorry." She wanted this strange man to go away and leave her alone.

He leaned in closer, making her flinch. "I'm sorry to have bothered you. My mistake." He slid his hand to hers, taking it and squeezing.

She realized he'd slipped a piece of paper in her hand.

"Have a good night." He stood, picked up one of the mugs, and disappeared into the crowd.

Brielle shoved the paper up her sleeve, figuring here was not the place to look at it. Not only was the lighting too dark to read, but there were far too many people around. Since he'd given it to her so stealthily, she should read it in private.

The lively music vibrated through the table. Brielle's headache turned into a throbbing pain, so she stood, eager to be outside where it was quieter. Declan couldn't have a problem with her not following his directions since he hadn't bothered to check on her. She pushed past patrons until she reached the door.

Someone pinched her right elbow and she yelped. No one heard her since it was so loud in the tavern.

"It's just me," Declan said in her ear. He opened the door and escorted her out into the pouring rain.

He wrapped his left arm around her, keeping her right arm tucked in close to her body. With his right hand, he covered her sleeve where she'd tucked the paper. She realized belatedly that he was trying to keep her sleeve from getting too wet and destroying the paper. She wondered how he even knew about it.

"The bridges will probably be closed," Declan said. "Not only is it late," he glanced up at the dark sky, "but it's too dangerous to cross in this weather."

The thought of crossing a bridge at night in the dark while a wave crashed over it, knocking her off, was enough to terrify her.

With the rain coming down so hard, she couldn't see much as they headed along the muddy street.

"In here," Declan said, reaching for a door. He opened it and shoved her inside.

Brielle wiped the water from her face. They were in a room of some sort with a single desk in the middle of it. Hallways lined with doors extended out on either side of the room. She suspected they were at an inn.

"We'll be needing one room," Declan said to the man working at the desk. "No windows."

Brielle wanted to insist that they needed two rooms. However, she didn't want to do so in front of the man. She'd wait until she was alone with Declan before asking about the sleeping arrangements. Perhaps it wasn't safe for her to be alone. Or maybe he planned on leaving her in the room while he went back out to another tavern.

The man nodded and handed Declan a key. "Room five. Down the hall there." He pointed to the right.

Declan led the way to the room, unlocking the door and ushering Brielle inside.

There was a single bed that took up most of the space. Nothing else, not even a wash table, could fit in the tight room.

"Read the note," Declan said, shaking the water from his hair.

Brielle carefully pulled up her sleeve and extricated the

damp paper. She unfolded it. "Midnight. Pier Fifteen." She turned it over, but nothing had been written on the back.

Declan's pants dripped water onto the floor of the room. He placed his hands on his hips. "We don't have much time. Midnight is in forty minutes, and it'll take us about fifteen minutes to get there."

"We're going to pier fifteen?" The sound of heavy rain pounded on the rooftop. "How do we even know this note was intended for me?"

"The guy had been following you. That's why I sat you at the table and left you alone. What did he say?" Declan started pacing at the end of the bed.

"He knew I was from Miervades."

"Did you recognize him?"

"No."

"I'm only going to ask you this once." He stopped pacing and turned to look her in the eyes. "Do you have any idea who would want you to go to pier fifteen?"

She hesitated. Lukas had told her to go to Oskar if she got into trouble. Maybe someone had been watching out for her. Then when she showed up today, they assumed she was running away. Her face warmed. When Declan had first offered to take her to the island, she had thought it was a good idea to go so she'd know where it was in case she needed to leave. He'd only been trying to spend some time with her, and she'd made a mess of things. "I'm not certain," she finally answered. "But I have an idea." Shame filled her. She didn't want Declan to think she'd planned this entire thing.

CHAPTER 14

DECLAN

The tips of Brielle's ears turned bright red. Declan didn't think she was an active participant in whatever was going on. However, she knew something. She needed to tell him because they didn't have a lot of time. And while he didn't trust anyone, he really wanted to at least be able to rely on her right now.

"I think it might be Lukas," she said, her voice soft and barely audible above the pouring rain.

"The guy you danced with at our engagement party?" The one from Miervades who Orson had been trying to get a tail on, and the man she'd said something about him wanting to marry her. Irritation grew. She was keeping things from him. However, Declan had given her no reason to trust him. His irritation turned to frustration—both with Brielle and with himself.

She nodded.

Declan folded his arms and asked as kindly as he could,

"Why do you think Lukas is involved with this note? Do you think he's at pier fifteen waiting for you?'

"I don't know if he'll be there," she said, playing with the edge of her sleeve. "It's just a hunch based upon a few things he said to me."

He pushed his wet hair back off his face. Keeping his temper in check, he calmly asked, "What do you think we should do?" He planned on going tonight to see who showed up. However, he wanted to know what she suggested. Maybe if he tried to at least give the appearance of trusting her and wanting her advice, she'd do the same with him.

"I think we should go to pier fifteen. You can hide, and I'll see who shows up. What do you think?" She looked up at him with her bright brown eyes, uncertainty filling them.

"I could go without you since it's raining." A strange urge to protect her filled him.

She bit her bottom lip for a second. "While I don't really want to go, if Lukas does show up, I want to talk to him. I need some answers."

Answers Declan probably had. He didn't know why he withheld the information Brooks had obtained about her father not having the money to pay Miervades's taxes. It probably had something to do with the look of worry and uncertainty on her face. A look he wished he could erase. "Okay," he said before he could change his mind.

She smiled.

Declan hid in the dark doorway watching Brielle stand at the entrance to the pier. Rain still came down steadily, though lighter than before. She hugged herself, shaking from the cold. Her hair clung to her face and body, making her seem too young and innocent to be out there all alone. Perhaps this was a bad idea.

A man approached from the west, heading straight toward Brielle. Declan slid the knife from his boot, gripping it in his right hand. He wasn't sure what he expected to happen. If the man turned out to be Lukas, he wouldn't hurt Brielle. Declan's instinct told him that Lukas wanted Brielle to run away with him. However, something more sinister than that could be at play here. Lukas could be using Brielle to lure Declan out. After all, there was a group of men here hunting the king, which meant there very well could be another group searching for Declan. Being on Oskar, unguarded, didn't seem like the best idea right now. His father had left him in charge, and he was already being reckless.

Brielle turned to face the approaching person. When the man reached her, he wrapped her in a hug before taking a step back and speaking. Declan wasn't close enough to hear what he said. It had to be that guy Lukas since he'd hugged Brielle. Hopefully she'd get her questions answered so she wouldn't have to deal with him again. For some reason, he rubbed Declan the wrong way.

Lukas grabbed Brielle's arm, and she tried to pull away. Fury filled Declan as he gripped his knife, aiming it at Lukas.

"No," Brielle said loud enough for Declan to hear from

where he stood. At first, he thought she'd been talking to him, but as he watched, he realized she'd been speaking to Lukas.

Lukas released her and started pacing, waving his arms back and forth like he was agitated. He gestured toward the pier. Brielle looked that way, then shook her head. Lukas said something else before storming away, going back the direction he'd come from.

Brielle stood there, watching his retreating figure.

Declan was about to head over to her, but something stopped him. A feeling that she was being watched. He remained in the doorway, scanning the surrounding area and not seeing anyone.

Brielle started walking the other direction, not once looking Declan's way. In fact, she seemed to make a point of avoiding him since she remained on the other side of the street. If someone was following her like he suspected, he wondered who and why. If Lukas was merely an old lover who wanted to steal her away, there wouldn't be anyone else involved. But someone had given her the note which meant there were more people here from Miervades than just Lukas.

Declan carefully trailed her, keeping to the shadows of the buildings. When she entered an inn, he hesitated. Even if she went in there to meet someone else, he didn't want her in there alone. Too many bad things could happen, especially this late at night. Just in case someone was still watching, he looped around the block and entered the building from the other side.

He found Brielle standing next to the front door. Their eyes met. "Is everything okay?" he whispered, not sure what was going on.

She shook her head.

"The inn we're staying in is two blocks over."

She shook her head again.

Which meant he needed to get them out of there without anyone seeing, and they couldn't return to the room at the inn that he'd paid for.

Since no one was currently tending to the counter, Declan reached over and grabbed a discarded cape that had been tossed on a chair. He wrapped it around Brielle, lifting the hood over her head, concealing her distinctly curly hair and hiding her face. Satisfied she wouldn't be easily recognized, he led her from the building. He made sure to keep his arm on her shoulder, as if they were a married couple.

The best course of action would be to go to an inn he didn't usually frequent. Something about the weather, the night, and Brielle made him overly cautious. Oskar had three different sections to the island—the wealthy area near the bridges, the poor area near the docks, and the in between which was literally between the poor and wealthy sections. He tended to stay away from the wealthy section, not wanting to attract attention by being recognized. Usually, he found the poorer areas teeming with information and activity. Tonight, he chose to go to the in between. Not only did he want a decent place for Brielle to stay where she could warm herself up, but he wanted to do something different. Unexpected. In case they were being watched.

They headed away from the docks, toward the interior of the island. The rain picked up, turning the streets into even more of a muddy mess. After another four blocks, Declan deemed them far enough away from the docks to be in a respectable area of Oskar. As soon as he spotted an inn, he led Brielle inside.

He quickly surveyed the room. A small empty tavern took up the left side with only a handful of tables for eating. The right side contained a hearth, the fire almost out, along with a man dozing at a desk. Declan walked over to the desk, gently knocking on it to rouse the attendant. He inquired about a single room large enough to accommodate two people for the night. He knew Brielle would prefer separate rooms. However, that would be too dangerous right now.

The man working at the desk lumbered to his feet and waved for them to follow him. He took them down the corridor to the right.

Brielle hovered behind Declan, so he reached back and took hold of her hand.

The man opened a door and went inside, lighting several candles. Then he bent and lit the kindle below the logs in the fireplace. "Do you need warm water or something to eat?" he inquired.

"No," Declan replied. He didn't want any servants coming to the room. The less people who saw them, the better.

"If you want anything, just come to my desk and let me know." The man left the room.

Declan ushered Brielle inside and locked the door. She went over to the hearth, her cape dripping water onto the carpet. Her teeth started to chatter. They needed to get out of their wet clothes or they'd both end up sick.

"Give me your cape," Declan said.

She immediately removed it, her hands shaking as she did so. He took it and hung it on the hook next to the door.

"Now remove your clothing. You can use the blanket on the bed to cover yourself." Declan pulled the top blanket back and found a softer one underneath. After yanking it off, he tossed it to her.

She caught it, staring at him with wide eyes.

"Keep your back to me," he said. "I'm going to face the other direction and do the same."

She nodded, turning away from him.

Sighing, he faced the wall, and started peeling off his wet clothing. He had to tug his pants over his feet to get the wet material off. Once naked, he took the sheet from the bed and wrapped it around his waist. Satisfied it would hold, he picked up his wet clothing and waited for Brielle.

"I'm decent," she said a few moments later.

He turned and saw her sitting in the chair by the hearth, wrapped in a blanket, her legs tucked up under her. She'd spread her dress out on the floor before the fire.

He went over to the hearth, laying his clothes out as well. "They're so wet I'm not sure they'll be dry by morning."

"I ripped my dress trying to get it off."

Chuckling, he climbed on the bed, being careful not to lose the sheet around his waist. He stretched out, leaning against the headboard. It killed him to sit there and not ask her all the questions swirling in his mind. But if he pushed, he feared she'd withdraw. So, he remained there, silent, hoping she'd talk to him and tell him what had happened tonight at the docks.

Brielle closed her eyes.

Maybe he should be the one to speak first. "The last time we talked, you apologized for not being the sort of wife you thought I should have. And I told you that I never even considered who I might want to marry since it wasn't an option."

She opened her eyes and nodded, her brows pulling together. Probably trying to figure out where he was going with this.

"Since then, I have been thinking about the sort of wife I want."

"And what did you conclude?" she asked, snuggling under her blanket.

"That I'd like to marry someone who is my friend. I look at my parents, and my mother isn't a political advisor to my father. She waltzes around court setting fashions. However, she looks out for my dad. She hears gossip that he's totally unaware of. And you'd never know it just by looking at them, but my parents are friends. They were friends long before they married. I think that's what has helped them remain together all these years." Never had he voiced his thoughts on the matter. He wasn't sure why he was trying to now.

Somehow it seemed appropriate. And if he wanted her to trust him, he needed to earn that trust.

Brielle considered him for a few minutes. "Can I ask you something?"

When people prefaced a question that way, it always put Declan on edge. "Sure."

"I'd like to know why you always do what you're supposed to. Is it out of loyalty to your family? Loyalty to your kingdom? Is it a moral obligation? Or is it something else entirely? I want to know why you're the way you are."

No one had ever asked him that, and he wondered if she somehow knew about the blood oath. "I'm definitely loyal to my family and kingdom. I want to be worthy of the crown I wear." Hopefully his generic answer would satisfy her.

"Let me ask you another question that may help clarify the heart of what I'm getting at. What if you learned that your brother had committed a crime, what would you, the crown prince, do?"

His heartbeat sped up and an anxious, unwelcome feeling took root. She had to know—but how? "Why are you asking?" His voice came out deep and rumbly.

"I'm just trying to understand you better since I don't know you very well. And…and I'm trying to decide something for myself. I'm trying to figure out how to handle a situation that may be morally ambiguous." She bit her bottom lip. He noticed she did that a lot.

However, her statement led him to believe this had nothing to do with the blood oath. He relaxed and considered her question. Since he needed her to trust him enough to tell him what happened or what she knew, he had to answer as honestly as possible. Trust was a funny thing. He wasn't worthy of hers, and she wasn't worthy of his. They barely knew each other. However, once married, they needed to find a way to work together. And somehow it all boiled down to trust.

Declan rubbed the side of his neck, considering how to answer. "If my brother broke the law, he'd be punished accordingly because it's the right thing to do."

She opened her mouth to speak, but he raised his hand, silencing her.

"Let me explain."

She nodded.

"Sometimes what I think or feel is the right thing to do, isn't the law. As the future king, it is my job to uphold the law. I spent years learning and studying our kingdom, the laws that govern us, and what happens to those who break them. Sometimes the rules feel harsh, but I know from studying my history why the laws we have are in place, and why the punishment for breaking a law is what it is. I know that for Valdis to function, be prosperous, and remain at peace, the laws must be upheld without question, regardless of what I think or feel." Because of the damn blood oath that he couldn't tell her about. "I can't give preferential treatment to my brother because it wouldn't be fair. All subjects are bound by the law."

Brielle sighed. "That's what I was afraid of." She turned away, staring into the fire.

He caught a glimpse of tears in her eyes. He wanted to

demand she tell him what had happened at the pier with Lukas, but he couldn't. She would tell him when she was ready. When she trusted him.

Declan moved to the edge of the mattress. "Here, come take the bed for the night. I'll sleep on the chair."

"I'm comfortable next to the fire," she whispered. "You can have the bed."

He didn't want to argue with her, so he laid back down. "We'll need to leave early tomorrow before the streets are too crowded." Since they didn't have papers, he'd need to reveal his identity to get back to the mainland from the bridges. It would cause a scene.

"I'll be ready first thing." Her voice wobbled as if she was crying.

Her sadness overwhelmed him. He wished he could make her feel better, but he couldn't. The lot they'd been dealt in life was set, and they couldn't change it.

Declan tossed and turned all night, unable to fall asleep. When he couldn't stand lying in bed another moment, he got up and dressed.

Brielle still slept soundly on the chair. The blanket had fallen from her shoulders, pooling on top of her crossed arms, revealing her bare neck, shoulders, and the top portion of her breasts. Knowing she'd be embarrassed if she woke in that state, Declan took his discarded blanket, placing it on top of her exposed skin, all the while trying not to stare at her. He'd seen a woman's breasts before, so he didn't know what the appeal was now.

Once she was fully covered, he stood there considering her for a moment. Now that he knew her a little better, she didn't seem homely anymore and he couldn't understand why he'd ever thought that. Even her hair, which at first, he'd considered wild and untamed, was one of the things he liked most about her. She was different from other women, and he could see why both of his brothers had taken to her.

Reaching out, he gently shook her.

She peeled her eyelids open, blinking.

"It's time for us to get going." He turned to give her privacy while she dressed. The fire had almost died out, bathing the room in a dim light. He tried not to watch the shadows her body cast as she dressed. His erratic thoughts had to be from a lack of sleep. He needed to focus and stop thinking so much about Brielle and her body. She was just a woman. A normal woman.

He didn't know for sure what time it was but it felt close to morning, and his intuition was rarely wrong. They needed to be on their way.

"I'm ready," she said a few moments later around a yawn. "My dress is still damp in a few places, but it'll do."

When he faced her, she pulled her hair over her shoulder and hastily braided it.

"When we're outside, I'd like for you to try and stay close to me." And not get sidetracked looking at stores, people, or goods being sold. The kid yesterday had almost swindled her.

She nodded and reached out, touching his arm and sending a jolt through him. "When we have more time, I need to speak with you about something."

"Of course." Relief filled him that she was finally going to confide in him. It would've been better for her to do it last night, so he'd have more time to figure out a solution, but at least she'd decided to tell him and that was all that mattered right now. Whatever it was, it had to affect her personally, otherwise she wouldn't have been so upset last night. He got the feeling it had to do with more than just Lukas wanting her to run away with him.

Declan opened the door and peered into the hallway. Not seeing anyone, he exited the room, Brielle close behind. When he usually returned to Valdis from Oskar, he went directly to the first bridge and informed the guards there of his presence. They always recognized him on sight and there were never any issues.

Today, however, he had Brielle with him. Not wanting to go into a lengthy explanation as to why she didn't have the necessary papers as the law required, he decided to head to the garrison where he could make such an explanation without causing a scene. Plus, he wanted an escort through the city to ensure her safety.

The two of them exited the inn without issue. The sun had not yet risen, and the sky had an eerie gray to it from the thick clouds. Thankfully the rain had stopped. Only a few people were out at this early hour, and those that were, were busy opening stores, baking, or setting up display tables for the day's trade. No one paid them any heed.

The garrison was located closer to the docks since that was where most of the trouble took place. They needed to travel east a couple of blocks to reach it.

A group of dock workers passed them, mumbling about some ship that had just arrived, several hours late, that needed its goods brought on shore. A block later, a couple of sailors walked by, searching for an inn.

Declan and Brielle were only a few buildings away from the garrison now. Peering toward the docks, Declan saw the ship that had recently arrived, people still disembarking. Three men headed their way having just gotten off the ship. Two turned down a street to the right while the third broke away from his companions, heading toward Declan. The man's walk went from slightly hunched over and slow to straight and fast.

An eerie sensation filled Declan.

The man turned down the street to his left. When Declan and Brielle reached that street, Declan looked to see if the man was still in sight.

At the corner, the man glanced back over his shoulder. A smile slid across the man's face before he turned and disappeared.

Declan cursed. It was the queen's personal assassin.

CHAPTER 15

BRIELLE

D eclan suddenly tensed, then grabbed Brielle's arm, pulling her along so quickly she could barely keep up.

"What's the matter?" she asked. She tripped on her cape, but Declan's grip was so firm, he kept her upright. "You're going to give me a bruise."

"I'm sorry." He released her arm, his eyes alight with panic. "But I need you to hurry."

Peering around, she didn't notice anything unusual or concerning. If there was some danger about, she didn't see it. "What's going on?" she asked since his entire disposition had changed. He was beginning to scare her.

At a rather bland looking building, Declan shoved the door open and rushed inside. Brielle followed him, wondering what he'd seen that had caused him to be so anxious. Inside, there were several desks along with a dozen or so jail cells toward the back of the room. This had to be the garrison for Oskar.

"I need immediate assistance," Declan demanded, holding up his right hand, displaying a large ring with the royal family crest on it.

The three men who'd been sitting at the desks all immediately shoved their chairs back and dropped to their knees.

"Rise," Declan said. "There's an emergency, and I need an escort to the palace. This is my fiancée, Lady Brielle, and she will be accompanying me."

One of the men returned to his desk. "Your Highness, I can log your ring in as proof of your identification. However, I need Lady Brielle's papers." He reached his hand out, clearly expecting her to turn them over.

Brielle looked up at Declan. She didn't even know if she'd brought her papers with her from Miervades to Sunder. And if she had, she didn't have the faintest clue where they'd be in the palace.

"She doesn't have them."

"That won't be a problem. I just need to write this down. I'll state that your word is proof of her identification."

"We are in a hurry," Declan said, leaning his hands on the desk.

"I understand. However, the law is clear. I have to log the two of you in." The soldier's quill started shaking.

"Write faster," Declan said, his words distinct and crisp, the command in them clear.

The man nodded and got to work. A few minutes later,

he turned the book to face Declan. "Your Highness, I need your signature, please."

Declan scribbled in the book.

The other two men sheathed their swords and stood next to the door. "We'll escort you both," the one on the right said.

The four of them exited the building. Declan started jogging, so the soldiers ran after him, one in front of the prince and the other behind him. As they jogged along the streets, they kept going in a northward direction heading toward the bridges. Brielle still had no idea why they had to hurry, but she could feel Declan's rising panic.

"Are there horses we can use?" she asked, trying to keep up with the men. She could tell they were running slower than they wanted to because of her. She lifted her cape and dress up a bit so she could run easier.

"Horses aren't allowed on the island," one of the soldiers said. "But there's no need to worry, Lady Brielle. We will get you safely to the palace."

Safety hadn't been her concern; getting to the palace as quickly as possible was her priority. Clearly something was the matter with Declan, and she wanted to help in any way she could. Right now, she was hindering him with her slow pace.

The four of them made their way through the city. Since it was early, not many people were out, and they could jog without attracting too much attention. When they reached the first bridge, they had to stop. Brielle used the opportunity to catch her breath as the two soldiers explained they'd already logged Declan and her in for passage across the bridges.

They were allowed to pass, and Declan took her hand, one soldier walking in front and the other behind the two of them. They couldn't jog due to the number of people heading to Oskar. They remained in line as they made their way across bridge after bridge. Since everyone had to show his or her papers to be admitted access, she was thankful Declan had gone to the garrison and obtained the personal escort. Otherwise, Brielle wouldn't have been allowed to return to Valdis.

Stepping off the last bridge, Brielle spotted the carriage from yesterday waiting for them. After Declan thanked the soldiers for their help, the two of them quickly climbed inside. He knocked on the roof, and the carriage took off, heading for the palace.

Now that they were alone, Brielle placed her hand on Declan's knee, demanding his attention. "What's going on?"

"I saw the queen's personal assassin." He rubbed his forehead and looked outside the carriage, away from her.

She blinked, wondering if she'd heard him correctly. She had to clarify. "The queen has an assassin?"

Declan turned to face her. "Yes. A man who only does the queen's bidding."

Revulsion filled her. She was going to be ill. She couldn't help but wonder who would choose such a job. Or, equally disturbing, that the queen needed to employ someone like that.

"My mother doesn't use him often. At least, I don't think she does."

"I'm not sure that makes it any better," Brielle mumbled. "I don't understand why seeing him has you so upset."

He fidgeted with his sleeve, rolling it up and then unrolling it as if it were the most important thing in the world. After a minute, he abandoned the task and sighed. "When I saw the assassin, I can't explain it, but I got the feeling he may no longer be loyal to my mother."

Brielle had to withhold her retort that anyone in that sort of profession couldn't be loyal or trustworthy since he killed people for a living.

Declan continued, "It doesn't make any sense. The assassin took an oath. He has no choice but to be loyal to the queen."

She had no idea if assassins took their oaths seriously. Instead of voicing that thought, she said, "Perhaps someone else is currently employing him?"

He shook his head. "It doesn't work that way. The assassin only works for the queen." Shifting his body on the bench seat, he faced her. "What I am about to tell you is not public knowledge." He reached out and took hold of her hand.

"I won't tell anyone," she whispered, shocked by his touch and that he was about to tell her something important.

"The king recently learned he fathered a child before he married my mother. Her name is Mabel, and she is a few months older than me, making her the true heir to the throne."

The statement sent shockwaves through Brielle. If Declan wasn't the heir, then what did that mean for their impending marriage? Nothing, she reminded herself. Since her father didn't plan on paying his taxes, her life would be forfeit. However, she had no idea what this had to do with the assassin.

"I think—and I don't have confirmation on this—but I think my mother discovered Mabel's existence and sent the assassin after her."

"To ensure you inherit the throne." Because Briar would never stand by while her husband's bastard child took the throne over her own son.

"Yes," Declan whispered. He turned Brielle's hand over and started drawing circles on her palm with his forefinger.

His face looked so vulnerable right now that she had the urge to reach forward and cup his cheek in her hand. She refrained from doing so, not wanting to completely embarrass herself. Focusing on their conversation, she asked, "If the assassin is here, does that mean his mission was successful?" She still didn't understand why if the assassin was supposedly loyal to the queen, Declan would be questioning that loyalty.

"No. I think he killed someone else. It was made to look like Mabel had been assassinated, but I think she escaped."

"Then why is he here?" she asked, getting to the heart of the matter.

"There is one rule the assassin can't break. He can't kill a member of the royal family. If my mother sent him after Mabel and he...figured out who Mabel is, I'm not sure if that severs the oath he made to my mother or not."

"Do you think he'd be upset once he figured it out? Upset enough to come after the queen?" She now began to understand Declan's panic.

"I do." He squeezed her hand and released it, facing forward again.

Brielle's head swam with all Declan had revealed. Rubbing her face, she tried to digest everything.

"I'm sorry I threw all of this on you," Declan said. "But since you're going to be a part of this family, you need to know what's going on."

Speaking of which, shame filled her when she recalled all that she'd learned when she spoke to Lukas at the docks. She would not be a part of Declan's family. Not now, not ever. After her conversation with Declan last night, she knew she couldn't tell him the truth because he had a duty to uphold the law. However, she wanted him to know without revealing the specifics in case there was a way for her to get out of this situation that didn't involve her dying. If she'd gone with Lukas last night, Declan would have followed her and killed her himself. Remaining with Declan, enlisting his help, was the only way she might have a chance at a real future.

"I need to discuss something with you." She'd spent hours last night thinking of how to do this. "Let's say I'm talking about a hypothetical situation involving a friend."

He raised a single eyebrow. "Okay." He gestured for her to continue.

"Let's say my friend's father owes a significant amount of money, and my friend has been taken as insurance so her father will pay. And then let's say the father doesn't have the money and can't pay." She'd already told him her fears about her father not paying, so this situation shouldn't be such a shock for him. "Is there any way for me to save my friend?"

"You mean legally?" he clarified.

"Yes, legally. Otherwise, my friend would have gotten on a ship last night and sailed away." She looked pointedly at him.

"Unfortunately, the law is the law," he mumbled, leaning his head back against the carriage. "I'd have to examine the contract in detail to see exactly what's written and if anything can be interpreted differently without breaking the law. Unfortunately, the king is excellent at writing iron-clad contracts." After a moment, he tilted his head toward her. "Why would your father offer you up as insurance if he knew he couldn't pay?"

Tears filled her eyes. "The king didn't give him a choice." Regardless, her father could have argued a bit. At least not given her over so easily. "I wish your father had thought of something else as insurance besides me."

Declan focused on the roof of the carriage, not looking her way. "That part did take me by surprise," he admitted. "I didn't know he was going to write a marriage contract that day."

"He didn't discuss it with you beforehand?" She thought

for sure the king would have mentioned it to his son and not sprung it on him.

"No. He didn't say anything." He rubbed his eyes. "And I'm not sure the king knows the financial state of your father. I think the king wishes for us to marry. He'll be sorely disappointed if it doesn't happen."

Brielle had no idea why the king thought she was a good match for his son. However, she didn't have time to consider that with more pressing matters at hand. "Let me ask you this," she said. "If I got on a ship tomorrow and disappeared, then what? Would I be hunted for the rest of my life?"

He nodded. "The king would personally track you down and kill you."

A shudder raked through her body. "That's what I thought," she whispered. She was running out of options.

"I have a hard time believing your father would give up your life so easily," Declan said.

Brielle happened to agree with him.

"Maybe..." He didn't finish his sentence.

"What?" she asked.

"Maybe your father has a plan. Maybe it involves Mabel."

"Why would you suggest that?" She didn't see how Mabel could be involved. Not only that, but her father had never been one to be involved with the mainland's politics.

"Mabel's mother was from Miervades. In fact, she came from a prominent family. One you probably know."

Panic started to set in. Her life was on the line, and she felt helpless.

"Do you know the Laris family?" he asked.

She felt like she was going to vomit. "Liam Laris runs the mines."

He nodded, clearly already aware of that fact. "And twenty-two years ago, Liam's son led the revolution."

Every time he spoke, it got worse. His words hung heavy in the air. Brielle didn't want to breathe them in because if she did, she'd have to acknowledge them. Acknowledging them meant knowing Liam's son had led a revolution and Liam's granddaughter had a child with the king. Since Duke Jaxon was good friends with Liam, this didn't bode well for her father.

Declan tapped his hand on his thigh. "My father thinks Mabel will go to Miervades searching for her family, but she hasn't turned up there yet. If she wants to be my father's heir, she'll have to eventually come here to Sunder. Once she does, she could be the new crown princess. On the other hand, she might want nothing to do with us. I honestly have no idea since we don't know anything about her."

The carriage pulled into the palace courtyard, making her remember why they were rushing to the palace in the first place.

"If the assassin is no longer loyal to your mother, then who is he loyal to?" Brielle asked.

He shrugged. "My guess would be Mabel since she is supposed to be the next queen. Unless I marry and produce a child before I turn twenty-four and Mabel doesn't. In that case, then I am the heir, and my wife would be the next queen."

Again, another law Brielle knew nothing about. Focusing

on the task at hand, she asked, "If the assassin is no longer working for the queen, what do you think he's doing here?"

"If the assassin is now loyal to Mabel, and he's here on her behalf, that means she's several steps ahead of us. I doubt she will be happy with my father for having her mother executed. I assume she'd want revenge."

"But the assassin can't kill anyone in the royal family?" she asked.

"It's against the law."

She wondered how the queen had sent the assassin after Mabel then. Maybe since Mabel hadn't officially been declared a member of the royal family, the law didn't apply to her.

"I know what you're thinking," Declan said as the carriage came to a halt. "And I don't know. If the queen broke a law, then the king will have to punish her. However, my mother isn't a complete idiot, and I doubt she would have knowingly and willingly broken a law." Declan reached for the handle. "And unless my father knows for certain and has proof," he looked pointedly at her, "he isn't bound to carry out the law."

Brielle nodded, taking a mental note to remember that tidbit for later. A thought occurred to her. "I'm not a member of the royal family. The assassin could kill me."

Declan's eyes darkened. "Especially if Mabel wishes to prevent our marriage. I'll see that you have added protection."

Brielle glanced outside the carriage, looking for anyone who appeared suspicious. She only had to keep herself alive for one week. At the end of the week, if she hadn't found a way around the law, she planned on leaving on her own.

Declan shoved the door open, exiting the carriage.

Brielle scooted across the seat and jumped out, crashing right into him.

"I was going to help you out," he said, his hands gripping her arms, trying to keep them both upright.

She regained her footing. "My apologies. I figured you'd be in too much of a hurry." Glancing up into his eyes, her breath caught. They were so close. Too close.

He released her and took a step back, putting some space between them.

Declan blinked before turning to face the sentries on duty. "You," he pointed at the one on the left, "go and find my brothers. Tell them I need to see them immediately."

"Yes, Your Highness." The sentry bowed and rushed away.

"Where's the queen?" Declan asked the other sentry.

"In the royal chambers, Your Highness."

"Have there been any security issues? Anything odd or out of place?" Declan demanded. "Anything I need to know about?"

"No, Your Highness," the sentry answered. "Everything has been quiet."

Brielle noticed Declan's hands shaking, so she grabbed hold of his right hand, squeezing it for support. "Let's go and check on your mother."

He nodded, and they hurried inside the palace. They went straight upstairs to the royal wing. When they reached it, they ran through the sitting room to the dining room where they found the queen seated at the table, eating by herself.

"Where have the two of you been?" Briar asked, her voice haughty. She glanced over and noticed Declan and Brielle holding hands. Her lips curled in disgust, as if the mere sight made it impossible to eat.

"Have you met with your personal assassin in the past day or two?" Declan demanded, releasing Brielle's hand and rushing to his mother's side. He inspected her plate, then began looking at her eyes and skin.

"What are you doing?" Briar snapped, yanking her arm away from him.

"Mother, answer me." He slammed his hand on the table, causing Briar to jump and water to spill out of her cup.

"No, I have not met with my assassin. Now explain yourself."

"I saw him." Declan sat on the chair to Briar's right, running his hands through his hair.

Brielle came farther into the room, hovering behind Declan, not sure what to say or do. Or if she should even be there.

"I sent him on a job," Briar said as she resumed eating. "I'm sure he's just here to report back to me."

Declan folded his hands before glancing at Brielle. "Lady Brielle, can I please ask you to leave the room and close the door. I must have a very private and confidential talk with my mother."

"Of course." She turned, about to go, when she noticed

something on the queen's plate. "Is that gratscot?" she asked, knowing full well it was. She'd recognize the plant anywhere.

"I have no idea what it is," Briar said. "But it's tasty and goes nicely with my eggs."

Brielle's eyes widened.

"What is it?" Declan demanded.

"That's a poisonous plant from Miervades."

CHAPTER 16

MABEL

Alone in her cabin below deck, Mabel stretched out on the bed rereading the contract the Lima government had drawn up for her. They'd been furious she'd refused to sign it on the spot. She had to point out that she wasn't a complete moron and if they wanted any hope of doing business with her, they'd let her have some time to consider their offer. They'd finally agreed.

From what Jorrg had explained, all trade had to go through Oskar. So having Miervades ship wheat and coal south to Oskar, then have Lima purchase it there, added to the cost substantially. If Miervades sold directly to Lima, Miervades made more money, and Lima spent less money, making it advantageous for both parties. However, Jorrg had also revealed that no one was allowed to trade on their own like that. Again, everything by law had to go through Oskar. No one seemed to know or understand why. Mabel felt like there was more going on, but she didn't want to deal with a foreign kingdom now since she had more pressing matters at hand.

Matsen had left her almost two weeks ago. After spending ten days in Lima, she'd boarded this ship and set out for a small town east of Monta on the island of Miervades. She was supposed to meet Matsen there—assuming his mission to Sunder had been successful.

Tossing the contract aside, she slid off the bed and headed above deck where Jorrg and the crew were. She squinted from the bright sun shining overhead as she made her way to the bow of the ship. Gradually, her eyes adjusted, and she stood at the bow, letting the fresh air wash against her skin.

Jorrg joined her a moment later. "I wanted to let you know that after we dock, you're going to disembark, and I'm going to sail back to Lima."

"You're not staying with me?" She hadn't anticipated being alone. Not that she minded.

"No. With the wind, it's taking us an extra day to get there. Your friend should be joining you shortly after you arrive. You'll be in safe hands. I think it best I return the ship to Lima so as not to raise any unwanted suspicions."

The original plan had been for the crew to return the ship and for Jorrg to remain with her until Matsen showed up. Sliding her hands over the rail, she tried to think of reasons the plan would have changed.

Jorrg fidgeted with a piece of rope he was holding.

She raised an eyebrow. "Is something the matter?"

"I'm supposed to take the signed contract back with me." He shoved the rope in his pocket.

Mabel returned her attention to the ocean, not looking Jorrg's way. An intense desire to slam her fist into his face inundated her. Honestly, she had no idea where his loyalties lay. He probably had none. "Very well," she said. She had no intention of signing the contract, at least not yet. But he didn't need to know that.

The wind whipped through her hair, tossing it around. She loved the messy freedom it offered. She closed her eyes and smiled, reveling in the feeling.

"I hope you'll make your way north to meet your family when it's safe," Jorrg said.

She opened her eyes and looked at him. Subtlety was not a trait he possessed. "The revolution that my...grandfather was involved and killed in, what was it about?"

He scratched the side of his head. "It was about the duke being tired of paying high taxes and having to trade through Oskar."

"Why did my grandfather get involved if it was about the duke?" she asked.

Jorrg furrowed his brows. "I was young back then, but I believe he was trying to help in whatever capacity he could."

"Why?"

He shrugged. "Easier trade?"

She really wanted to ask him if he had any knowledge of blood oaths, but it felt wrong to do so. Somehow, she knew it was a secret and she couldn't discuss it with him.

He withdrew a small satchel and handed it to her.

"Here's some money. It should cover food and a room at the local inn."

Mabel took the bag, tucking it in her dress. "Thank you."

He patted her on her shoulder. "Just make sure to meet your family."

"I will." Though she didn't think of or consider the strangers in Miervades her family. The man and woman who raised her were the only family she knew. Even if they weren't of her blood.

Jorrg smiled and then went back over to the man steering the ship, talking with him.

Mabel faced forward, once again enjoying the feel of the wind as it caressed her.

She hadn't even dealt with the royal family yet and already political issues were bogging her down. Her so-called family wanted something from her, Lima wanted something from her, even Matsen probably wanted something from her as well.

When she'd met with Cecel and the city leaders, they'd been clear. If Mabel claimed her birthright, Lima would send someone to Valdis to deal with the king. Cecel wouldn't go into specifics, but she'd said Mabel would be sitting on the throne within a year. Then all Mabel had to do was open trade with the other kingdoms.

Her instinct told her there was more to it than that, so she didn't want to hastily enter a bargain without thinking it through. Especially when she knew so little of the kingdoms and their politics. Mabel kept going back to her conversation with Matsen about blood magic and oaths. She couldn't help but wonder if magic was more common in other kingdoms. Maybe other royal families had blood oaths as well. It seemed logical to conclude that people in positions of power, like the ruling families, would enter into these agreements to gain more power or to hold onto it.

The fact that the Lima kingdom still had a royal family even though they didn't do anything seemed suspicious. Especially since the rules and laws were made and enforced by the governing board, not the royal family. Perhaps Lima was trying to work around the blood oaths their kingdom had taken. Not only had Mabel not signed the treaty because she wasn't well-informed enough, but she felt as if they were trying to pull something over on her. As if having her sign the treaty before she was crowned meant something. By signing in ignorance of Valdis's laws, maybe she was unknowingly working around a treaty. Or perhaps there was some sort of blood oath in place. By signing, she could end up dooming herself for doing something wrong—even if she didn't know it was wrong. The best course of action would be to claim her birthright, then learn the laws so she didn't violate a treaty or blood oath and get herself killed.

Most likely, she was overthinking all of this. She blamed it on her father—well, the man who'd raised her. He'd always had her look at things from multiple angles and insisted she be suspicious of people and their motives. He was a good man, and she missed him dearly.

As the sun crested the horizon, Miervades came into view. Mabel stood at the side of the ship, observing the land before her. When she'd come here with Matsen, they'd only docked. And that had been in the larger town of Monta. Here, on this part of the island, she didn't see any buildings or homes. Nothing that indicated that people actually lived there.

All she saw were miles upon miles of low rolling green hills. It was beautiful, but somehow not what she'd been expecting. She vaguely wondered where all the wheat was grown.

Jorrg joined her. "The town where you're going to meet your friend at is south of where we're dropping you off. We don't want to pull into port and attract attention."

She nodded, understanding that she'd be on her own from here on out. Somehow, she preferred it like that. Glancing sidelong at Jorrg, she wondered why he kept calling Matsen her friend. He was an assassin—nothing more.

"Is there anything you need before we part ways?" Jorrg asked.

"No, but I do want to thank you for your help." Although he hadn't really done much.

"You're welcome." He smiled, apparently pleased with himself. "Where's the signed contract?"

"I set it on the desk in the cabin below deck," she lied.

"Thank you. And make sure to wait for your friend. You shouldn't be going anywhere without him. He'll keep you safe."

She found it appalling that Jorrg thought so little of her.

She was perfectly capable of keeping herself safe. The only reason she wanted Matsen around was because of his unique skill set and his knowledge of the kingdom and royal family. Instead of responding, she smiled at him, all the while thinking that he was a complete idiot, and she had no idea how she was related to him.

The ship slowed as it got closer to the shore. One of the men on board tossed a rope ladder over the side of the ship. He waved Mabel over.

Glad to get away from Jorrg, Mabel joined the crewman, peering over the side of the ship at the rough water below and wondering what he wanted her to do.

"There's a dock," he assured her. "Just a little ways down. When we get close enough, you'll climb over the side of the ship, down the ladder, and onto the dock." He nodded in encouragement, moving his hands to try and explain what he wanted her to do. His smile revealed several missing teeth.

Mabel tried not to cringe. "I can do that." She'd just have to be careful her dress didn't get caught on the way down.

The ship turned, and a wooden dock level with the water came into view. Several of the boards were missing or warped, and the water lapped over portions of the structure.

"Is that it?" she asked. There wasn't even a railing. Just some boards slapped together.

"Aye."

Her eyes narrowed. It looked like it hadn't been used in years. Mabel wasn't confident the thing would hold her weight. She very well may end up having to swim to shore.

"This is as close as we can get," the man said.

Instead of questioning if there was another option, she quickly said goodbye to Jorrg, thanked the men for bringing her, and then climbed up and over the railing. The sooner she was done with these idiots, the better. Grabbing onto the rope ladder, she climbed down, keeping her eye on the dock. When she neared it, she twisted her body around so her back faced the ship. She stuck her right leg out, testing the dock. It stayed in one place. Not wanting to jump onto it and risk having the thing collapse, she gently placed one foot and then the other onto the dock. Once she had her balance, she released the rope ladder. The ship immediately moved away from the dock though it remained close by, probably waiting to make sure she reached land about forty feet away.

The dark water lapping over the wood boards made it difficult to see where to place her feet. She assumed the structure went straight to the land, but she didn't want to make a false assumption and step right off it. Lifting her dress, she slowly slid her feet forward, making her way toward the island. Every so often she had to stop and wait for the swell to go down so she could see where to go. The frigid water soaked into her shoes and socks, making her cold. A few times, it felt as if the dock swayed, but she couldn't be sure if it was actually moving or just the water currents throwing her off.

Finally, she reached dry land and jumped from the dock onto solid ground. She waved to the ship, letting the crew members know she'd made it. The ship raised its sails and headed away from her.

The town she needed to reach was supposed to be about a mile south from her current location. The best course of action would be to keep the coastline in view so she wouldn't wander inland and get lost. Since it was too rocky here to walk, she needed to climb up the small rise to where the green grass coated the land. Scanning the area, she looked for the best place to climb up. After a minute, she spotted stone steps that had been carved into the side of the nearby cliff. They were small and worn with age but would work.

Lifting her dress, she quickly ascended the slick steps until she reached the top. She released her dress and marveled at the view before her. As far as she could see in one direction, the endless ocean. In the other direction, green rolling hills. The wind kicked up, tossing her hair every which way.

She started walking south, thankful the sun had risen more and was starting to warm her up. Hopefully her socks, shoes, and the bottom portion of her dress would dry quickly.

After about ten or fifteen minutes, an odd sensation filled her. She stopped and looked around to see what could be causing it. Goosebumps covered her body, a slight pain thrummed in her head, and her stomach rolled with nausea. Not seeing anything of concern, she had no idea why she felt so ill at ease. Perhaps it had something to do with being on the ship and now walking on land. Although, she'd sailed before and didn't have an issue. She just needed to force herself to keep moving. When she reached the town, she could lie down and rest for a bit. That would help her feel better.

Mabel took a step forward, and the land beneath her feet pulsed. She froze. The air around her seemed to vibrate, and a low humming sound came from her right. She looked toward the low rolling hills in the distance, but she didn't see anything.

She took a couple of steps closer to the cliff, wanting to glance over the side to see if there was something down there causing these bizarre things to happen. As she moved closer to the water, the eerie sensation went away, and everything returned to normal. She blinked, wondering if she'd just imagined the entire thing.

Now was not the time to investigate. She needed to stay on course, so she continued walking. A few minutes later, she glanced to her right. A lone figure cloaked in a black cape stood at the top of one of the hills in the distance. Mabel squinted, trying to see the person better. Only the figure disappeared. One of the crewmen must have slipped something in her food. Whatever he'd given her was causing her to hallucinate. She needed to get to the town and eat something to get the poison out of her system.

Not deviating from her path, she headed along the shoreline. After another ten minutes, she came to the edge of a cliff cut into the island. Glancing over the side, she saw a small town nestled at the base next to the water. Several small fishing boats were docked in the tiny harbor. There appeared to be one main street with several small houses situated on the outskirts of that one street. A path had been carved into the cliff, leading down, so she took it, thankful it was gradual instead of steep like the streets in Lima.

At the bottom, she headed directly to the main street, searching for a place to eat. She found a tavern and entered. The door squeaked as it shut behind her. Not wanting to sit at a table, she went to the bar and took a seat.

"What'll it be?" a large man behind the bar asked, eyeing her warily. He probably was wondering why a woman was all alone at a tavern so early in the day.

Looking him directly in the eyes, she replied, "Stew, bread, and a cup of ale." Hopefully the food and alcohol would absorb or kill whatever was in her system. She had no idea why one of the crewmen would have slipped something into her food, but it was the only logical explanation for what she'd experienced on her way to the town.

The bartender nodded and went in the back room.

Mabel rubbed her face while taking note of everyone in the tavern. Two men sat conversing at the table behind her and to the left, a single man sat eating at the table closest to the door, and five chairs to her right a lone man sat at the bar nursing a mug of ale.

A few minutes later, the bartender returned carrying a bowl. He set it on the counter and then shoved it toward Mabel. She took it and pulled it closer to her, noticing the slice of bread soaking in the stew. Apparently, she wouldn't be getting bread on the side. The man picked up a cup and filled it with ale. When he plopped it before her, a bit spilled over the side.

Pursing her lips, she took her spoon and started eating the lukewarm food.

"You passing through?" the bartender asked, his voice gruff.

She lifted a single eyebrow and observed him standing on the other side of the counter. "What I am or am not doing is none of your concern."

The man sitting a few chairs to her right chuckled. "Leave the woman alone, Kert."

"We're all supposed to be on the lookout for a young woman," the bartender, Kert, said. "You heard the man."

"What man?" Mabel asked, trying not to appear too interested. Maybe Matsen had gotten here before her.

"One of the king's soldiers. He passed through delivering a message from the king. If a young woman shows up, it's supposed to be reported." Kert picked up a towel and started wiping the counter off. "I suppose we'll have to report you."

She chuckled. "I'm sure my husband will appreciate that," she lied. The last thing she wanted was to be taken into custody. She didn't want to meet the king until she was well and ready.

"You're married?"

"I am. And I've come here while I wait for my husband who's running an errand for me." She took a bite of her stew, trying to act as if she had nothing to hide. As if she wasn't the heir to the throne.

Kert scratched the side of his face. "We're not supposed

to bother with the married women. Only the unmarried ones." He hung up his towel before going into the back room.

Mabel continued to eat her stew, now in peace.

"No one ever comes here," the man to her right said.

"Funny," she replied. "I could have sworn Kert just said one of the king's soldiers was in this town." She could feel the man staring at her. "My husband and I are only passing through. We're headed north to visit family."

"Why didn't you take the main road?" the man asked.

"My husband prefers to sail." She figured that was a safer answer since she didn't know if there was a main road and perhaps this man was trying to catch her in a lie.

"There're rough waters around here."

"That there are," she agreed. "And docks in dire need of repair."

That seemed to appease him as he went back to sipping his ale.

When Mabel finished her food, she put three coins on the counter before exiting the tavern. Outside, she'd intended on going to the town's inn. Glancing up at the sky, dark clouds had rolled in, covering the sun, promising rain. She suspected she had an hour or two until the storm hit, so she decided to explore the area before being stuck in a room all afternoon.

Since there weren't any stores for shopping, she headed back up the path carved into the cliff. At the top, she stood near the edge, letting the wind whip around her body as she watched the ocean below. The waves had picked up, crashing against the cliffs in roaring delight. Mabel breathed it all in. She much preferred this than the sticky humid weather typical on the island of Karlis.

A tingling sensation fluttered up her spine, so she spun around to see who or what had caused it. About a quarter of a mile away, on the peak of a hill, stood the cloaked figure she saw earlier. The person's face remained completely hidden beneath the hood of the cape. They stared at one another for an uncomfortable minute. Then, suddenly, the cloaked figure turned and strode away, disappearing behind the hill.

The odd sensation filling Mabel evaporated. She shivered, knowing nothing about the cloaked figure was normal. She felt a soft tug, as if she had a rope tied around her waist and someone had gently pulled on it. Without a doubt, she knew the mysterious person was the source of the pull. Two options stretched out before her. One, she could ignore it, as the rational part of her brain told her to do, and return to the inn where she could secure a room for the evening. Or two, she could follow the pull to see where it led.

It really wasn't a choice.

Mabel followed the pull, letting it lead her inland. She scaled the hill where the cloaked figure had been. At the top, she spotted a small village about a half mile away. The pull increased, coming from the village. Heading that way, an odd sensation swept over her again, making her feel ill. Regardless, she continued, wanting—needing—to figure out what was going on.

She stopped at a narrow dirt road. The road encircled the

village which consisted of fifteen huts arranged in a circle. Smoke came from the chimney of one of the huts while the others appeared lifeless.

She couldn't explain it, but there was some sort of barrier preventing her from taking another step forward. Reaching out with her left hand, she felt an invisible wall of some sort. When she looked closely, she could see something shimmering in the air.

Mabel took a step back; a mixture of fear and wonder filled her.

A tingle brushed her spine again, as if spiders were crawling up her back. She spun around and saw the cloaked figure hovering a few feet away. As the cloak fluttered in the wind, Mabel realized it didn't have any feet or hands. The reason she didn't see a face beneath the hood was because there wasn't one.

"What are you doing here?" a woman's voice asked from behind Mabel.

She spun around and saw a woman on the other side of the invisible barrier. The woman appeared to be in her forties and had light brown, curly hair. She wore a simple brown dress. "I'm just out exploring the area," Mabel replied. "I saw the," she pointed over her shoulder at the floating cloak, "and followed it."

The woman smiled. "My eyes and ears since I can't leave. It can only go about a mile, but it's enough."

Mabel wondered if the woman was stuck inside the invisible barrier. "Who are you?"

"I think the more important question is who are you?"

"Mabel Bakken," she answered before even realizing she'd spoken. Confusion washed through her.

The woman tilted her head to the side. "That's not a name I recognize. I assumed you'd be from one of the five royal families since you're here."

"I am the daughter of King Rhett Forberg." Mabel knew there were five known kingdoms, and she wondered if those were the five royal families this woman was referring to.

"Ah," the woman said, as if that explained everything. "Did he send you?"

Mabel shook her head.

"Then why are you here?"

"I don't know," she whispered. "I felt drawn to this place." Because there was some sort of magic here. Powerful magic. "What are you?" she asked, already knowing the answer. This woman had to be a witch.

"I already told the man how to end it. Until he has everything I need, I don't want to be disturbed. Now be gone." The woman flicked her wrist.

Everything went black.

CHAPTER 17

DECLAN

Brooks snapped the book shut. "Brielle is correct."

Declan had figured as much.

"According to what I read, a hundred years ago, gratscot was frequently used in Miervades as a form of torture." Brooks set the book on the table and started pacing. Which meant he was thinking.

Declan went over to the window in the library and stared outside. Brielle had told him that Miervades parents gave their children very small doses as a punishment. Her father had even given it to her when she snuck away from home once. Brielle said she'd been in such pain and discomfort that she never even considered running away again. He hadn't thought to ask why she'd run away in the first place. "Brielle said the queen would be fine." He clasped his hands behind his back. No, his mother wouldn't die, but she would suffer greatly for the next week or so.

"You said you saw the queen's assassin?" Brooks asked as he took a seat, stretching out his bad leg.

"Yes. On Oskar. I think he did this to her."

"To send a message?"

"Exactly." Declan wondered if he should send a message of his own.

"You never considered that Brielle might have done this to the queen?" Brooks asked.

Declan couldn't help but laugh. "Brielle?" Doing something so evil and manipulative wasn't in her nature. "She was with me. She didn't do it."

Brooks nodded. "And there's no one here at the palace who would help her. No one like Jenice?"

Declan looked pointedly at his brother. "Why would you suggest such a thing? I thought you liked Brielle."

"I do like her." He started massaging his bad leg. "But Mother was given a plant from Miervades. It makes more sense that it would be Brielle. Think about it. If the assassin had just arrived in Oskar, how did he get to the palace so quickly? Not only that, but how did he manage to slip gratscot onto Mother's plate? It's a bit of a stretch. Plus, I wouldn't consider Mabel a Miervades native."

All valid points. However, Declan knew Brielle hadn't done it. He focused outside the window again. "There is one other thing I need to tell you." The sun shone on the water, allowing him to see straight to the ocean floor. The storm yesterday had made everything crystal clear today. "I met with one of our informants in Oskar. He said there are men from Lima's army here hunting the king. Apparently, there are rumors they intend to assassinate him." Information from this particular source usually turned out to be accurate.

"Have you sent word to Father?" Brooks asked.

"No." Declan had been waiting for the king to return so he could tell him in person. He didn't want to send a message and have rumors start circulating. When dealing with something of this magnitude, discretion was best. "We need to find Mabel." She was the key to everything right now.

"If the king can't find her with his extensive resources, I doubt the two of us will be able to."

"I've been thinking."

"Oh no." Brooks chuckled.

Declan ignored him and took a seat across the table from Brooks. "I'd like to find a way around Father's contract with Duke Jaxon. I'd like to marry Brielle, regardless if the duke pays his taxes or not." He had to marry and produce an heir by the time he turned twenty-four, only three years from now. Brielle seemed like a smart, reasonable person he could spend his life with. In addition, he didn't think Brielle should die simply because her father didn't have the money for his taxes. If the blood oath wasn't in place, the duke could bring his books to the king and re-negotiate the terms to something he could afford to pay.

"Hmm," Brooks said, his eyes narrowing. "Why the change of heart?"

"I don't know," he admitted. "It just feels right."

"I already told you what I think you should do about the contract."

Declan had been giving it a lot of thought. "I just want to make sure I'm not violating any laws."

"You're not. So long as you do it before the king returns."

Declan tapped the table twice. "I need to be going." He stood. "Do you have any idea how the queen communicates with her assassin?" The only reason he even knew about the assassin was because Orson had been snooping around in the military archives a few years back and stumbled upon it.

"I have no idea," Brooks answered. "However, I'm sure in Mother's current state, you could ask her, and she'd tell you."

A good idea.

"Why do you want to know?"

"I want to ask him if he's working for Mabel now." And discover if the assassin had been the one to poison the queen.

"Some things are left better off alone. I believe this is one of those situations."

Declan patted Brooks's shoulder. "Perhaps."

"Before you go," Brooks said, "Can you hand me those two books on the shelf over there?" He pointed behind Declan.

"Sure." He grabbed the books, sliding them on the table. He didn't usually bother to take notice of what his brother was reading, but one of the titles caught his attention. *The Witch's Cove.* "Still researching that children's story?"

"Something like that." Brooks opened one of the books.

The page on the left revealed a faded drawing while the story had been written on the right side. Declan glanced at the picture, wondering how the children's story depicted witches. There was a beautiful woman with long, wavy hair reaching out toward a child. There was a mark on the woman's wrist. A mark Declan was certain he'd seen before, but he had no idea where.

"If I discover anything interesting, I'll let you know," Brooks said, looking up from the book and effectively dismissing Declan.

Declan nodded and hurried from the room, all the while trying to remember where he'd seen that mark before.

Dressed as a common foot soldier, Declan kept his hood up and his head angled down while he strode across the bridge leading to the military island of Jargis. There were enough people crossing midday to allow him to blend in without there being so many he'd have to worry about someone recognizing him.

At the end of the bridge, he discretely showed his ring to the soldier on duty. The man waved him through. Stepping off the bridge and onto solid ground, Declan headed north. It always amazed him how large Jargis was since it was so close to Sunder. Often it felt like a different kingdom entirely. Probably because this island's sole purpose was to house Valdis's military. He found it strange that his father maintained such a large army when there hadn't been a major war with another kingdom in over five hundred years. Every time he asked his father about it, the king merely said it was better to be prepared than taken by surprise. Still, it cost an enormous amount of money.

The only city on the island was located at the northern end. It consisted of shops, taverns, and a theater. It was like any other city in Valdis except that military families owned, operated, and shopped at all the places. The western section of the island was where the barracks and homes could be found. In the middle of Jargis, the training facilities, armories, and offices were situated. The docks were on the east side of the island. The only people allowed to step foot on Jargis were military personnel and their immediate family. Even though anyone in the army could live on the island, not everyone chose to do so. Jargis did have a school for children, but a lot of the families decided to live on Valdis and have their kids attend classes there.

Declan didn't care for the island. The dirt streets made everything dusty, and all the buildings were tan and plain. Nothing in Jargis had any color. There weren't even any plants or trees on the island. And the buildings were all square, single-story structures with nothing distinct about them. Orson had said it had to do with sight lines and making sure they could see so many miles out at any time without obstructions.

It was here, on this regimented military island, that Declan's grandfather, General Sullivan, lived. The general's home was the one and only two-story structure on Jargis. While the military families lived in simple homes with only four or five rooms, the general's house consisted of over twenty rooms. Sullivan had bedchambers to spare, dining rooms, ballrooms, a library, and even an atrium. Supposedly the house had been built hundreds of years ago, before the military took over the island. Declan found it insulting that the person leading the army lived in excess while the soldiers were denied so much. However, it wasn't his place to complain since he lived in a palace while most of his subjects had homes a fraction of the size. So, he chose not to question the way things were done. Sometimes it was easier to go along with the status quo rather than to try and change it.

Declan kept his hood up, trying to look like every other off-duty soldier. He hoped no one got a good look at his face. If his grandfather got wind of his presence on the island, the general would be sure to seek him out. And the last person Declan wanted to see right now was Sullivan. He wanted to speak with his brother privately without anyone else knowing about his visit.

Traversing along the streets, he headed in a zig-zag pattern toward his grandfather's home, knowing the general wouldn't be there at this hour. Sullivan would be at the training facility, overseeing the new recruits being brought in. Declan had chosen to come at this time for that exact reason. Technically, Orson should be at the training facility as well. However, Declan knew his brother had been out drinking last night, so Orson was at his future home recuperating from his wild endeavors. At least that was the appearance Orson gave.

At the gate to the general's home, Declan lifted his chin,

allowing the guard to catch a glimpse of his face. The guard opened the gate, granting him entrance.

When he reached the front door, he didn't bother knocking and just strode right inside. Sullivan's house felt vastly different from the open and airy palace Declan had grown up in. The stone walls only had a few scattered windows here and there which gave the place a warm, dark feeling. That, coupled with the richly colored decorations and furnishings, made it seem masculine. Apparently, his grandmother had passed before the general moved into this house. Growing up, Declan had always thought it lacked a woman's feminine touch.

He headed up the wide, wooden staircase to the second floor. How someone like his mother had grown up here, he didn't know. He never could picture a little girl running through these halls or playing in these rooms.

At the last door on the right, Declan knocked before entering.

Orson sat shirtless on the bed, reading. When he spotted Declan, he smiled. "I was wondering when you'd show up. We have a lot to discuss."

"Grandfather?" he asked, needing confirmation the man wasn't home.

Orson set his book aside and then stood. "He's working with the recruits at the docks. I made sure there'd be a few problems, so he'll be needed all afternoon." Orson smirked, confident in his scheming as always.

Ever since Orson was a child, he'd always been thinking a few steps ahead to be sure he never got caught doing whatever it was he shouldn't have been doing. It was one of the reasons Declan loved his brother so much. "Excellent. What do you have for me?"

"First, how's Mother doing?" Orson grabbed a shirt, pulling it on as he headed over to the bookshelf. "Nasty poison, gratscot." He shuddered.

"She's not doing well." After she'd ingested the plant, it only took about fifteen minutes until she started having severe stomach cramps. Declan and Brielle dismissed the royal servants and took the queen to her bedchamber. Since Declan needed to make sure no one discovered the queen's condition, Brielle offered to remain at her side, tending to her. The queen didn't seem thrilled with the idea, but when she started vomiting, her protests stopped.

They'd need to come up with a better story as to why the queen wasn't parading around court like usual. Brooks had suggested they tell people she missed the king and was sulking in her room. Not that Briar would ever sulk, but it was the best excuse they'd come up with so far. They couldn't afford for anyone to know she was ill from poison. It would be seen as a direct threat to the crown and make the king look weak. With the possibility of the assassins here from Lima, Declan needed to keep the queen's condition quiet.

"I'm surprised the food taster didn't get ill as well." Orson swung the bookshelf open, revealing a secret passage behind it.

"I agree." If the gratscot had been added to her plate

after the food taster inspected it, that meant someone intimately involved with the queen had poisoned her.

"Isn't gratscot from Miervades?" Orson asked.

Declan groaned. He'd already been through this with Brooks. "Yes. And no, Brielle didn't have anything to do with it. She was with me the entire time."

"Might be worth questioning her." He shrugged. "She could have been involved somehow."

Declan dismissed the idea since it was preposterous.

Orson grabbed a candle from his nightstand and entered the dark passageway. Declan followed him, closing the bookshelf door just in case. Their grandfather didn't keep servants in the house on a full-time basis, but a handful did come to cook and clean at certain designated hours of the day. Regardless, it was best not to take any chances and have someone accidentally discover the passageway.

At the other end, Orson pushed on part of the wall, and it swung open, revealing Grandfather's room. "If he ever found us in here, I'm not sure we'd survive," Orson mumbled as he stepped inside.

Declan had been thinking the same thing. They'd never been permitted in their grandfather's room. In fact, Declan hadn't even been allowed upstairs until Orson started staying in the house. And the only reason Orson insisted on living here was because the house was designated for the general of the army. It was well past time for Sullivan to retire. Even the king had begun issuing hints that Sullivan needed to step aside and allow Orson to take over. Their grandfather had always claimed Orson was too young and inexperienced. So, Orson started screwing around, being irresponsible, claiming he had too much free time on his hands. They hoped to force Grandfather's hand into retiring. The problem was that Sullivan loved control. And power. He wouldn't relinquish his position until he was good and ready to do so.

Declan had no qualms about being in his grandfather's room because they didn't have a loving relationship filled with trust and respect. Rather, it seemed Sullivan prided himself on Declan's position as the crown prince, not Declan as a person. All Sullivan cared about was his own position as the general, the queen's place in the kingdom, and that his grandson would be the king one day. There had never been any fondness between them.

"Over here," Orson said from across the room.

Declan joined his brother at the armoire.

Orson pulled out a key, unlocked the doors, and then opened them, revealing several military tunics meticulously hung up. He reached underneath the clothing, feeling around until he found what he was looking for. Smiling, he pulled out a journal. "Here." He handed it to Declan.

"Did you read this?" he asked as he peeled back the cover.

Orson rolled his eyes. "No. I glanced through it. When I saw our grandfather's name—and I want to clarify, our father's father's name—I read that section." He reached out, fingering through the pages until he came to the place he wanted Declan to read. "Here." He pointed to a page. "This is the part you need to see."

Declan read the words, not quite comprehending them. His ears rang, his hands shook, and he could scarcely see the writing on the page any longer. He was going to be ill.

"It makes sense," Orson said, folding his arms. "Once our grandfather, the king, was out of the way, our father ascended to the throne, making Briar the queen. It's all General Sullivan wanted. His daughter as the queen. And you, his grandson, as the heir."

Declan's head thrummed from the implications. The writing in this journal belonged to General Sullivan. All the particulars were there about where their paternal grandfather would be and when. It had all been made to look like an accident. Declan slid the journal under his vest, wanting to keep it as evidence.

"His daughter was a princess," Declan said. "She would have been queen one day. I don't understand why Sullivan had to hurry the process along." Why he had to commit treason to get his daughter on the throne sooner, forcing Declan to do something about it now that he knew the truth. When a law was broken, he had to enforce it. Unless they could find a way to end the blood oath which didn't seem likely.

"Read the rest of the journal when you get a chance. It offers some insight into Grandfather's head. It's a scary place to be."

"He's never going to let Mabel live," Declan mumbled, thinking out loud. Since Mabel was not of Briar's blood, Sullivan would do anything to make sure she didn't ascend to the throne. Declan rubbed his face and looked at his brother. "You're coming with me. I won't leave you here. If Grandfather discovers his journal is missing, you'll be in danger."

Orson shrugged. "Would he kill me? I'm not so sure. He'd be furious, yes. He'd be wild with rage. But kill his own blood? I'm not certain he would."

"It's not a chance I'm willing to take."

"And you don't have to. It's a chance *I'm* willing to take. I want to keep tabs on him, and I can do that from here. Besides, I'm too lazy to pull off something like discovering a hidden journal. No, that's for someone far cleverer than me." He winked. "That's why he's the general, not me."

Declan pursed his lips, trying to think through everything. He needed to discuss this with Brooks.

"Do you think Mother knew?"

Declan shrugged. "I hope not." If she did, she'd be an accomplice to treason and would be put to death. However, he knew his mother and her unending thirst for power. The fact that she'd sent her assassin after Mabel only made her look more guilty. Once she was better, he'd have to question her about both events. When Father returned, Declan would have to tell him. The king wouldn't handle the news well.

"One last thing to consider," Orson said as he shut the armoire and locked it. "Grandfather controls Jurgis. I'd hate to see a civil war—king against general."

A scary thought indeed. "Be prepared to give the order to sink the bridge if necessary." It would buy them time if it came to that. They'd still have to deal with the forces that attacked by boat, but the immediate assault from foot soldiers would be halted.

"I will. And Declan, watch your back."

"I always do."

After bidding his brother farewell, Declan exited his grandfather's house and headed toward the center of the island. When he reached the buildings containing the offices, he went straight to the records room. The people he passed didn't bother to ask what he was doing there. It was one of the benefits of outranking every single person on the island.

Thankfully the records room was empty. Declan closed and locked the door. He scanned the rows and rows of shelves containing hundreds of boxes filled with papers. It would take him some time to find what he wanted since he couldn't ask anyone for help. If he did, it would raise unwanted suspicions. Then his grandfather would find out. This task he had to do on his own and as quietly as possible. He got to work.

CHAPTER 18
BRIELLE

The last thing Brielle wanted to do was nurse the queen back to health. Not only did she not like being around sick people, especially when they were vomiting, but she did not care for Briar. And she was certain the woman did not care for her either.

Yet here Brielle sat on a chair next to Briar's bed. Declan didn't want anyone finding out about the queen's condition. He feared people would panic, especially with the king gone. And he didn't want word to get back to Mabel that the assassin had been successful.

Brielle eyed the sleeping queen. Drool slid from the corner of Briar's mouth, along her cheek, and down to her neck. There was no point in wiping it up since the drool didn't stop and it would only wake her. Then Briar would start barking out orders and tell Brielle how worthless she was.

A sleeping queen was a quiet queen.

Brielle stood and went over to the balcony doors, opening them up to allow the fresh air in. The dark gray curtains on the four-poster bed rustled from the gentle breeze. Earlier in the day, Brielle had pulled the curtains back so she could see the queen at all times. Briar had protested, but Brielle had simply ignored her. She wondered if the queen had always been such high maintenance and used to people doing whatever she wanted. She'd probably always been that way. Being the queen couldn't have changed her that much.

At least Brielle had never allowed herself to get caught up in the fantasy of marrying Declan and becoming a princess. Everything had happened so quickly that she hadn't had a chance to settle into the idea of being a member of the royal family. She'd been so caught up with leaving her family, her home, and marrying a stranger, that she hadn't ever thought about what her future could look like with Declan. And now, she had no future with him. She might not have one at all if she didn't figure something out.

"Do you plan on standing there all day, blocking the air flow?" the queen asked, startling Brielle. Briar had managed to sit up and was leaning against the headboard, watching Brielle.

"Can I get you something to drink?" she asked, returning to her chair beside the bed.

"No. My stomach is calm for a change, and I don't want to upset it." The queen closed her eyes, breathed in deeply, and then opened her eyes again. "For the first time in days, I don't feel like death." She delicately lifted her right shoulder in a half shrug. "I'm sure it'll only last a few minutes before I want to scream again."

Brielle didn't bother saying anything since the queen didn't really want a response. Briar treated her like a servant rather than a future daughter-in-law. Maybe the queen somehow knew Brielle would never marry Declan. Tears filled her eyes. The one thing she had hoped for coming here was that she might find a mother figure in Briar. She tried not to laugh at the absurdity of it. The queen was as far from a mother as could be. Again, there was no use wishing for things that could never happen.

"I didn't think you had ingested the poison as well," Briar said, a snide tone to her voice.

"I didn't," Brielle said, confused.

"Then I don't see why you're on the verge of tears." Briar rested her head against the headboard. "No one tried to kill you. You're not in severe discomfort."

"You're right," Brielle whispered. "I'm not in any physical pain like you are. It doesn't feel like a knife is stabbing me in the stomach, I'm not nauseous, and I'm not running a fever."

At that the queen lifted her head, studying Brielle. "Tell me, have you ingested this plant before?"

She folded her hands together. "I have," she admitted. "Not on purpose. It was a punishment."

Briar's eyes narrowed. "I doubt you're teary-eyed because you sympathize with me."

A snort escaped Brielle's mouth before she could think better of it.

The queen lifted an eyebrow.

"Sorry," Brielle mumbled.

"That…noise…you made is answer enough." Briar pushed herself up a little more, adjusting the pillow against her back. "Since there's nothing else for me to do but…*talk*, tell me why you look like you're about to cry."

If this were any other person, Brielle might think she cared about her. But that was not the case here. With her emotions under control, and the tears no longer threatening, she could talk to the queen though she would not reveal anything personal that could be used against her. "I'm not about to cry. I'm fine." Her voice even sounded confident.

"You weren't fine a moment ago," the queen purred, as if she enjoyed making Brielle squirm.

Knowing Briar wouldn't let up until she had an answer, Brielle said the first thing that came to mind. "I miss my family." Because there was no way she could admit to wanting a mother figure in Briar. She also couldn't mention that her father didn't have the money to pay the taxes Miervades owed. So basically, Brielle would either be dead on Walpurgis, or she'd be on the run, hunted by the crown. She blinked, forcing the tears to remain at bay.

"I'm sure your family will come for the wedding," Briar said, sounding utterly bored with the topic.

She tried not to roll her eyes. The queen had probably thought something juicy was going on, and she'd wanted in on the gossip. "Yes." Brielle forced a smile on her face. "I'm sure my family will come for the wedding." The words tasted like dirt to say since they were lies. Wanting to move the conversation away from herself, she asked, "What was your wedding like?" She expected the queen would gladly reminisce about her own special day. "I'm certain it was quite grand."

Briar's attention went to the canopy over her bed, a smile gracing her lips as her mind went to a distant place, a distant time. "I had the most spectacular wedding."

Only half listening, Brielle shoved the sleeves of her dress up to her elbows and snuggled on her chair, thankful the attention was no longer on her and that she didn't have to respond. The queen really didn't want to know anything about her anyway.

Briar explained what her dress had looked like, how her hair had been done, what flowers were arranged in the chapel, and all of the food that had been served. All in great detail, as if it had happened yesterday.

Silence filled the air, and Brielle realized Briar had stopped talking. "How old were you when you married?" she asked to keep the queen rambling on about herself.

"Nineteen. And I was very much in love with Rhett."

She'd never heard the king addressed by his first name without a title attached to it. It somehow made him seem more human—like a person instead of the king. "You were in love with him even though it was an arranged marriage?" No royal person ever married simply for love; it always focused on power, land, or prestige.

"My family has been serving the king for generations," Briar said. "My father and the late king were the best of friends. The two of them arranged for Rhett and I to marry, wanting to unite our families. Since I'd grown up with Rhett, I knew him well. By the time I was twelve, I was already madly in love with him." She smiled, her eyes focused on something in the distance, a memory perhaps. "I became pregnant with Declan right after we wed. The king died in an unfortunate accident before Declan was even born. Such a tragedy. Rhett ascended to the throne before he was truly ready."

"That must have been a huge responsibility for you," Brielle said. "To be newly married, crowned queen, and then become a mother."

"Everything happened so quickly," Briar said. "My own mother died when I was young, so I had no guidance." Briar hunched forward, moaning.

Another bout must be about to start so Brielle reached out, taking the queen's hand, and squeezing it. It was all the comfort and support she could provide. Sweat broke out along Briar's forehead, and her breathing turned laborious.

With her free hand, Brielle grabbed the washcloth out of the bucket of water, using it to wipe off the queen's forehead. "Just breathe," she said. "Deep breath in, deep breath out. Nice and slow."

"What's that?" Briar asked through gritted teeth.

Brielle had no idea what the woman was referring to.

"Your bracelet." The queen turned Brielle's bracelet around. "There's no latch to remove it from your wrist?"

"No."

"Who gave it to you?"

She shrugged. "I've always had it. My father said it was

one of the few things my mother had given me." It was such a part of her that she often forgot it was even on.

"It's not very fitting for a princess."

"Then I guess it's a good thing I'm not a princess."

Briar looked into Brielle's eyes, making her feel oddly naked. "I see sparks of myself in you at times."

That was the last thing Brielle expected her to say. She had no idea how to respond. However, she did know that she was nothing like the queen—and she never would be.

Someone shook Brielle awake. She peeled her eyelids open and found Declan standing above her in the queen's now dark room.

"Why aren't any candles lit?" he whispered.

"I fell asleep when it was still light out." She glanced at the sleeping queen. "What time is it?"

"Just after supper." Declan went over to his mother, feeling her forehead. Turning to Brielle, he waved for her to follow him.

She trailed him out to the queen's balcony.

"Have you eaten?" he asked.

"No."

"Excellent."

She didn't see how that was excellent at all.

"Wait here." He left her standing on the balcony while he went back into the queen's bedchamber.

In the darkness, she could no longer see him.

He returned a moment later with two plates of food. Smiling, he set them on a small table on the right side of the balcony. "My mother occasionally takes her breakfast out here," he said, as if that explained what he was doing. He sat on one of the chairs. "Aren't you going to join me?"

Stunned, she took the seat across from him. "This plate is for me?" She had no idea why he'd do something so nice for her.

"It's the least I can do. I want to thank you for helping my mother and for your discretion." He pulled utensils out of his pocket, handing her a fork. Then he took his own fork and started eating.

"I'm happy to help." Truth be told, she was pleased to do this for the three brothers, not the queen. She looked at the assortment of food on her plate and began eating.

"There's something I need to tell you."

She glanced up at him across the table from her.

"I read through the entire marriage contract. It's solid, and there aren't any areas that can be negotiated or misinterpreted. Which means, when your father doesn't pay, you will be killed."

It felt as if she'd eaten stones instead of grapes. Shoving her plate aside, she stared out at the ocean. "Then I have no choice but to run." She didn't know why she'd held onto hope that something could be done. Lukas had told her as much, yet she hadn't wanted to believe him.

"There's always a choice."

"What would you do in my situation?" The turbulent ocean below mimicked her own worrying stomach that churned with what lie ahead. If she wanted a chance at a normal life, she would have to go to another kingdom. Try and blend in. Build a new life. And every single day, look over her shoulder to see if the king or one of his assassins had finally found her.

"If I were you, I'd run. Go back to your father. See if he has anything planned for you. If he doesn't, go to Lima and hide."

She absently nodded, already making plans. Since the king was gone, she'd have to leave as soon as possible to give herself time to hide. Her hands started shaking.

"I'm sorry I can't do more to help you," he said gently.

Brielle shrugged. The laws as written weren't his fault. He was the prince and had to enforce them. She understood the precarious position he was in.

They ate in silence for a few minutes. Then Declan sighed and ran his hands through his hair. "I don't believe your father would do this to you without having a plan in place."

Her eyes filled with tears. Her father had never been one to plan ahead. Both him and Kenna always did things on a whim. "If he doesn't have the money, there isn't much he can do." The blame should be with the king who'd backed her father into a corner with no way out.

Declan drummed his fingers on the table. "Can I ask you a question without you getting upset?"

"Of course." She couldn't imagine what he'd ask that would upset her.

"Do you and your sister have the same mother?"

She had no idea why he'd ask that. "Yes. She died delivering me. Why do you ask?"

"I think it's strange my father chose you over Kenna." He continued drumming his fingers on the table. "Don't get me wrong," he glanced at her, "I'm glad he chose you and not her, but it makes me wonder if I'm missing something."

She thought they'd gone over this already on the day the king had shown up at her home. Since her sister was the heir, she couldn't marry the crown prince and leave Miervades. Reaching out, Brielle took hold of Declan's hand, stilling it. "I wouldn't stress over too much," she said. "It doesn't matter anyway. We'll never marry."

He squeezed her hand back. "It's an unfortunate situation. I think we would have gotten along nicely."

"Me too." The more she got to know Declan, the more she liked him and could see a life with him.

"You're thoughtful and put others before yourself. You would have made a great queen one day."

She pulled her hand free and wiped the tears that started falling.

A sound came from the queen's bedchamber. Declan held his finger to his lips. Brielle nodded in understanding.

"Mother?" Brooks said.

Declan's shoulders relaxed and he opened his mouth to say something when Brooks spoke again.

"I received word from your assassin," Brooks mumbled.

Declan grabbed Brielle's wrist, his eyes going wide. She immediately understood that she was not to make a sound.

"And?" the queen asked.

"He has everything that is needed."

"Except the girl." The queen sighed. "I don't know what else I have to do to get her there since this brilliant plan of mine didn't work."

"I told you not to do it," Brooks said. "If you'd just let me tell her the plan, she might have gone along with it without you suffering needlessly."

"I'm not certain where her loyalties lie," the queen said.

"I think she'd side with us," Brooks replied.

"*Think* is not good enough. We're running out of time, and we can't leave anything to chance."

"I understand. I have a plan that will work. There's nothing to worry about, Mother. Everything is under control. How would you like me to respond to your assassin?"

There was a brief pause before the queen asked, "With this plan of yours, when do you expect her to be there?"

"In a week."

"Then let him know that's when he should have the last piece. He has as much to gain from this as we do." There was a shuffling noise.

"Where's Brielle?" Brooks asked. "I thought she was supposed to be watching you so we could keep tabs on her."

"The little twit ran off. She's probably reading in her own room."

Brooks chuckled. "There's nothing wrong with reading, Mother. It improves one's mind."

"Don't even get me started on how ill-educated she is."

"Be nice. She is kind and you owe her. Do you need anything before I leave?"

"No. Just get this wrapped up before your father returns. If he catches wind of what we're doing, he'll put an end to it."

Brielle heard footsteps and then a door close. She dared not move. They sat in silence for a long time. Declan remained so still, she feared he wasn't breathing.

After what felt like an hour, Declan stood and gestured for Brielle to remain where she was. He went and peered into his mother's room. He returned to Brielle and whispered in her ear, "She's asleep. I think. We're going to enter her room and remain in the shadows against the wall. There's a door to the king's room not far from where we are. We'll go in there and then you can exit the suite."

She nodded and stood, being careful not to move her chair and make a noise. She followed Declan to the open door. He reached back and took hold of her hand, leading her into the queen's room. They moved slowly along the wall. Declan released her hand and then reached forward, opening a door. All the time she'd spent in this room with the queen, she'd thought this door led to a dressing closet and had no idea it went to the king's room. Declan pulled her through the doorway before carefully shutting the door.

Taking her hand again, Declan led her through the room and to another door. He stopped before it. "Go down the hall to the right. You'll find yourself at the entrance to my mother's room. You should know how to exit the royal suite from there. Don't talk to anyone or make any noise. If someone asks where you're coming from, tell them you napped in my room."

Brielle nodded, suddenly wondering what Declan's room looked like.

"Be safe." He leaned down and kissed her forehead.

She nodded and did as he said, making her way through the royal chambers and exiting them.

Brielle headed toward her own room. She had no idea what was going on with Brooks, but she could tell it had upset Declan. Given her conversation with him tonight and everything going on, now would probably be a good time to run away. However, exhaustion consumed her, and she wanted nothing more than to crawl into bed to sleep for a few hours.

This late at night, the palace was eerily silent since those staying at court were all in bed sleeping. Brielle only passed a handful of sentries on duty, and a strange feeling of abandonment set in, making her shiver. Her footsteps seemed loud in the quiet palace.

Brielle entered her room and went over to the side table to light the candle. A tingling sensation crawled up her back and she swung around, coming face-to-face with Lukas. "What are you doing here?" she hissed, her heart pounding from fright.

"Shh," he whispered. "We don't want anyone to hear us." He placed both his hands on her shoulders. "I'm going to get you out of here."

She vaguely wondered how he'd managed to get in there in the first place. Her tired brain tried to process everything.

Without waiting for her to respond, Lukas took hold of her arm, dragging her from the room.

"We're leaving right this second?" she asked as they headed down the hallway. She hadn't grabbed any clothing or supplies for their journey. She didn't even have a cape on.

Lukas pulled her down another corridor, one she'd never been in.

"What's the plan?" she asked, trying to yank her arm free. It almost felt as if he was kidnapping her. They couldn't just leave in the middle of the night without any supplies. Unless he planned to charter a boat. The mere thought made her stomach roll with nausea.

"I'm taking you home." He didn't look at her when he spoke. Instead, his grip on her tightened. "Your father wants you there."

Something was wrong—she could feel it. "Let go of me."

Lukas spun around, his face mere inches from hers. "I'll carry you out of here if I have to," he replied, a hard edge to his voice.

This was not the Lukas she knew; the boy she'd grown up with. Even if he was there on her father's behalf, he didn't have to treat her so illy. "You will do no such thing. Now release me."

He resumed walking, dragging her along after him. "I'm not letting go until we're out of this place. Now stop fighting me and let's be on our way before someone finds us."

"Perhaps someone has already found you," Orson purred from a dark archway ahead of them. He stepped into the light, blocking the way, a wicked gleam to his eyes. "Lady Brielle, who's your...friend?"

Relief coursed through her. Orson could help her with Lukas.

"You shouldn't be dallying around the hallways late at night with another man when you're engaged to my brother," Orson commented. "It doesn't look good."

"You have the wrong idea," she said, trying to explain.

Lukas released Brielle, stepping in front of her, shielding her from Orson so he couldn't easily reach her. "I'm leaving with Lady Brielle," Lukas insisted, folding his arms across his chest.

Brielle rolled her eyes. Orson could knock him over in a second.

"I'm sorry, I don't believe we've been properly introduced," Orson said, tilting his head to the side.

"Prince Orson," Brielle said, trying to stand next to Lukas, "this is my friend, Lukas, from Miervades." She knew Orson was aware of Lukas since he'd seen him at the engagement ball. He'd even said he had men watching him —which was why Orson was probably here. One of his spies must have told him Lukas was in the palace.

Orson raised a single eyebrow. "You're a long way from home."

Brielle pushed Lukas to the side so she could see Orson. "And that is exactly where Lukas is returning. Right now."

Orson narrowed his eyes. "Do you wish to visit your home?" he asked her, his voice softer than before.

Her heart pounded, considering her options. There

wasn't much that happened without Orson knowing about it, so he had to be aware that she intended on running away to avoid being executed. Strange that both Declan and Orson were letting her go. She swallowed. "Yes, I wish to visit my father." Everything here was based on rules and laws. If the king believed she'd left to visit her father, it would buy her additional time to hide. Now she could return home, come up with a plan, and then run away all before anyone suspected anything.

"Then go. When you return on Walpurgis, bring your father's taxes along with the wheat he owes."

She bit her bottom lip, her brows pulling together. "Are you sure?" she asked before she could think better of it. He knew her father didn't have the money, which meant he was letting her go under the guise of her visiting her father.

The corners of his lips pulled up. "I'm certain." He stepped to the side of the hallway, granting them passage.

Lukas took hold of Brielle's arm, pulling her along. When Brielle passed Orson, he reached out, slipping something into the palm of her hand. Her fingers curled around the paper as she followed Lukas out of the palace and into the dark night.

CHAPTER 19

DECLAN

Standing at the window, Declan watched Brielle and Lukas run from the palace, disappearing into the night. When he could no longer see them, he returned to the royal chambers where he found his brother stretched out on the sofa in the sitting room.

"Well?" Brooks asked. "Did everything go as planned?"

He nodded. Orson did what needed to be done. "Now tell me why Brielle had to go home?" Once the king learned of her disappearance, it would be the first place he'd check for her. As far as hiding places went, it wasn't one.

"I can't tell you that."

Because of the blood oath. Declan unbuttoned the top of his shirt, pulling it away from his neck. After pouring a cup of ale from the side table, he sat on the sofa across from his brother. Earlier tonight, when he'd heard Brooks talking with their mother, he'd known there was more going on than he was privy to. He had a feeling it had to do with the blood oath and Brooks was working around it. However, it was one of the only times he'd ever questioned his brother's loyalty. Perhaps it had to do with the fact that their mother was involved. Briar always had ulterior motives. But Brooks wasn't stupid, and if he believed this plan—whatever the plan was—would work, then Declan had to trust him.

Orson entered the room. "It's done." He plopped on the chair. "I gave her the note. You know, that Lukas is a real idiot."

Declan didn't want to hear anything about Lukas right now. Not when the man was traveling with Brielle and responsible for her safety. "I hope this plan of yours works," he mumbled. "How many of your men are following them?"

"I sent four."

Declan took a sip of ale. Maybe if he drank enough, he wouldn't be so worried about Brielle. There was no reason for him to feel so uneasy. She wasn't his wife, and they wouldn't be marrying. He may very well never see her again.

"Any luck hunting down the men from Lima?" Brooks asked. "I still can't believe another kingdom had the audacity to send assassins here."

"I think we have them all. I don't want to kill them yet and have Lima get worried. I'll do it when the time is right."

Declan needed to know one thing. "Sending Brielle away...is it for her own safety? Or is there more to it than that?" While he knew his brothers liked her, he didn't think they'd risk their necks like this just to save her.

"There's more going on," Brooks revealed. "A lot more." He looked pointedly at him.

As Declan suspected, it must have to do with the blood oath. Maybe they were using Brielle as a distraction. He rubbed his forehead. The last time he'd talked to Brooks, his brother hadn't found a way to end the blood oath. He doubted something had changed between then and now.

"I wouldn't get your hopes up," Brooks said. "As far as plans go, this one has a lot of elements that could go wrong."

"True," Orson said, agreeing with his brother. "But in this case, I think the risks are worth it."

"Risks?" Declan asked. "You're not putting Brielle in danger, are you?"

Brooks chuckled. "I assume that means you've come to care for her."

Orson slapped Declan's shoulder. "She managed to get under your skin?" he said around a large grin. "It's about time a woman whips you into shape."

"I don't believe you need to concern yourself with Brielle's safety," Brooks said. "It shouldn't be a problem."

"There is one problem, though," Orson said, extending his arms over the back of the chair. "Mother. One of you has to sit with her because it's not going to be me." He chuckled.

Declan looked to Brooks.

"Sure," Brooks said, standing. "Send the disabled man. He has nothing better to do than sit around tending to the sick." He lumbered to the queen's room. "Let me know if either of you hear anything."

Orson tilted his head back, glancing up at the ceiling.

"What's the matter?" Declan asked. There had to be a problem; otherwise, Orson would have left the room by now.

"I don't know how to say this..." Orson's focus remained on the ceiling above him. "You know Father chose her for a reason, right?"

"Yes." He'd known it from the day the king had signed the marriage contract. However, he'd never figured out why. "Wait, you know, don't you?" With Orson's extensive resources, he would have been able to figure it out.

Orson stood, sliding his hands in his pockets. "I do."

"And?" Declan asked, half afraid to know.

"I'm surprised you haven't figured it out. You have one of the key ingredients. Really, Brooks and I each had parts and when we put it together, we realized we have everything we need."

The room seemed unnaturally silent. For years, they'd been trying to figure out a way to end the blood oath. Now, it seemed as if his brothers might actually be on to something. What that had to do with Brielle, he couldn't imagine. It was hard not to ask the details; however, if his brothers could've told him, they would have done so by now. Which meant he needed to remain in the dark.

"What do you need me to do?" he finally asked.

"Be prepared for all outcomes."

"With regards to?"

"Brielle." He headed toward the door.

"I don't understand."

"Didn't Brooks give you a way to save her?" Orson asked over his shoulder.

"Yes." Brooks had suggested finding a way to alter the contract. Declan been thinking about it, considering it, but hadn't come up with anything. That was why he'd sent Brielle away—so she could live. "The only person who can alter the marriage contract is the king." And they both knew their father wouldn't do such a thing.

Orson smiled. "Too bad you're the acting king while father is away."

"He'd be furious if I altered the contract." Yet, Declan's heart beat frantically with the possibility.

"He might be more upset when the duke doesn't pay his taxes and Father has to execute Brielle." Orson shrugged. "If I were you, I'd alter it and make sure you still marry her." He exited the royal chambers, whistling as he went.

Declan took one last sip of his drink before setting it down and stretching. He went to his room and grabbed his grandfather's journal. Since taking it, he hadn't had time to read through it. He slid the book in his vest and then exited the royal wing. Thankfully it was late so no one was out. He didn't feel like dealing with people at the moment. When he reached the king's office, he went in and lit a candle. Plopping on the chair, he pulled the journal out and set it on the desk, staring at it.

Ever since he learned that his maternal grandfather had killed his paternal grandfather, he'd been numb with disbelief. It was another element in an already complicated series of things he needed to deal with. Orson wanted General Sullivan arrested and tried for treason. It would force Sullivan to step down as general, allowing Orson to officially take over.

Declan rubbed his forehead. He didn't know what to do. If he arrested everyone who needed arresting, half the royal family would be in the dungeon. Even though he was currently the acting king, he felt it more prudent to wait until his father returned to handle the situation. The law required Declan to deal with the matter swiftly. However, he wanted more proof than just the journal. He still had several boxes in the records room he needed to go through. He knew he was stalling to prevent a major rift in his family and the kingdom. Arresting the general couldn't be done quietly. Everyone would know. And then his family would be dragged through more gossip and scandal.

His head pounded. He didn't know what was right anymore. It seemed that the truth changed depending on one's perspective.

In his heart, he knew Brielle shouldn't be killed for her father's transgressions. Declan wanted to marry her. Opening the top drawer, he looked through the papers until he found the marriage contract. He set it on the desk and examined it.

At the time the contract had been written, he didn't bother reading the particulars. He'd been so upset with his father for tying him to someone so insignificant, that he hadn't been involved in its creation. But now, he wanted to know the details, including why his father had really chosen Brielle. The king wanting to unite Declan to Brielle was no accident.

The king just hadn't intended on the duke not paying. It probably never crossed his mind that Jaxon didn't have the money. Pulling out a quill, Declan realized he had a unique opportunity to solve more than one problem. His hand shook as he read through the contract. When he got to the part where it said that if the duke failed to pay his taxes and provide the required wheat, Lady Brielle would be executed, Declan crossed out that part and changed it to something else. Something much more productive. Should Duke Jaxon fail to send the required taxes and wheat to the king, he will forfeit his dukedom which shall then pass to Liam Laris and his direct descendants, including Mabel Bakken, daughter of Willa Laris, father unknown. Declan then signed his name, placing his seal next to it.

He leaned back in the chair, examining the contract. Maybe he shouldn't have added that part about Mabel, but it was done now. Since he removed the part about Brielle being executed, it meant that no matter what, Declan and Brielle would marry. There weren't any stipulations which could prevent the union from happening. When he'd first met her, he thought her not worthy of marrying into the royal family and completely insignificant. Now he feared he may not be worthy of her.

Once the ink dried, he replaced the contract in the drawer.

Exhaustion consumed Declan. He ran his hand over the journal, too tired to read it now. He stood and opened it, fingering through the first couple of pages to get an idea of when Sullivan wrote the first entry. It seemed like it was a few months before he'd plotted to kill the king. Curious, Declan flipped to the end, wanting to see when he'd stopped writing. The last few pages were different from the others. They contained mostly symbols and strange words Declan didn't recognize. Walpurgis night was mentioned several times which he found odd. And on one of the pages, a symbol that looked familiar. It was the same symbol he'd seen in the book Brooks had been reading that day in the library.

Declan traced the symbol with his finger, trying to remember where he'd seen it before. When he completed the last line, a dull vibration started. He quickly closed the book, and the sensation went away. He blinked. He needed to get some sleep since he was imagining things. He placed the book in the drawer on his right. He'd return tomorrow morning, after a few hours of sleep, and read through it then.

Declan snuffed out the candle and left the office. Turning a corner, he came face to face with Sasha. "What are you doing here?" He hadn't seen her in days.

"We need to talk," she whispered.

She wouldn't have sought him out late at night like this if it wasn't important, so he led her to an empty storage room. "What's going on?" For a moment, he feared she was pregnant. If so, he didn't know what he'd do. Now he understood how his father had gotten into the situation he had and fathered a child before he married Briar. Declan should have realized the repercussions and not entered into a physical relationship with another woman before he married. Now this child would be Declan's heir. He'd have to take the baby away from Sasha and raise the child in the palace. How would Brielle feel about raising a child that was not her own? She probably wouldn't care and would love the child regardless. But Declan never should have put her in this position. Shame washed over him.

Sasha rested her head on Declan's shoulder. "I've missed you."

"What did you come here to tell me?" he asked, needing to know and get the shock over with.

"I just want to be with you. Feel you. Love you." She nuzzled into him.

Relief coursed through Declan like a tidal wave. She wasn't pregnant. He wrapped his arms around her. "I've missed you, too." The familiar smell of her stirred something inside of him.

"Be with me tonight." She started kissing his neck. "I need you."

He slid his hands up, one winding in her hair, the other pressed against her back. Her lips moved to his as she unbuttoned his shirt.

"I can't." Especially not after the scare he just had. He leaned back and another realization dawned on him. He didn't want to be there with her—he wanted someone else. Declan dropped his hands and cursed. Somehow, someway, he'd fallen for Brielle. He actually wanted her to be here with him, throwing herself at him. Pinching his eyes shut, he hoped altering the marriage contract had been the right thing to do and not a result of his feelings. This was why he never wanted to fall in love—it clouded one's judgement.

Sitting in the king's office with the journal opened before him, Declan stared out the window, considering Orson's note. It had been hand delivered about five minutes ago, and from the moment he'd read it, he knew there was a problem.

Brother—

I need your assistance at the training grounds.

O

Declan rubbed his face. While the note sounded normal, reasonable even, he knew otherwise. Orson rarely asked for help—especially with matters involving the army. The fact that Orson had addressed the note to his brother, not mentioning Declan by name, meant Orson needed his brother, not the prince or ruler of Valdis.

Declan had a feeling this had to do with their grandfather. Declan hoped Orson hadn't gone and done something stupid. Or worse, done something to try and prove he deserved the position as general of the Valdis army.

Since Orson was four years younger than Declan, he always seemed to be trying to prove himself. Declan suspected it had to do with the fact that Brooks should be the one leading the army and would be if it weren't for his leg. Growing up, Orson had always been weaker, less skilled with the sword, and not as advanced in his tactical studies as Declan. In a sword fight, Declan still had the upper hand, though Orson was quickly gaining on him. In another year, Orson would be far superior since Declan's time was now spent at court, leading their people, and not training or practicing daily.

Declan stood, a feeling of dread consuming him. It was best to just get it over with. He exited the office and found the soldier who'd delivered the note waiting for him in the hallway.

"Prince Orson asked me to escort you to the training grounds," the soldier said.

"Very well." They exited the palace and headed to Jurgis. The entire time, different scenarios played out in his head. Everything from Orson being injured to Grandfather having discovered his journal was missing. With each possibility, Declan walked faster and faster until he was practically running.

Crossing over the bridge leading to the military island, Declan wondered if perhaps Grandfather had figured out that they'd uncovered his secret. If the general had confronted Orson on the matter, Orson may have decided to be preemptive and arrest him. Doing so at Sullivan's house seemed the most logical place since there wouldn't be a lot of people around, fighting inside would be difficult, and escape wouldn't be easy. But Declan wasn't heading to Grandfather's house—he was going to the training grounds. He groaned. The training grounds were always crowded, they contained several entry and exit points, and there were dozens of hiding places. Arresting Grandfather there made little sense and would be difficult. Which was why Declan believed something bad may have happened which required his help.

No matter where Orson chose to arrest their grandfather, one thing was certain—he wouldn't go down without a fight. Sullivan loved power, craved it even, and he wouldn't relinquish it easily. It would be a battle to the end. General Sullivan would rather die fighting than die a disgraced man.

They passed under the archway leading to the training grounds. The square-shaped area had been built into the ground to allow spectators to watch from above. Not only did new recruits learn basic hand-to-hand combat here, but the more seasoned soldiers would often come here to hone their skills or challenge someone. If a lower ranked officer challenged a person and won, they took that spot while the loser went to the lower rank. It encouraged people to maintain their edge when it came to fighting. Declan had spent many days here working with his father. The king was an excellent swordsman and fighter. Declan wasn't half the man he was. He wasn't sure he'd ever be.

At the edge of the arena, Declan glanced down. Two flags had been raised which meant someone had challenged another person to a fight, and the challenge had been accepted.

Declan blinked; certain his eyes were playing tricks on him. Staring at the flags, a sick feeling overcame him.

General Sullivan's flag had been raised as the challenger.

The royal family's flag flew as the defender.

Declan cursed. Orson couldn't fight Sullivan—they weren't evenly matched. Grandfather was too experienced. Not only that, but it wouldn't look good for the incoming general to fight the outgoing general. Also, this could be a political nightmare for the royal family. Grandfather and grandson shouldn't be fighting publicly to the death.

After dismissing the soldier who'd escorted him there, Declan headed down to the individual training rooms, searching for his brother. The fifth room he stuck his head in, he found Orson.

Declan went inside. "What's going on?"

"I've been challenged to a fight." Orson stretched his neck from side to side.

"I got that part. What I don't understand is why. Just arrest Grandfather and end this."

"I did." Orson removed his shirt and swung his arms, loosening them up.

Declan blinked. "Then why are you fighting him? Just have him transported to Karlis for his trial."

Orson laughed, shaking his head. "Did you know there's an old law that prohibits the incoming general from arresting the outgoing general?"

Declan's blood went cold. He'd never heard of such a law.

"Apparently it's to prevent someone from being subverted unnecessarily."

"As the acting king, I can officially give the order to arrest him." His voice sounded weak to his own ears.

"You and I both know the law is absolute. Grandfather had a grand old time pointing all of this out to me."

There was nothing they could do then. Unless the blood oath ended within the next hour or so. "You're fighting hand-to-hand?" The sword would be a better choice. Orson would last longer with the sword and could at least wear Grandfather out some.

"The general is sixty-five. I'm seventeen. I've fought him enough times with a practice sword to know I'd lose in under ten minutes. I'm hoping I can survive hand-to-hand."

His brother would be able to hold his own for the first five minutes. However, the general was ruthless and weighed considerably more than Orson. It would only be a matter of time until Sullivan bested him. Now, if it was a knife fight, Orson would win in less than a minute.

Declan started pacing. "I don't think you should fight General Sullivan without the king present." Something occurred to Declan. As the acting king, he could postpone this duel until his father returned. It might give Brooks enough time to at least research the law to see if they could find a way around it. He came to an abrupt halt. "As the acting king, I hereby declare that this fight shall not take place until King Rhett returns from his journey."

"I don't want anyone to think I'm too afraid to face him," Orson muttered. "It would ruin my reputation."

"I understand." And he did. But he wouldn't allow his brother to sacrifice himself. "However, the law is the law. You will not fight until Father returns. It'll also give you more time to get the soldiers involved. They can place bets, and we'll make a big production of it."

"You don't want me to just fight him and get it over with?"

"No, I don't. Now if you'll excuse me, I must go and find

the general to inform him of the change in plans." Declan left before Orson could say another word.

A few doors down, he spotted two soldiers standing guard. The general had to be in that room preparing himself. Declan went to the door and knocked. Without waiting to be granted entrance, he opened the door and went inside. For this to work, he needed to act like a king.

The general stood in the middle of the room dressed in his uniform. "Did your welp of a brother send you to plead his case?"

"That's no way to address your prince and acting king." Declan stopped a few feet away from his grandfather.

Sullivan shook his head in disgust. "If your brother wanted my job so badly, he could have just asked me to step down. He didn't have to resort to arresting me. Now look at the mess we're in."

Declan kept his face neutral, not revealing his thoughts on the matter. They'd been asking the general to step down for months now. Sullivan had refused each time. And he'd arranged for the former king to be killed so his daughter could be the queen. He deserved to be in prison. However, saying any of that would only fuel the man's rage, especially since he didn't like to be challenged.

"I'm here to let you know the duel will take place once King Rhett returns. That's an official decree. Until then, you'll be held at the local dungeons, charged with murder. As the acting king, I can—and just did—make that official. If you refuse or don't comply, you'll be executed."

Sullivan's face turned red.

"Guards!" Declan said, calling the two soldiers who'd been standing outside the door into the room. "Did you hear my orders?"

"Yes, Your Highness," the guards said in unison.

"Excellent. Escort the general to a holding cell."

"Your brother violated the law," Sullivan snarled. "If we don't carry out the duel, you know what'll happen."

Declan raised his eyebrows. "I am carrying out the law. Do not disrespect me by speaking right now." He turned and strode from the room, wondering how much his grandfather knew about the blood oath. It seemed as if the general knew more than he should.

Declan sat on the throne chair listening to a nobleman air his grievances about not receiving the correct horse he purchased a fortnight ago. Declan tapped his fingers on the arm of the chair, trying to pay attention to the man as he complained that the horse he received was far inferior to the one he purchased. At the end, Declan would have to give his verdict. Honestly, it seemed like a mix-up with the breeder.

"Lord Haren, thank you for your insightful comments," Declan said, trying to sound interested in the proceedings at hand. "I suggest you contact the breeder—"

The door flew open and the king stormed into the throne room, his cape floating behind him. Everyone in the room curtsied or dropped to a knee, heads bowed low.

When the king reached the dais, he spared one quick

glance at Declan before turning to face those present. "Dismissed," he said curtly.

Stunned, Declan kept his mouth shut. He'd been in the middle of a verdict. Not only that, but this was the time for petitioners to come forward. At the very least, the king should have addressed his people to let them know the proceedings would be rescheduled.

As soon as everyone started rushing out of the throne room, he turned and faced his son. "We have a problem," the king said. "My office. Now."

Dread filled Declan. The king had either learned about the general's arrest or he had discovered their plan to end the blood oath. Trying to keep his face free from emotion, Declan stood and followed his father. "We have more than *one* problem." He wanted to try and keep the mood light by offering the joke.

"Don't be coy with me."

"There are several issues we need to discuss." So much had happened since his father had left. "However, before we do, you need to know about the queen." And Declan needed a moment to compose his thoughts.

The king came to an abrupt halt. "The queen? Did something happen? Why is this the first I'm hearing about it?" The concern in his voice leaked through, softening the furious undertones he'd been emanating.

"The queen is in her room." Declan turned and headed toward the royal wing, not wanting to discuss her condition in the hallway where servants could overhear. "Come with me." It was best to explain everything in private. The king would be upset word wasn't sent to him right away, but it would have been too risky if the situation became known to others.

Without another word, the two of them went directly to the queen's bedchamber.

Declan stopped at her door. "I believe Mabel sent an assassin to poison Mother. She is going to be fine but has been in quite some pain. Brielle knew of the poison used and has been diligently tending to her." He opened the door, escorting his father inside.

"I have questions," the king murmured.

"I'm sure you do. I will answer them all once you're done here."

Brooks was sitting on a chair beside the queen's bed, reading a book out loud to her. Briar was propped up, her long blonde hair flowing around her face. For the first time in days, her coloring appeared normal.

The king rushed to her side.

Brooks stood. "We'll leave the two of you alone for a bit." He joined Declan and they went to the sitting room to wait.

"Father is going to kill Mabel himself," Brooks said. "I haven't seen him look that furious since you set the garden on fire."

"I only did that once and it was an accident." He hated when Brooks brought that up. "And Father was furious the second he got to the palace. He said there's a problem." Declan looked pointedly at Brooks.

"There's no way he knows. Trust me."

"I hope so. Otherwise, this plan will have failed in spectacular fashion before it even gets off the ground."

Brooks started pacing, lost in thought.

Declan went over to the window and stared outside.

A moment later, Rhett exited the queen's room. "Brooks, go and find Orson. I need to see him immediately."

"Of course, Father." Brooks left the room, shooting Declan a concerned glance on his way out.

"You're worrying me," Declan said. "What's the matter?"

"Besides someone trying to kill your mother?" The king pulled out a piece of paper and handed it to Declan. "I received this letter from Mabel. She wants to meet."

That was the last thing Declan expected to hear. He plucked the letter from his father's hand and opened it, quickly reading its contents.

Mabel proposed meeting in one week's time at Edvin, a large town to the east. She demanded the king come without soldiers. She said if he brought anyone other than a handful of guards, there would be no talking, no negotiations, and the king would regret it.

"Have you sent her an answer?" Declan assumed his father would agree to meet with her.

"Yes." He folded his hands behind his back. "She doesn't know about the blood oath. I have to tell her before she does something she'll regret. If she announces a bid for the throne, she's bound."

"Do you want her to be the crown heir?" If so, then Declan would no longer be the next king. Mabel would become the queen, and Declan would just be in line for the throne. Most likely, he'd never take it because Mabel would marry and have her own children.

"I've regretted signing that decree. I was young. I could have stopped myself from demanding she declare the father. I knew it was me."

"Did you push because Mother wanted to know?" Declan asked, suspecting, and fearing his mother had a hand in this.

"Yes. And I wanted to please her and not cause problems so early on in our marriage. She said it could be the wedding gift I forgot to give her."

Declan pursed his lips. He needed to tell his father about the general ordering the previous king's death. But he didn't know how to tell his father something like that. The words seemed stuck in his throat. As of now, Declan had to assume the blood oath would remain in place. Every decision he made had to reflect that, so he didn't mess anything up.

Brooks and Orson entered the room.

"Good," the king said. "Now that the three of you are here, I have an announcement. The four of us are leaving in one hour. We will travel to Edvin to meet Mabel. Dismissed." He turned and went into the king's bedchamber.

Brooks raised his brows. "I sure hope he doesn't expect me to travel on horseback."

"We're not all going," Orson said. "If we all die, Mother will take the throne. And we can't have that now, can we? Brooks, you'll stay here. That way, should Father, Declan, and I die, you can be the king."

Brooks folded his arms, observing his brother. "You're always so blunt."

Orson shrugged. "Blunt and practical. Now get out of here. We'll let Father know you're not coming."

"And by *we*, I assume you mean me?" Declan said dryly.

Orson wrapped his arm around Declan's shoulder and smiled. "Of course. He likes you better anyway."

CHAPTER 20
BRIELLE

itting astride the horse, Brielle kept nodding off. She and Lukas had been traveling on horseback for two days without stopping. The only food they'd consumed had been the bread he'd packed in one of the saddlebags. If she didn't rest soon, she'd topple off her horse. At this point, she wouldn't mind if she did. At least then she could sleep.

The sky started to lighten, and she felt ill at ease for some reason.

Lukas led his horse from the road. Brielle did the same, following him.

"Let's stop and rest the horses." He dismounted under a maple tree.

Thankful, Brielle climbed off and slid to the ground, her eyes closing of their own accord. Birds chirped and a soft wind rustled the leaves of the surrounding trees.

"I'll water and feed the horses," Lukas said.

Brielle ignored him, already half asleep.

And then she remembered Orson's note. Forcing herself to open her eyes, she spotted Lukas off to the side tending to the animals. She quickly pulled the note out from her dress, unfolding it.

His messy handwriting made it difficult to read: *I have four soldiers trailing you. If you're in danger or want to return to the palace, all you have to do is scream and they will assist you. I let you go because you owe me. I'm calling in my favor from the bet you lost. We believe Mabel is working with your father. I think they need you for something. If it's what we're hoping, we'd like you to go along with it. We're trying to prevent a coup and save countless lives. You may be the key.*

Shocked by what she'd just read, she quickly tore the note into small pieces, scattering them on the ground. Closing her eyes, she went over Orson's letter again and again. She had no idea what he meant by her father and Mabel possibly working together. Her father didn't even know about Mabel's existence. And she had to disagree with Orson believing Brielle could be the key to saving the kingdom. She was just an ordinary woman who wanted to stay alive. As far as helping the royal family, she didn't know about that. Sure, they'd let her go. But the king could still send men after her. She shivered knowing that Orson had four soldiers trailing her. She hadn't seen anyone following them.

Once she slept and could think rationally, she'd consider everything again. Right now, she was too tired to sort through it all.

The days passed in a jumble. Riding, stopping to eat, and more riding. Brielle had nothing but her thoughts to keep her company. Thoughts about what to do, who to trust, and the four soldiers following her. Thoughts about her father, sister, Mabel, and the royal family.

The strangest emotion she felt happened to be longing—she missed Declan. She had no idea why. The man drove her insane with him constantly overthinking everything, his never-ending brooding, and his lack of conversation. It seemed like he never said what he wanted to and instead, he adjusted his conversation depending on who he was speaking to. But underneath all that, there was an intelligent, thoughtful man who seemed to care for Brielle's wellbeing.

"We're going to stay at Edvin tonight," Lukas said, interrupting her thoughts. "Tomorrow we'll board a ship for Miervades."

Dread filled Brielle. The last thing she wanted to do was get on a ship.

"It's only a day to Miervades," Lukas assured her. "Then we'll be on horseback to your house."

One day. She could handle one day of sailing. Especially if it meant she would see her family.

"Is that Edvin?" she asked, pointing up ahead to the town against the backdrop of the setting sun. They'd been riding alongside a forest for the entire day, but now the trees had lessened, replaced by low rolling hills. Situated next to the hills, there was a large town. To the east, the ocean stretched as far as she could see.

"It is."

Brielle couldn't help but glance behind her. She didn't see anyone. If Orson's men trailed them, she had no idea where they were. A shiver ran down her spine.

Over the past few days, thoughts of what to do had consumed her. Should she speak to her father and report back to Declan? Whose side was she on? Were there even sides? All her life, she'd been either shielded from or avoided politics. Now, she was thrust full center and had no choice but to be involved.

They descended the hill and entered the town. "Why can't we just leave now?" That way she could sleep while they sailed. Maybe then she wouldn't vomit all over the place.

Lukas glanced back at her. "You're joking, right? Surely, you're not that daft."

She swallowed. Apparently she was since she didn't know why he'd responded that way.

"You know we can't leave the harbor at night because it's too dangerous." He spoke to her as if she were a child who knew nothing of the world. Well, she was not a child, and she simply didn't know that much about sailing. He didn't need to treat her so disrespectfully. Instead of responding, she kept her mouth shut. There was no use arguing with him.

When they were younger, she used to think Lukas knew so much about the world that he'd fascinated her with his knowledge. She no longer cared for his company. Something had changed between them, and he no longer felt like a friend.

At the first public stables, they dismounted and left their horses there. Then they found an inn. When Lukas requested one room for the night, Brielle protested.

"Two rooms," Brielle insisted to the innkeeper, even though she had no idea how Lukas planned on paying for the rooms. However, she would not share a room with him, especially knowing Orson's men were following her. The last thing she wanted was word getting back to Declan. She didn't want him to think she cared for Lukas at all, not that it mattered since she wouldn't be marrying Declan. Regardless, it was important to her that he not think illy of her.

Lukas tensed. "We only need one room."

"I understand, but we will be taking two." She smiled, trying to lessen the sting. However, she wanted to be perfectly clear that she wouldn't budge on this matter.

"Do you have two rooms that connect?" Lukas asked the innkeeper. "My...sister needs to be close to me."

"Yes, of course." The man handed them two keys.

After thanking the innkeeper, they went to the second floor where they found their adjoining rooms. Lukas made her promise to knock on the connecting door if she needed anything. Once he left her alone, she locked both doors. She peeled off her dirty dress and climbed into bed. Minutes after lying down, she drifted into a peaceful sleep.

Someone pounded on the door, startling Brielle awake.

"Lady Brielle," Lukas hissed, still pounding on the door. "Wake up."

She jumped out of bed and wrapped a blanket around her body. Opening the adjoining door an inch, she found Lukas standing there, his hair a mess. "What's the matter?" She yawned, glancing over her shoulder at the still dark window. "It's not even light out."

"Get dressed. We're leaving. Now."

She thought the ship was to leave in the morning once it was light out. But maybe the sun would rise soon. "Give me a minute." She closed the door and dressed.

Still feeling half asleep, Brielle followed Lukas out of the inn and to the docks about a block away. He maintained a brisk pace even though no one else was out at this hour.

He pulled out a piece of paper. "We need to find slip twenty-two." He took her hand, pulling her to the left.

When they located it, Brielle froze at the sight of the small boat barely big enough for four people. "I thought we'd be taking a larger vessel." One that wouldn't rock from the turbulent ocean. This one would be even worse than the one she'd traveled in before. Her stomach rolled with nausea just thinking about it.

"There's been a change in plans," Lukas mumbled. "We must depart immediately."

"Why? What's changed?" The wind rolling in off the ocean had a chill to it. She wrapped her arms around herself, trying to stay warm.

Two men joined them, jumping deftly onto the boat. One

started loosening the rope attached to the berth while the other adjusted one of the masts.

"I'll tell you once we're on our way." Lukas took hold of Brielle's elbow, helping her climb on board.

She sat on one of the two bench seats, wondering if this boat would even make it to Miervades. If they encountered rough water, a wave would surely crash right over them. She never thought she'd die by drowning, but now it seemed a real possibility.

The boat gently left the berth, heading for the jetty as the sky began to lighten. Brielle could just make out a couple of other ships outside the jetty, probably waiting for it to get a little lighter before entering the harbor.

They were just about to reach the exit when a large ship pulled into the jetty, preventing them from exiting the harbor.

The two sailors steered their small boat off to the side, waiting for the larger ship to enter first.

"Why are there so many ships so early in the morning?" Brielle asked. As the large ship passed, she thought she caught sight of a soldier on board. While the vessel was large, it was nowhere near the size of the king's warships. However, it didn't mean the ship didn't belong to the king.

Lukas cursed.

"What's going on?" she demanded.

"The king and prince are here," he answered.

She didn't think that could be the case since when she'd left Declan a couple of days ago, the king hadn't returned yet. Even if he had, she didn't think he could have sailed here that quickly or that he would have chosen a ship of that size instead of one of his warships.

Lukas nervously ran his hands over his thighs. "It'll be fine. Once the ship is out of the jetty, we can still set sail." He spoke more to himself than to her.

"Once the green flag is waved, we'll be on our way," one of the sailors said.

"Here." Lukas pulled out a muffin. "I got this for you to eat for breakfast." He handed it to Brielle.

She took a bite, tasting something familiar in the muffin, something she'd had before. Memories flashed and she recalled being on board the king's ship for the first time, sailing from Miervades to Sunder. The sailor had given her something to knock her out so she could make the trip without being ill the entire time.

Her eyes widened and she looked at Lukas.

"Sorry," he muttered.

Her world went black.

Brielle peeled her eyelids open; her mouth felt sticky and dry. Her skin hurt as if she had rubbed against stinging nettle. She sat up, looking around. She was at home, in her bed. She had on clean clothes, her hair had been brushed, and she smelled of honey and lavender.

She breathed in the familiar scent of her room. She looked out the windows to the low rolling hills cast in sunlight. Standing, she stretched. It felt good to be home.

Maybe everything that had happened over the past few weeks had been nothing but a dream. She trailed her fingers over her books. When she noticed her favorite ones missing, she knew it hadn't been a dream. Her missing books were in Sunder at the king's palace.

Lukas had drugged her to get her here. She would never forgive him for doing that. He hadn't asked permission. By doing that against her will, he'd violated her.

She went over to the window. How she'd missed this view. Glancing down at the courtyard, she wondered about the prince's soldiers who'd been trailing her. Had they also boarded a boat and sailed after her to Miervades? She didn't know how they could have done so without Lukas noticing. Perhaps the soldiers had known she would end up here in Miervades so they'd come another way.

A soft knock resounded on her door before it opened. "You're awake," Kenna said, coming into the room. "I was starting to worry. I think that idiot Lukas gave you too potent of a dose."

"He told you he drugged me?" Brielle asked.

Kenna rolled her eyes. "He did. When he showed up with you in his arms, he explained quickly so Father wouldn't kill him."

At least her own father hadn't ordered Lukas to drug her. That would have been another violation she wasn't sure she could handle right now.

Kenna hugged Brielle, then held her at arm's length. "I really could kill Lukas for being so daft."

That made two of them.

"It's good to see you. Father is downstairs anxiously waiting for you."

Brielle nodded. While she wanted to see him, something made her pause.

"What's the matter?" Kenna asked, taking Brielle's hand. "Were you mistreated in any way at the palace?"

"No." At least not by the royal family. The only person who'd mistreated her was Lukas.

"Then what's the matter?"

"I'm just tired is all," she said since she couldn't figure out what made her feel uncomfortable.

"I don't know how that's possible," Kenna replied, heading for the door. "You've been asleep for over a day; you should feel refreshed and invigorated."

Smiling, Brielle followed her sister out of the room and downstairs. "Did anything important happen while I was gone?"

They were just about to enter the sitting room when Kenna turned to face Brielle. "A great many things. It's good you're home. We need you."

Brielle didn't think she'd ever heard those words come out of her sister's mouth before. "Then I'm glad I'm here so I can help." She pushed open the door and entered the sitting room. Her father stood out on the balcony, his back to the room. "Papa!" Brielle rushed to him.

He turned, wrapping her in a hug. "My baby girl is home."

Tears filled her eyes. After everything she'd been through, it felt wonderful to be in her father's arms again.

Duke Jaxon released Brielle. "Come, there is much to discuss." He led her over to the sofa where Kenna was sitting.

Brielle sat sandwiched between her father and sister. She hadn't realized how much she truly missed them until now. "It's good to be home." Even if she didn't care for the means used to get her there.

"We've missed you," the duke said. "Did you have a safe journey?"

She nodded, a few tears sliding down her cheeks.

"What's the matter?" he asked.

"I know you don't have the money to pay our taxes." She wiped her tears with her sleeve. "How could you send me away knowing I'd be executed?"

"You're here, aren't you?" Kenna huffed. "You're not dead. And we have no intention of letting you die."

Brielle didn't take her focus off her father.

His eyes softened. "I'm sorry about all of that. But never doubt my love for you. The king had backed me into a corner."

"What's the plan? I run away and hide for the rest of my life?"

He shook his head. "I made a deal with the other kingdoms. I'll have the money needed to pay our taxes. But you must do something for me."

Orson's note came back to her. He'd said he thought the duke had a plan for her. Not only the duke, but Mabel as well. "What do you need me to do?" she asked, her voice almost a whisper. She feared what he'd say because she knew Orson was right. And if she did this, and her father paid the money he owed, did that mean she would marry Declan? At a time like this, she shouldn't be thinking or worrying about Declan.

Kenna stood and went over to the door, closing it. Then she went to the balcony doors, closing them as well.

The duke twisted on the sofa, so he faced his daughter. Taking her hands, he said, "Before I tell you, there is something you must know." He glanced at Kenna.

"Would you like me to leave?" Kenna asked.

"That won't be necessary." He squeezed Brielle's hands. "There's no easy way to say this, so I'm just going to come out and say it. When my wife gave birth to Kenna, she died. I was devastated." His eyes turned glassy.

Brielle didn't understand what he said. She thought their mother had died birthing her, not Kenna. And if her mother had died delivering Kenna, then how was Brielle sitting there? She suddenly felt ill.

"The woman who'd helped deliver Kenna was named Josephine. She stayed to tend to the baby while I dealt with my grief." He took a deep breath, releasing it slowly. "I came to care for Josephine."

"I don't understand," Brielle said. "Kenna and I have different mothers? Why didn't you ever tell us before now?" It made no sense.

"After Josephine delivered you, she had to go away for a little bit. She had to see her sisters. She had two of them. They both ended up dying, and Josephine had no choice but to stay at her family's land, tending to it since she was the only one left."

"My mother is alive?" Shock and confusion swirled inside of Brielle.

"She is. And she would like to meet you."

She nodded. "But why now? Why didn't she want to meet me when I was younger?" She had a feeling her father wasn't telling her the entire story. It was the first time she ever felt herself doubt him. She wondered if she could trust this man sitting before her.

"That is a question your mother can answer better than me," he replied.

Her mother. Just hearing the word sent shivers through her. Brielle had no idea how she felt on the matter. She needed some time alone to process everything. "Is she here?" If her mother had shown up to see her, then that would explain why her father decided to finally tell her the truth. She couldn't think of one feasible reason for her mother to have concealed her existence from Brielle. Hurt, fury, and confusion warred within her.

"No." The duke stood. He went over to the door and opened it.

A young woman entered wearing a simple dress. She had beautiful long, silky black hair and chocolate brown eyes. She appeared to be in her early twenties. Brielle thought she might be a friend of Kenna's, especially since the woman looked slightly familiar.

"Brielle," the duke said, "I'd like for you to meet Mabel Bakken."

She knew that name—Mabel. This was Declan's half-sister. The reason this woman looked familiar was because she greatly resembled the king.

"Mabel, this is my daughter, Lady Brielle Tranum."

Mabel came farther into the room. "We finally meet," Mabel said, stopping before Brielle.

While there was nothing rude or hostile about Mabel, Brielle got a weird feeling and instantly felt on edge around her.

"Well don't just sit there like a blob," Kenna said, rolling her eyes.

"Oh." Brielle tried to get her wits about her. "It's nice to meet you."

Mabel lifted a single eyebrow. "You know who I am, don't you?"

Brielle nodded. "What are you doing here?"

The corners of Mabel's lips pulled into a half smile. "I'm here for you."

The duke sat next to Brielle again. "Mabel is headed south to meet up with someone. Your mother is that way. I thought the two of you could travel there together."

"Why?" Something wasn't adding up. They were keeping things from her. It could just be that Orson's note put her on edge or it could be her intuition. But something was amiss. She was certain of it.

"Because I don't want you traveling alone," the duke answered. "You want to meet your mother, don't you?"

"Of course, I do."

"Mabel has a friend that will escort the two of you."

"Yes," Mabel said. "And we do need to be on our way." She tilted her head to the side, watching Brielle.

"I've already packed a bag for you," Kenna said. "I'll go and get it."

Everything was happening so quickly. "But I just got here."

The duke took her hands again. "I hate to ask this of you. But I need you to cooperate and go and do this for me. Once you've met your mother, I can collect the money I need. We're running out of time, so that's why I need you to leave now."

"How is meeting my mother going to get you money?" The more her father spoke, the more confused she became.

"It's a long story," he said. "And your mother will explain all of it to you. She asked for me to refrain from telling you anything until she was ready. She wants to be the one to do it, and I agreed. I hope you can understand that." He leaned forward and kissed her forehead.

Kenna returned with a satchel and a cape. "Here are your things for the trip."

"If this will help our family and keep me from being hunted by the king and executed, then I'll do it." Even though a sense of dread filled her.

"Excellent," the duke said. He stood, pulling Brielle up alongside him. He wrapped his arms around her. "Be safe." He took a step back. "There's a carriage waiting out front to take you to the ship."

"Ship?" How far were they going?

"Your escort is on the ship waiting for you." The duke kissed Brielle's forehead again. "Have a safe journey."

Mabel chuckled. "Don't tell me you get seasick."

Brielle didn't answer. She liked Mabel less with each passing minute.

"It won't take you long to get there," the duke assured her. "You'll be there by nightfall."

She nodded. A day was better than a week. She just had to keep telling herself that.

Kenna wrapped the cape around Brielle's shoulders. "Have a safe journey. I'll see you when you return." She kissed Brielle's cheek.

Brielle took her satchel and followed Mabel out of the room, downstairs, and to the front of the castle where the carriage waited for them. She climbed in after Mabel. There was something she really didn't like about her even though she couldn't say what it was specifically.

The carriage set out. "What did you think of the king and his sons?" Mabel asked as she looked out the window, away from Brielle. Her casual posture didn't fool Brielle.

"I only met the king a couple of times and very briefly. It wasn't long enough to form an opinion." She didn't need to reveal that she'd come to care for each of the princes and found them to be exceptional men.

Mabel chuckled. "Yet you have an opinion on me, and we've only just met."

Brielle bit her bottom lip to keep herself from saying something nasty to this woman.

"It's obvious you don't like me," Mabel continued. "Your face gives your emotions away."

She tried to keep her face neutral, not revealing her feelings. Mabel didn't need to know anything about her, so the less she said and expressed, the better.

Mabel turned and looked right at her. "What I don't understand is why. What have I done to make you dislike me so? If you marry Prince Declan, we shall be sisters."

She almost said something. Almost. Something about Mabel claiming her birthright or going to meet the king.

A slow smile spread across Mabel's face. "Wait, did you come to care for Declan?" She chuckled.

"That's no concern of yours," Brielle ground out, irritation rising.

"Oh, that's rich." She shook her head and ignored Brielle for the rest of the drive.

The carriage pulled to a stop before a ship that was much larger than the one she'd just been on with Lukas. However, it was significantly smaller than one of the king's warships. The two of them exited the carriage. Brielle followed Mabel onto the ship. On the top deck, she went to the front, remembering how Declan had told her it would help with motion sickness.

"I'm Matsen," someone said from behind her.

She spun around and found a young man with his arms folded across his chest.

"If you need anything let me know." He shoved his hand in his pocket. "And here, this is for you." He extended his arm and opened his hand, revealing some sort of root. "It'll help with the motion sickness. Mabel told me."

Brielle took the root. "What do I do with it?"

Matsen smiled. "You just chew on it. We'll be there in a couple hours." He winked and turned away, heading to the steering wheel.

Brielle chewed on the root—which tasted awful. However, as the ship set out to sea, she never felt the need to vomit. Relief filled her. At least one thing had gone well today.

The ship pulled into a tiny harbor at Witch's Cove. Brielle had to be mistaken—no one lived at Witch's Cove. Scanning the area, tucked behind the harbor she spotted a town of no more than fifty homes. It was more village than town. They had to be just north of Witch's Cove then.

It had only taken them a couple of hours to get there. If this was where her mother lived, then she very well should have been able to come and see Brielle. It made no sense that her mother had to stay here on the family's land and tend to it. Surely there would have been a time she could have visited her daughter. And then another thought occurred to her—maybe her mother had married and had a family here.

She glanced over her shoulder and noticed Mabel and Matsen talking with their heads close together. They looked as if they were conspiring. They probably were. She didn't trust either one of them. Even if Mabel had mentioned her motion sickness and Matsen had given her the root to help.

Brielle picked up her satchel, slinging the arm over her head and shoulder. Then she went over to join the two of them.

"Your mother isn't far from here," Mabel said. "We have to climb that hill, so I'd leave your bag and anything valuable here." Without waiting for a response, she turned and exited the ship.

"Aren't you coming with us?" Brielle asked Matsen as she removed her engagement ring and slid it in the pocket of her satchel.

"I have to do a few things on the ship, and then I'll catch up to you. Here," he extended his arm, "give me your bag and I'll put it below deck for you."

Brielle handed it to him and then looked over the side of the ship to where Mabel waited, tapping her foot impatiently. She hesitated.

"You have nothing to worry about, I promise," Matsen assured her.

For some reason, those words sent a dose of strength into her that she desperately needed. She exited the ship and joined Mabel.

"Let's just get this over with," Mabel mumbled. "I'm tired and hungry and desperately need a bath." She set out, leading the way up a narrow pathway carved into the steep cliff.

As Brielle followed, she wondered what had happened to Orson's men. If she screamed now, they wouldn't be anywhere nearby to help. There was no way they could have followed the ship. And if they had managed to procure a boat, she didn't see it in the harbor. The only ship was the one she'd sailed in on.

At the top, Mabel led the way. "We're close," she said.

They traveled on a dirt road a little bit farther until they came to fifteen huts arranged in a circle. It appeared to be a small village, but it didn't look inhabited.

Mabel stopped walking. "We're here. Your mother is in one of the huts."

"You're not coming with me?"

"I can't."

Frowning, Brielle continued without her. A few steps later she bounced against something and stumbled backward. Confused, she reached out with her hand and felt a soft, squishy thing that she couldn't penetrate.

"You can't walk through it?" Mabel asked.

"No." She wondered what in the world it was.

A woman exited one of the huts and approached.

Brielle couldn't help but stare at the woman. She knew, without a doubt, that it was her mother. They had the same hair, skin, and eyes.

"Hello," the woman, Josephine, said.

"Hi." She suddenly felt awkward standing there meeting her mother. She didn't know what she expected to feel, but this wasn't it. She pointed to the barrier to ask what it was.

"It's a protection ward. Or at least it was," Josephine said. "Now, it keeps me locked in here."

"Is it of magical origin?" she asked. There was no other way to explain it.

Josephine smiled. "It is."

Brielle glanced around, wondering if they were indeed at Witch's Cove and if the bedtime story she'd been told as a child had any truth to it. She cleared her throat and asked, "How'd you get stuck in there?"

"Someone of my...nature...is required to be in here at all times to ensure stability. I used to split my time with my two sisters. However, they were hunted down and killed. Now it's just me."

"I'm so sorry," she whispered, a voice in her head screaming that this couldn't be happening. That this woman who looked almost identical to Brielle couldn't be a witch. Because if she was...

"I want to be free of my bonds so I can bring the man responsible for killing my sisters to justice."

"How do you get out of there?" Brielle couldn't comprehend the power or magic that kept Josephine trapped in there. However, at least now she understood why her mother never visited before.

"You must come in here and help me. Together, we can lower the barrier and fix everything."

Brielle swallowed, trying to summon her courage to ask the question she needed but was was afraid to. "Why me?"

"Because you're of my blood. You're the same as me. You're a witch."

And just like that, Brielle's world turned upside down. "I don't understand." She didn't think witches existed. Or magic. She reached out and touched the barrier again to try and convince herself this was really happening. "I don't have anything special in me."

"You do. It's just being blocked."

Brielle grabbed her bracelet, turning it on her wrist.

"Yes," Josephine said. "That keeps your magic hidden so no one knows what you are. I didn't want the man who killed my sisters to kill you."

"If I remove this bracelet, what'll happen to me?" She didn't even know how to take it off.

"You'll be able to access your magic."

Brielle took a step back, away from the barrier and her mother. She didn't want power. She just wanted to be normal. Herself. No one special.

"At least let me explain it to you," Josephine said. "It's not what you think it is. There are spells you have to say to access your magic. If you choose not to use it, you don't have to. But at least free me."

Brielle didn't know if she could trust her mother. After all, she didn't know this woman and she could be lying. Or, she could have evil intentions. But then she remembered Orson's note. He'd said they needed her to help them with something. Maybe this was it.

"Why the hesitation?"

Everything was happening too fast, and she was overwhelmed. She didn't know how she felt.

"Didn't Brooks ask you to come here to help me?" Josephine whispered.

Brielle's head snapped up. Josephine had her attention

by using Brooks's name. She shook her head since he hadn't said anything to her.

Josephine motioned for Brielle to move closer to the barrier.

She went up as close to it as she could.

"The royal family is bound by a blood oath they created centuries ago. Brooks sent you here to help end it."

"What blood oath?" She'd never heard of such a thing.

"Each of the five kingdoms had been at war for so long, they got together and made a treaty. To ensure its success, and that no one would be taken advantage of, they sealed it in blood magic. Each king gave his blood to me, and I mixed it together, binding each kingdom to their laws. No kingdom is allowed to go to war with another kingdom, all trade must go through Oskar, all laws must be enforced as written and approved by the other sovereigns. If a king disobeys, he is killed by the magic binding him, and a new heir takes his place." She said it all so matter of fact, as if discussing the weather and not some powerful blood oath.

Brielle had a hard time comprehending what it all meant. "That's why the law is upheld so rigidly." It all started to make sense. Declan had said he had no choice but to enforce the law. She'd thought it was some moral obligation, not his life on the line.

"Yes. And ending the curse will allow them to modify the laws."

"And go to war." That part couldn't be forgotten. Brielle hesitated. While the laws might be strict, at least they prevented war. But Orson had asked her to do this for his family, and apparently Brooks was involved as well.

"Yes. If that's the road a sovereign should choose to take for his people. Don't you believe everyone should have the freedom of choice?"

"Why is Mabel here?" Brielle asked. "What does she have to do with it?"

"There are a lot of things I need to perform the spell. She's been helping me get what is required since I'm stuck here." Josephine's head turned slightly as she looked at something behind Brielle.

She glanced over her shoulder to see what her mother was looking at. Matsen had arrived though Josephine didn't look surprised to see him. Her mother must know he was helping Mabel.

"Do you have everything?" Josephine asked.

"I do," Matsen replied.

Josephine closed her eyes and smiled. "Finally." She opened her eyes, looking at Brielle. "A spell of this magnitude has to be cast when magic is at its strongest. We must do it on Walpurgis. It's only a few days away, and you have a lot to learn before then."

In Orson's note, he asked Brielle to go along with this to help the royal family. Not only that, but her father had sent her there as well. So, this had to be the right thing to do. As scary and uncertain as it was, she was meant to be there. "What do I need to do?"

"First, we must remove your bracelet. Then you can

enter through the barrier, and I can teach you the spells we will use."

"Okay." She couldn't imagine the piece of jewelry being removed from her body. "What do I do?"

"Put your free hand over the bracelet and repeat after me."

Brielle did as instructed.

"Notem vu corba hir lastrita."

She repeated her mother's words. As she said them, they felt foreign on her tongue, but right somehow. Then a warmth inside of her sprouted.

"Greta von kirum."

Brielle said the words, only this time, a light blue glow emanated from her hand.

"Lluvba."

"Lluvba." The bracelet came off, falling to the ground with a soft *thud*. Brielle stood there, stunned. And then it felt as if her legs melted into the earth. When she looked down at them, they were fine. "What's happening?"

"The magic in the world is getting to know you," Josephine answered, a look of pride radiating from her. "Now come through the barrier."

Brielle wasn't sure her legs would work. However, when she thought about moving forward, her legs felt normal again, and she took a step as if nothing had changed. She took another step and went right through the barrier like it didn't exist. She knew it was still in place because she could now see a pale blue shimmering dome shielding the small village.

"How do you feel?" Josephine asked.

Brielle looked at her wrist, still shocked the bracelet wasn't there. She'd never seen her wrist without it. "I feel... the same." A lie. She felt alive, confused, vibrating with energy. Things looked clearer, sounded crisper.

"Are you tired?"

She shook her head.

"Good. Then using your power didn't drain you. You'll stay here with me. We'll get to work right away." Josephine rubbed the side of Brielle's arm. "Oh." She turned to face Matsen. "Bring everyone to me on Walpurgis in the morning so I can prepare them."

"Who's everyone?" Brielle asked.

"One person of royal blood from each of the five kingdoms. Their blood sacrifice is needed to end the oath. Now come, let's go inside." They turned to leave.

"What's the sacrifice part?" Mabel asked. "I know the blood is needed. And I'm here on behalf of the royal family to give blood, but no one ever said anything about a sacrifice."

Josephine and Matsen glanced at one another.

"The sacrifice is your blood," Josephine explained. "Each royal had to give blood to form the blood oath, and now you're all giving blood to end it."

Mabel nodded. "Very well. I'll be back on Walpurgis." She turned and left, Matsen trailing her.

CHAPTER 21

MABEL

After waking, Mabel went to the deck of the ship, happy to find it had docked already. She stood and observed the town before her. With the sun cresting the horizon, it cast the buildings in a soft glow. They were mostly old, weathered single story brown structures. Like all the towns she'd come across in Valdis, it was dull.

"Your...Highness," a sailor said as he approached her. "Matsen went into town to see the state of things. He said once you wake, I'm to take you to the inn where you'll meet the king. That's where Matsen will be waiting for you."

She cringed every time he said Matsen's name. This entire time, Matsen had been using her. They needed the blood from a royal family member from each of the kingdoms. She suspected they needed *all* of their blood. Well, she would not sacrifice herself to end the curse. The blood oath was their problem, they could deal with it. The issue was, she feared she was bound to it as well. There was no way she could live with those chains. No, she would help end the blood oath so she could be free. If it meant luring Declan to Witch's Cove so he would be the sacrifice in her place, so be it.

However, she did need to figure out how to get Matsen out of the way. Luckily, she had an idea for that.

"Very well," she said to the sailor. It was time for her to get this meeting over with. "Let's go."

After disembarking, Mabel followed the man two blocks to the inn that had been emptied specifically for this meeting. Her palms became sweaty, and nervousness filled her. Part of her was curious to meet her birth father and half-brothers. Another part of her expected to be stabbed in the back during the encounter. Matsen had assured her he'd be at her side during the meeting, and nothing would happen to her. But he was trained in the art of killing, not protecting. And now that she understood how to end the blood oath—with blood—she knew they wouldn't kill her. They needed her alive to use as a sacrifice.

She had a plan to make sure she came out on top at the end of this. If it meant burying her so-called family in the process, so be it.

After all, her birth father had ordered her birth mother's death and signed Mabel's execution as well. She owed him nothing. He was nothing to her. And this man she was about to meet still wanted her dead. He thought he could toss her aside to end some blood oath. Well, little did he know, she would not be the sacrifice. One of his sons would. She would claim her place as his daughter and heir. And then the king would die, and she would inherit the throne.

A little voice inside her head tried consoling her by saying that she already had a father who loved her. She didn't need to meet her birth father. Running away and starting a new life could be a viable option. Peerson, the man who'd raised her, had always treated her like his own daughter. At least she thought he did since she had nothing to compare it to. Maybe he'd intended on using her in the future but had died too soon. She'd never know. The woman who'd raised her, Sanda, had taken off the moment she'd discovered Mabel wasn't her own flesh and blood.

It seemed no one alive loved or cared for her.

That would all change. She would make them care. Make them love.

Another voice in her head said that she needed to come face to face with the king. She needed to stare into his cold, brutal eyes so she could know her enemy. It still surprised her that he'd written to her requesting she meet him here today.

They reached the inn where Matsen stood waiting for her. "We're all set," he said, his eyes focused intently on hers.

As if he cared. She wanted to spit on him.

Facing the king required her to be calm, collected, and strong. She could do this. "Then let's proceed." Holding her head high, she followed Matsen into the inn.

Inside, the room to her left contained a bar with a dozen or so tables. In the room to her right, several sofas had been situated around a low table. Straight ahead, a wide staircase led up to the second floor. All patrons and people who worked there had been removed from the premises for today's meeting.

Matsen gallantly escorted her to the sofas. She saw through his lies now. He'd been sent to the dungeons not to assassinate her, but to lure her to Witch's Cove so she could be a sacrifice. And if that was his job, and he worked for the queen, then the queen could die right along next to her husband. Thankfully Mabel wasn't some naive, trusting woman who knew nothing of the world. Peerson had seen to that. He'd told her that people always had ulterior motives and not to trust anyone.

Mabel refused to sit until the king and his sons had arrived. Footsteps sounded on the stairs. Mabel lifted her chin higher, waiting for the king and princes to join her in the receiving room.

Three men came around the corner, stopping at the threshold. The oldest of the three, standing in the middle, had to be King Rhett. The young man to his right had a severe look on his face as he assessed Mabel. The young man on the left wore a cocky grin. All three had dark hair and eyes and were unmistakably related to one another.

"Mabel," the king said, bowing his head slightly. "I'm honored to finally meet you."

She had no idea how to address him. King felt too formal, especially since he hadn't used a title when speaking to her. And he wasn't a father to her in any way, so she couldn't bring herself to call him that either. She decided to remain silent and let him take the lead.

"These are my sons," he continued. "Declan." He pointed to the severe looking man. "And Orson." He indicated the smiling one on his other side.

Mabel glanced behind them, trying to see if anyone else lurked around the corner. "Don't you have three sons?"

"I do." Rhett stepped into the room. "Let's all be seated." He and Declan both sat on one of the sofas while Orson remained standing near the threshold, almost blocking it.

The entire thing felt rehearsed, putting Mabel on edge. However, if the king didn't want to see and talk to her, he wouldn't have bothered meeting her. Therefore, she could conclude that he wouldn't render her unconscious and have Matsen drag her back to Witch's Cove. Most likely, he'd let her return with Matsen assuming she didn't know what was going on. Feeling relatively safe for the moment, she took a seat on the sofa across from the king and prince.

Rhett cleared his throat. "My middle son, Brooks, remained at home."

Mabel tried not to laugh at that. They'd left one at home in case something happened here today. As if they feared her. Good, because they should be afraid.

"Brooks fell ill as a child," Rhett explained. "One of his legs doesn't work properly."

More likely, they were embarrassed of him. "You don't like for him to be seen in public," she commented. They were ashamed of him like they were ashamed of her.

"No," the king replied, shaking his head. "Not at all. The travel here would have been too difficult for him."

Excuses. Mabel didn't believe him.

"Why is the queen's assassin here?" Rhett asked, pointing at Matsen, appearing genuinely confused.

She glanced over her shoulder at Matsen standing in the corner. "He's accompanying me." As if he didn't already know. The assassin was simply doing his job—leading her to her death.

Orson began pacing at the threshold. "What do you hope to gain through this meeting?" he asked. "Matsen could have escorted you to the palace. Why here? Why now?"

On the journey there, Matsen had informed her that Orson was training to lead the king's army. When she first saw him, she thought him rather young for such a position and figured it would be years before he became the general. However, after watching him prowl over there, the forced casualness in his demeanor, she knew he was the one she had to watch. Orson was the real threat in the room. His questions also got to the heart of the matter—but she couldn't reveal what she wanted. At least, not yet.

She forced herself to smile and say, "I wanted to meet all of you since we're family." She focused on the king and Declan before her, ignoring Orson. She didn't want him to know that she'd figured out their plan. Otherwise, they might tie her up and drag her back to Witch's Cove. If that happened, she would be the sacrifice. She had to play this right if she wanted to stay alive. The weakest one here was Declan which worked out quite nicely for her plan.

Neither Rhett nor Declan's expressions changed, making it hard to discern what either one was thinking.

"I'm glad you wanted to meet us." Rhett leaned forward,

resting his arms on his legs, folding his hands together. "You look so much like your mother."

Anger boiled inside of Mabel. How dare he tell her that? Swallowing the nasty retort she wanted to say, she took a calming breath and responded, "I wouldn't know since you had her killed." Silence hung heavy in the room as all eyes were on her, assessing her every move.

Out of the corner of her eye, she noticed Declan shift on the sofa—the first hint at an emotion since stepping foot in the room. Satisfaction filled her. She would not let them have the upper hand. This man sitting before her had tried killing her once before. It wouldn't happen again.

"Listen, Mabel," the king said. "I'd like to get to know you better. I want you to be a part of my family."

She cocked her head to the side. "Why?" So he could use her as a sacrifice?

"Because you're my daughter."

The word *daughter* made her cringe. "You signed the warrant for my execution. You wanted me dead minutes after I was born. You're a monster, not a father." Even now, he still intended on killing her.

Orson abruptly stopped pacing, his focus solely on Mabel. "The law is the law," he said. "You must understand that the royal family has a duty to uphold the law whether we agree with it or not."

Mabel had to force herself to remain pleasant instead of snarling at him. He was testing her to see if she knew about the blood oath. Clever, but she was cleverer.

Orson continued, "Besides, all your mother had to do

was reveal who the father of her child was, as the law dictates. She had the power to prevent her death—and yours." He resumed pacing. "So really, your mother is responsible."

Mabel clasped her hands together, squeezing hard to keep her temper under control. She wondered if he really believed that or if he was simply trying to get a reaction out of her, testing her. She would not fall for his antics.

Rhett leaned back on the sofa, rubbing his face. "Sometimes the law can be...harsh. Since I married Briar, I think Willa was afraid I'd take the baby away from her to raise as my own without her. Plus, her father had just led a rebellion against the king and was killed for it. I'm sure she hated my family and didn't want any child of hers to be a part of it."

Rhett's frankness stunned her, forcing her to look at things from another angle. She'd never stopped to think about the strength and courage it must have taken her mother to stand up to the king. Pride filled Mabel's heart. Her mother had loved her enough to die for her.

Mabel crossed her legs. "You say pretty words, telling me you want me to be a part of your family, but you signed a warrant for my execution. You haven't mentioned anything about fixing that." The law was the law, and it was absolute. It was something Peerson had repeatedly told her, explaining that was why so many people were in the dungeons. Now that she knew about the blood oath, she understood. It still didn't excuse the king for what he'd done. And she still needed him to publicly acknowledge who she was and pardon her. Otherwise, it would be a lot more difficult for her to take the throne. It was the only reason she'd shown up today.

"I'm investigating ways to remedy the situation," Rhett said. "I'd like for you to come to the palace with us. Let me announce you to the kingdom as my daughter."

She waited a moment, giving him enough time to add anything else should he want to. When he didn't, Mabel said, "And heir." The room went absolutely silent, and she wondered if anyone was even breathing. Her focus remained on the king, not daring to look at Declan, the current crown prince. But as Orson so eloquently and needlessly explained, the law was the law. Mabel was the firstborn and therefore, the true heir.

"That is something we'll need to discuss," Rhett replied.

"What's to discuss?" she asked, trying to keep her tone even and calm.

"Do you even want to be the heir?" he asked. "You were raised away from the palace. There is much for you to learn if you want to be the queen one day. I wouldn't force it upon you. You don't deserve that."

As if leading and being the queen would somehow be a burden and not a privilege. More likely, he didn't want to announce her as the heir and then explain to the kingdom how she'd died. "This meeting is over." Enough of her life had been taken away from who she truly was, and she would stand for it no longer.

"Will you come home with us?" the king asked.

She wanted to tell him he could lick the dirt off the

bottom of her shoes. Instead, she said, "No. I need some time to process everything. I do, however, want you to declare that I am your daughter and eldest child, making me the rightful heir."

"I'll declare you're my daughter right now if you'll come with us."

"Write the decree. Then, and only then, will I go with you." She stood and left the room, not looking back.

Now that she'd met her enemy, she had no qualms about what needed to be done.

/ / CHAPTER 22
DECLAN

"Pack your things," the king said to Declan and Orson. "We leave in ten minutes to return home."

Declan immediately went up to his room and gathered his belongings. He still couldn't get over how angry Mabel had looked—her eyes alight with rage, revenge, and shrewd intelligence. He feared they'd all pay the price.

After shouldering his bag, he went back downstairs where he found his father and Orson already in the sitting room waiting for him.

"I still can't figure out why Matsen was there," the king said. "He's the queen's assassin. He works for her and only her." He eyed his children. "Is there something going on that I don't know about?"

"I'm as confused as you are," Declan mumbled. He'd been surprised to see Matsen there as well. He looked at Orson.

"It's nothing either of you need to concern yourselves with," Orson said.

Declan knew his mother would never allow Mabel to take the throne, which led him to believe Matsen was working around the blood oath that prevented him from killing a member of the royal family. While he couldn't make the kill, someone else very well could.

"We need to figure out what to do with Mabel." The king scratched his chin. "She seems a bit wild, and I'm not sure I want to declare her as my own yet. Not until I know her intentions."

"Don't forget, she's claiming to be the heir based upon the word of a dungeon guard," Orson said. "Willa never publicly named you as the father." He shrugged. "As far as you know, she isn't yours."

"I don't want to alienate her; she is my child."

"Is she?" Orson asked. "You don't know that."

Declan found it interesting that his brother was working so hard to get their father to believe Mabel wasn't a part of the family. Orson was up to something, so he decided to play along. "I concur. And I believe she's trying to have you killed. My sources say she was in Lima. There is now a group of assassins here from Lima and you're the target."

The king's face turned white. "Why am I only hearing about this now?"

"I was going to tell you but when you showed up, we left right away to come here. There hasn't been time."

"We've been waiting here for days," the king pointed out.

Orson ignored the comment and said, "As soon as you claim her as your daughter, the assassins will kill you." He sat on the sofa, stretching his arms across the back of it. "And that's not all."

Declan knew Orson was going to tell their father about their grandfather. He went over to where Mabel had been sitting, about to sit down, when he noticed something on the floor. Bending over, he picked it up. His hands started shaking. It was the engagement ring he'd given Brielle—and it was covered with dried blood.

"What's the matter?" Orson asked, immediately at his side.

He showed his brother the ring.

"Brielle's?"

Declan nodded.

"Okay," Orson said, "I know this looks bad, but you need to think rationally."

His hands shook, and he could barely think straight. If Mabel had done something to Brielle, he would kill her. As soon as he thought it, he realized something. "She wants me to try and kill her. If I do, the blood oath will kick in and I'll die. Clever."

"Now you're getting it." Orson patted his shoulder. "But I do believe Father has to declare her as his child before she is bound."

"Why would Mabel do something like that?" the king asked, pointing at the ring and Declan.

"Obviously she knows about the blood oath," Orson said. "Maybe Matsen told her." He shrugged. "The point is, she had us meet her here for a reason. Otherwise, she would have come to the palace."

"Mabel grew up on Karlis. She was raised by a dungeon guard and knows little of the world. I think you're reading too much into it," the king said.

"You're probably right," Orson said. "And we need to be on our way."

"I'm going outside to give the orders." Rhett left without waiting for either of his sons to respond.

"She wants you," Orson said. "So, I'll go after her to see what trap she has set."

Declan slid the ring in his pocket. "I think you already know what she's doing. Or at least what she's up to, don't you?"

"I do."

"And we're trying to work around the blood oath?" He assumed that was why his brothers had kept so much from him.

"We are."

"Then I need to be the one to go," Declan said.

Orson took hold of Declan's shoulder. "I don't think you should. If she has Brielle, you don't want to do anything stupid."

Declan didn't know if Orson would sacrifice Brielle to end the curse. He had a feeling he would. "You're right. Let's let your original plan play out. Neither of us will go."

Orson released his hold of Declan. "Very well. Let's go and meet up with Father."

The two of them exited the inn. They joined the king and headed to the ship.

"Once we're on board," Rhett said, "I'll write an official decree stating Mabel is my child." He looked at Orson. "Don't argue with me." After a few more steps, he said, "The two of you are my witnesses should anything happen before I can make the official announcement. Mabel is my child and part of the royal family."

Declan couldn't explain it, but he felt some sort of pulse. As if the king's words had just bound Mabel in magic. He glanced at Orson to see if he'd noticed. His brother studiously ignored him. However, Declan could have sworn he saw Orson smile.

The three of them reached their ship.

"I didn't sleep well," Declan said as he climbed on board. "I'm going to my cabin to lie down. Do either of you need anything before I turn in?"

"No," Rhett replied. "I'll give the order to set sail, and we'll be out of here within ten minutes. Then I'm going to my cabin to compose the official decree." He walked away from his sons.

"Don't worry about Brielle," Orson said. "I'm sure she'll be fine."

"Yeah," Declan said. "You're probably right." He left his brother and went down the ladder to the lower deck. He quickly made his way to his room. Inside, he fluffed the bed to make it look like someone was sleeping in it. Then he changed clothes into plain pants and a tunic. He grabbed a simple cloak and exited his room. Not seeing anyone in the hallway, he made his way to the stern of the ship. He could hear men yelling as the anchor was being hauled up which meant he didn't have much time.

He waited until everyone had moved to the mast and busied themselves with raising the sails. When no one was looking, Declan climbed over the side and down the rope ladder in the back. He just needed to make it to the dock before they pulled up the ladder. He was almost there. And he reached the dock. He hurried and lifted the hood of his cape up as he walked away from the ship with a slight limp, hoping no one noticed or recognized him.

When no shouts rang out, he relaxed. Now all he had to do was find Mabel. She would lead him straight to Brielle.

As he headed along the dock, his head down, he heard a familiar voice. He kept walking, not wanting to bring attention to himself. Angling his head lower, he listened as he passed the man and woman, being careful not to look in their direction.

He glanced back and saw Mabel and Matsen board the ship on their right. He spotted them arguing with one another on the top deck, so Declan casually turned and headed toward their ship. Once he was close enough that they couldn't see him, he jumped and caught hold of the anchor. He climbed up the chain and into the ship. Knowing someone would enter the small area to raise the anchor, he immediately exited and found a tiny storage area to hide in.

He hoped it wasn't a long journey.

It felt like the ship had docked. While Declan wanted to stand and stretch from his extremely uncomfortable position that he'd been forced to maintain for a few hours, he feared being seen. He stayed there waiting until he didn't hear any voices. Carefully, he exited the storage area, trying not to make a sound.

Declan decided to get off the ship the same way he'd gotten on it. When he stuck his head out the back hole, he spotted Mabel and Matsen heading along the dock toward a dingy looking town. Once he could no longer see them, he exited the ship and climbed down the anchor, jumping onto the dock.

He was just about to head the direction Mabel and Matsen had gone when he noticed a second boat anchored nearby. He recognized it as one of the dinghies belonging to his father's warship. More specifically, the warship they'd left behind in Monta. He glanced around, not seeing the warship. This harbor was much too small for a ship of that size, so it was probably anchored just off the coast which was why the dinghy was here. But why?

Since it was almost dark out, not many were out at this hour, making it easier to get around unnoticed. Not wanting to lose Mabel and Matsen, he went after them. He spotted them up ahead entering a building. When Declan reached it, a small wooden sign indicated it was an inn. From the size of it, there couldn't be more than four rooms. It wouldn't be safe for him to go in.

Most likely, the two of them had gone in there to spend the night. He wondered if Brielle was in there.

"You here for Walpurgis too?" someone said from behind him.

Declan turned and found an elderly lady standing a few feet away.

"Oh, no," he said. "I'm just passing through."

She nodded. "You won't find any rooms in there." She pointed at the inn. "You can stay in my house if you need a room. Twenty greveks for the night." She smiled, revealing several missing front teeth.

"That's a bit much," Declan said. "I'll just sleep out on the street." He didn't need to be swindled.

"Ten."

"Deal." He might as well try and sleep for a few hours.

The elderly woman led him to her house a few doors down. It was a simple home with only two rooms. She gave him her bed to sleep in while she remained in the kitchen. Not wanting to argue, he paid the woman and took the bed.

Unable to fall asleep, he tossed and turned. Tomorrow was Walpurgis. The deadline for the duke to pay. He glanced out the window. It had to be well after midnight. He stood and exited the room.

The elderly woman sat in a rocking chair, knitting. "Do you need something?"

"No. I can't sleep. I'm going to go for a walk."

She kept rocking. "Stay away from the cliffs. Strange things happen up there. You remember what your mother told you as a bedtime story when you were a child. Well, here's the place that story happened, so you best be careful."

"Thank you." He exited the house. The crisp air felt

refreshing. As he walked, he turned over the old woman's words about a childhood story. He remembered the one Brielle had told him. About a boy, a cove, and witches. The woman had said this was the place where it happened. Which must mean a child had fallen from the cliffs, so the story was created to scare children away.

Curiosity got the better of him and he wandered over to the steep cliff. A path had been cut in the side of it, wide enough for two people to walk side by side but narrow for how tall the cliff rose. Something compelled him to go up. A pull of some sort. Putting one foot in front of the other, he was halfway up before he realized this was a stupid thing to be doing in the middle of the night. However, going back down seemed like an even worse idea, so he continued. At the top, his legs burned, and he was slightly out of breath. He stood far enough away from the edge, marveling at the sight before him. Under the full moon, the ocean glistened, stretching on for miles and miles. He spotted the king's warship.

A tingling sensation crawled up his spine, and he turned around. In the distance, he could see a soft glow, as if from a fire. He headed that way, feeling drawn to it. The closer he got, the more certain he became that there was a fire. He started running in case people were in danger and needed his help.

CHAPTER 23

BRIELLE

Brielle repeated the words her mother said, trying to get the pronunciation correct. Since the words were foreign to her, she found it difficult, especially with the crackling fire in front of them.

"Say it sharper, crisper," Josephine instructed.

"I'm trying." She was exhausted from working at it all day. "I'll do it better the next time. I promise." The heat of the fire was starting to get to her. "Let's try again."

"We can't." Her mother walked away from the fire, over to a small well where she lifted a bucket of water and drank from it. "It's after midnight."

"It's Walpurgis?" The day magic was its strongest. She shivered.

"It is. We don't want to risk playing with magic on a day like today. It's too dangerous."

"But you think I'm ready to help you end the blood oath?" She didn't feel ready.

"I do." Josephine came over to Brielle, placing her hands on her shoulders. "You're my daughter; you're strong, you'll do well, and I'll be here with you every step of the way."

Brielle was about to ask her more questions, wanting to understand how the magic flowed beneath the ground and why this spot in particular acted as a direct conduit to the magic when something caught her eye. She squinted, looking past the raging fire to a lone man standing there.

Declan.

His face was a mixture of horror, astonishment, and relief.

"Who's that?" Josephine asked.

Brielle's chest tightened. "Prince Declan." She had no idea what he was doing there, but just the sight of him caused tears to fill her eyes. A sense of completeness filled her.

"I'll leave the two of you alone for a minute. I must get more wood for the fire. We can't let it die today. It must burn to ward off the evil spirits now that we've dropped the barrier."

Brielle ignored her mother and headed straight toward Declan, half relieved and half scared to see him there. She didn't know if something had happened or if he'd simply come to be with her. When she reached him, she said, "I got Orson's note." As if that explained everything. "He asked me to help. So here I am, doing what you want to end the blood oath."

His eyes widened. "I knew Brooks and Orson were up to

something, but never in my wildest dreams did I imagine it was this." He pointed at Josephine. "Is she a...witch?"

She nodded. "And my mother. Which makes me a witch, too." It felt foreign to say that out loud—both the mother and the witch part.

"I don't understand." He shifted his weight from foot to foot, as if prepared to bolt at a moment's notice.

"The bracelet blocked my powers," Brielle said, hoping that explained enough. This was the first time that she'd spoken to him since knowing she cared for him, and the entire conversation seemed awkward.

Josephine approached. "There are a few things I must do to make sure we're prepared for today. Why don't the two of you go inside and talk?"

"I don't believe we've met," Declan said. "I am Prince Declan Forberg, your soon to be son-in-law." He held out his hand.

Josephine took it and smiled. "It's a pleasure to meet you. Thankfully your brother figured out how to end this oath. I've been stuck here for quite some time."

After he released Josephine's hand, Brielle led the way to one of the huts. She turned over her mother's words in her head, wondering how it all worked. For instance, upon Josephine's death, what would have happened? Would the blood oath have imploded on its own? During the course of their conversations during the day, Josephine had revealed that the general had hunted down and killed her two sisters while they were out on their break. Since Josephine had been here when that happened, she became stuck, unable to leave. But who had been here before Josephine and her two sisters? Who'd created the blood oath in the first place? Brielle still had so many questions she wanted to ask her mother.

"Josephine," she called out over her shoulder. "Are there others like me?"

"There are. My sisters had children of their own who would one day replace them. However, they all wear their bracelets."

"So, they don't know who they really are?"

She shook her head. "I don't even know who they are."

Feeling an overwhelming amount of sadness, she reached back, took Declan's hand, and led him into the round hut.

"My father must know about you," Declan said. "That's why he wants to unite your blood with mine in marriage. He wants our children to have my blood and your power."

"I'm so sorry," she whispered. "I had no idea. I didn't know about the bracelet or anything." She reached for her bracelet, but it wasn't there.

"I believe you."

His words sent a jolt of relief through her. She didn't want him to think she'd withheld information or hadn't been honest with him.

A low fire burned in the hearth. On the one side of the room, there was a bed. On the other side, a basic kitchen along with a table and three chairs. Brielle didn't know what to do. She went to sit on one of the chairs when Declan reached out and grabbed her bare wrist.

"It's been a long day, and I'm exhausted. Let's sit on the bed. It looks far more comfortable." His eyes glistened in the firelight.

Words suddenly became difficult to say, getting stuck in her throat, so she nodded and went to the bed, sitting on it.

Declan sat next to her. His hand rubbed her back. "Are you okay?" he asked, his voice husky.

"I don't know." Everything had happened so quickly. "If I pull this off, I'm not going to die." When she'd set out, that had been her goal.

"About that." His hand dropped from her back. "I sort of altered the marriage contract. You're not going to die, no matter what happens. You do have to marry me though."

She turned her head, her eyes meeting his. "I get to marry you?" Not once had she allowed herself to think what it would really be like to be this man's wife.

"I'm sorry if that upsets you. I just wanted to save your life, and I moved some words around..." his voice trailed off. His focus went to his hands, no longer looking her in the eyes.

"I'm happy to be marrying you," she revealed, shocked by her own honesty. Of course, that assumed she made it through this oath breaking ceremony she would perform in a few hours.

"You are?" He sounded genuinely shocked.

And then she realized she'd been so focused on herself,

she hadn't considered his own feelings. "I'm sorry you don't wish to marry me and are now stuck." That lump in her throat got larger, making it hard to breathe.

"Why do you think that?" he asked.

"You don't seem like you wish to marry me." She chewed on her bottom lip, heat rising to her face in embarrassment.

"Hmm." He leaned forward, his eyes focused on hers. Then he glanced at her lips. "There's something I've been wanting to do."

Shock rolled through her as she realized his intentions. Brielle held absolutely still, unable to believe what was about to happen. No one had ever kissed her before. She closed her eyes, and his lips gently brushed hers. Warmth spread throughout her body. Her heartbeat sped up, her toes curled, and she wrapped her arms around Declan, pulling him closer.

His hand slid up her side, cupping her face.

"Brielle!" Josephine shouted.

She jumped, startled.

"I hear voices outside," Declan murmured. "Are you expecting anyone?"

"No." Since she did that spell to drop the barrier, they could have a problem on their hands. She stood and rushed to the door. She and Declan hurried outside toward where her mother stood next to the bonfire. Now, a second fire blazed, encircling the entire village.

She reached her mom's side. "Did you do that?" She pointed to the fire encircling them.

"Yes." Josephine reached out and took her daughter's arm, pulling her to the other side of the bonfire. "We have company."

Brielle looked past the flames and into the eyes of someone she hated.

CHAPTER 24
MABEL

Mabel stared at Brielle and Declan on the other side of the flames. With Matsen at her side and the four royals from the other kingdoms behind her, she said boldly, "We're ready to begin." It was Walpurgis, and Declan would serve as the fifth and final royal family sacrifice.

Honestly, the look on Brielle's face was priceless. Part stunned and part horrified. Mabel tried not to smile or act too smug. After all, she still had Matsen to contend with. She'd hoped the king would have had Orson kill him for being there with her. But the king had been too dense, his mind elsewhere.

No matter. She'd had a conversation with Matsen a few hours ago. After she'd told him she knew exactly what he was doing—leading her to slaughter—he'd told her she had it wrong. They literally just needed her blood, nothing more. She informed him since that was the case, if one of the princes showed up, they'd use his blood instead of hers. Matsen immediately agreed, not even phased by what she'd said. Mabel still didn't trust him fully. Throughout this entire ceremony, she'd have to keep an eye on him, just in case. At least he was bound by his own blood oath, and he couldn't kill her.

"I thought we were going to do this tonight, not this morning," Josephine said.

Mabel raised a single eyebrow. It certainly didn't look that way with the ring of fire. The witch couldn't possibly expect a response from her.

"We'll do it now," Matsen said. "Everyone is here and eager to get this over with. Besides, the duke has a deadline to meet, and the money isn't to be delivered until the oath is ended."

"Okay." Josephine looked at her daughter. "We're ready."

Mabel certainly hoped Brielle was ready since she appeared so frail and weak. How that skinny thing with wild curly hair had any power was beyond her.

Declan remained hovering in the background like an incompetent, uncertain idiot. If he cared for Brielle like Mabel suspected, he would be at her side, holding her hand, protecting her. Mabel found it hard to believe she was related to him, the fool.

"Brielle and I will go through a series of chants," Josephine said loud enough for everyone to hear. "You'll notice the fire in the center here changing colors as we call upon the magic of the earth." She stopped and looked at the four royals to make sure they understood what she'd said.

"When it's solid green, each of you can pass through the exterior fire and no harm will come to you. Except for you Matsen since you aren't of royal blood."

"Then I'll remain out here," he said with a chuckle.

"Once you've crossed through, I'll tell you what to do next. Each of you has a strategic role to play. We are undoing what our ancestors did. Which means, each of us must perform the same sacrifice they did hundreds of years ago." Josephine looked at each royal there. "Any questions?" When no one said anything, she nodded. "Then let's begin." She instructed Declan to stand a few feet back while she and Brielle went to the north side of the interior bonfire.

The witch started singing unrecognizable words, Brielle joining her. Their eyes turned black as a blue fog rose from the fire and encased each of them. Mabel shivered. This was not normal. Not natural. And the two of them shouldn't exist. She half wondered if Matsen would kill them for her once this was over.

The center fire suddenly turned green. The wind kicked up, ruffling everyone's hair.

"Time to go through the fire," Matsen said.

"I'll go first," an elderly gentleman said. Clutching his bag filled with coins, he took a tentative step toward the outer fire ring. When he was inches away from the green fire, he stuck one hand out, as if testing it. Seemingly satisfied, he walked straight through it. His back stiffened, and then he was on the other side. "It feels strange," he said over his shoulder. "But it doesn't hurt." He joined Josephine at the bonfire.

A young woman went next. Holding her chin high, she closed her eyes and went through the fire, not once hesitating. Her shoulders relaxed when she reached the other side. She also had a bag of money that she carried slung over her shoulder.

A middle-aged woman went and stood before the fire. Biting her bottom lip, she took a deep breath and ran through the flames. "It doesn't hurt!" she exclaimed on the other side.

The last person, a young man with strange scabs on his face, didn't hesitate as he walked straight through it.

The five royals and two witches stood around the bonfire.

"I need you in here, too, Mabel," Josephine called out. "The magic can feel your royal blood, and you're throwing it off so it can't focus."

Mabel considered leaving. However, she wanted to be there to make sure the oath ended so she didn't wind up accidentally dead.

"You won't have to do anything," Josephine continued. "Just be inside the ring so the magic is contained and responsive."

Rolling her eyes, Mabel decided not to argue or make a big deal out of it. The wind had kicked up even more, giving the air an electric feeling. Something strange was happening, and the world around them was reacting to it. Balling her hands into fists, Mabel trudged through the flames. As she did, hissing erupted all around her, enveloping her. Instead of being hot, the flames were cool to the touch, almost caressing. And then she was on the other side, sucking in the clean air.

The exterior fire ring flashed bright red, the heat returning full force. The interior bonfire suddenly lowered to only two or three feet off the ground, shifting to a vibrant shade of blue. Josephine and Brielle started chanting again; this time the words sounded harsher.

Mabel wondered if they were saying the original spell backwards since she didn't recognize any of the words.

"One at a time, you will put the body part I tell you over the fire, cut open your skin, and allow the blood to drip into the flames. Once the flames flash red, you're finished. You'll take a step back and wait for everyone else to go." Josephine looked to the man who'd walked through the fire first. "The royal from Bireta will go first. And you will sacrifice your arm."

The elderly man put his bag of coins on the ground before stepping up next to the fire. Brielle handed him a sharp looking knife. He took it, placed the blade against his forearm, and slowly cut open his skin a few inches. It couldn't have been that deep. The man twisted his arm, letting the blood drip into the fire. It took several long minutes until the fire turned red. The man withdrew his arm, pulled down his sleeve, and stepped back.

The young woman took the knife from him.

"You will sacrifice your leg," Josephine said.

The young woman stepped up to the fire, lifted her dress, and cut the bottom of her calf. She held her leg over the fire, letting the blood drip into the flames. After a minute, the flames turned red and she took a step back, her part done.

"Torso."

The middle-aged woman took the knife and went up to the fire. Once it turned blue again, she knelt. She cut straight through her clothing, cutting open a section of her stomach.

Mabel flinched. That had to hurt.

The woman leaned forward, allowing the blood to flow down into the flames. They immediately turned red. She scooted backward, took her shawl, and pressed it against her wound. Her entire body shook.

"Head."

The young man with the scabs took the knife and went right up to the blue flames. He slowly cut each cheek, then leaned forward, letting the blood drip into the fire. It took a few minutes for the flames to turn red.

"Hands."

Declan reached for the knife. He sliced open his palm then made a fist over the fire. His blood fell into the flames which immediately turned red.

Josephine and Brielle began chanting again, this time louder and faster than before.

The flames dropped even lower, hovering mere inches above the ground now. Josephine waved her arms and the flames turned purple.

Sweat broke out over both Josephine and Brielle's foreheads. Mabel wondered if the spell was working or if Brielle was too weak. It seemed like they should be done since there wasn't anything else to do.

Mabel's feet suddenly left the ground as her entire body shot up ten feet into the air.

She was about to ask what was happening when she glanced over at Matsen.

He mouthed, "I'm sorry."

She tried to scream, but she had no voice. She tried to fight, thrash out, do something, anything, but she was frozen, unable to move of her own accord.

Her body hovered parallel to the ground, and she now faced the stars and full moon above. She hovered over the flames though she felt nothing.

The young man with the scabs came over and stood at her side. He handed her the knife. "It's your turn," he said. "You will sacrifice your soul."

Of its own accord, her hand reached out and took the knife. In her mind, she screamed every curse word and horrible thing she could think of. Mabel didn't want the knife. It felt heavy and wrong. She watched in horror as she placed the tip of the knife over her heart. With sudden clarity, she understood everything. She'd been born for this reason—to have royal blood and to be the sacrifice needed to end the curse. A single tear slid from the corner of her eye. That was why her mother hadn't claimed who the father was—she was trying to protect Mabel.

So much evil lurked beneath the surface of the king—her father.

And the knife plunged into her heart. The excruciating pain became unbearable, but she couldn't even scream. No sound escaped her lips. She couldn't fight. She couldn't move. Blood flowed like warm milk over her hand, down her sides, and into the flames. The fire grew, consuming her entire body. She felt the magic's pleasure as her skin burned. Pain like she'd never felt before raged within.

Everything went black.

CHAPTER 25
DECLAN

Declan stood there, frozen, unable to comprehend that he'd just watched Mabel stab herself and then burn to death.

The fires died completely, sending the area into darkness. The air around them stilled.

Mabel's body had vanished.

Brielle fell to her knees, sobbing. Her mother patted her back.

The four other royals didn't utter a word. One by one, they dropped a bag of money next to Brielle and then left.

Matsen came and squatted before Brielle. "I'm supposed to give Declan the amount the king is owed, and then escort you and the remaining amount home to your father."

Brielle looked at him, blinking, as if trying to comprehend his words.

Declan had a million questions for him starting with

who set this up. Brooks? The queen? But he went with the most pertinent one first. "Is the blood oath undone?"

"It is," Josephine said. "The royal families are free to do as they please."

Matsen stood.

"Brielle isn't going anywhere with you," Declan said. Especially after what Matsen had just done to Mabel. Whether the woman deserved her fate or not, it was an awful way to die and Matsen had a direct hand in it.

"I said that's what I'm *supposed* to do," Matsen said. "For once in my life, I'd like to decide for myself."

"You want Josephine to end the blood oath between your family and the line of queens?" Declan asked.

"I would prefer to live a life that isn't filled with killing," Matsen admitted.

Declan thought that wise. His mother didn't need someone like him tied to her. Having a weapon that dangerous was too appealing for the queen.

"I can easily undo it," Josephine said. "It doesn't require Brielle's help. Come." She reached out and took Matsen's hand. She led him away from the area.

Declan sat next to Brielle. "Are you all right?" He didn't know if she cried from the magic she'd just used having drained her, or if it was from watching Mabel die so violently, or if it was something else entirely. He barely knew her. But what he did know, he liked.

She wiped the tears from her face. "Did we do the right thing?"

Declan shrugged. "I don't know. The problem with

things of this magnitude, we'll never know if we made the right decision or not. Something bad could come of it, but how do you know something worse wouldn't have happened if we had allowed it to stay in place?"

Brielle's fingers slid into the dirt, grabbing it. "At first, all I could think about was my own predicament. I figured that if I ended the oath, I wouldn't be executed, so I was willing to do it. Then you told me you altered our marriage contract. Everything became confusing then. I know Orson wanted me to go through with it." She looked into Declan's eyes, seeking an answer he couldn't give.

"I've had years to think about the blood oath," he admitted. "While I had no idea what was going to happen here tonight, I've considered ending the oath and what that would mean for our kingdom and for future generations. The problem I had with it was that the blood oath didn't allow for human compassion. It was too strict, too regimented. Laws couldn't change though they might need to because people change. I'll give you one easy example— your father. The amount he owes in taxes is too much. It should be amended."

"Josephine told me my father can't mine as much as he needs to because of the magic supporting the blood oath. Now that the oath is out of the way, he can mine this area and will be able to produce ten times as much coal and diamonds for selling. He'll be in a much better position." She wiped her tears again. "I've never seen a person die before." Her body shook as she started crying again.

"It was a lot to watch, even for me." That must have been

what his family sacrificed all those years ago to make the blood oath. The life of a family member seemed a steep price to pay.

"In all the books I've read, when the hero or heroine saves the day, there's always a happy ending. This doesn't feel very happy."

Declan nodded. "But this also isn't the ending of your story either." He stood and pulled her up along with him. "Don't forget, we're supposed to marry tomorrow."

Her lips pulled into a smile, and she looked him in the eyes. "If you don't want to marry me, you don't have to. Now that the curse is over, I'm sure we can find a way around it."

"Just because you've ended the blood oath doesn't mean I'm going to stop upholding the law." He leaned in closer, putting his forehead against hers. "Besides, I want to marry you. I think we'll make a great team."

She pulled back. "Because of my power?"

"It has nothing to do with your power. I want to marry you, Brielle, the woman I've come to know these last few weeks."

"Are you certain?"

"Yes." He took her hands, squeezing them. "But I do have one request."

"Okay," she said wearily, swaying on her feet.

He wondered when the last time she'd slept or had something to eat. As soon as they finished up here, he'd have to make sure she was taken care of. "I don't want my father to know about your ability to wield magic."

"I think that's a wise decision," Josephine said as she joined them, Matsen trailing slightly behind her.

Declan's focus went to Matsen. Something told him not to trust the man.

And then it all happened so quickly.

Matsen withdrew a dagger and lunged at Josephine's back. Brielle screamed, and Josephine threw a shield over her body, Matsen's dagger bouncing off it. Before the assassin could regroup, Declan ran at him, throwing himself at Matsen and knocking him to the ground.

The two men grappled. Declan rolled, trying to get his legs locked around the assassin. Matsen's body went stiff, frozen by magic. Declan plucked the dagger from Matsen's hand and then plunged it into him, rendering a killing blow. He scooted out from under the man, setting him gently on the ground.

He stood, his hands shaking.

"Thank you," Josephine said. "I couldn't have taken him on my own. And my daughter—I'm sure he would have killed Brielle next."

Brielle backed away from the body. "Is this how our lives are going to be? We'll be hunted for our magic?"

"No," Josephine said. "This is how it's going to be. I'm going to run away and hide. You will tell everyone that the magic was so powerful, it ended all the blood oaths. Matsen dropped dead because of it. Same with me. You tell them I'm dead, and you're drained. When we performed the ceremony, you barely had anything at all to begin with. You'd been stifled too long. Do you understand?"

Brielle nodded. "I won't use my magic."

"That's not what I said." Josephine went closer to Brielle, making eye contact. "I want you to use it. Your children will have your power. You will have to teach them how to wield it. I just don't want anyone stealing you and making you do their bidding. That's why you're going to keep quiet."

"Your mother's right," Declan said. "Especially now, when things are so new and tentative." He was thankful his father had maintained such a large military presence. Hopefully it would deter other kingdoms from messing with them. He still needed to do something about Lima sending their assassins.

Josephine's head snapped to the right. "A large ship just pulled into port," she said. "I think it's the king and his son."

Declan had been expecting them. "If they're here, you must go. Brielle and I will head them off. We'll try and keep them away from here."

"Thank you. I'll gather my things and be gone." She looked at the huts. "It's been so long."

"I'll leave the two of you alone to say goodbye," Declan said. "I'll be just over there. Don't take too long."

He left Brielle with her mother and went to where the path cut into the cliff so he could look at the harbor. Sure enough, his father's ship had just pulled in and was docking. It probably hadn't taken them long to realize he wasn't on the ship. It wouldn't have been hard for Orson to figure out where Declan had gone.

He still felt shaken from Matsen trying to kill Josephine. It made sense. The queen, or whoever was behind this, probably never wanted it to happen again. Getting rid of Josephine and Brielle made sense. Which meant he'd have to make sure Brielle had extra protection at all times.

Panic suddenly gripped him and he spun around, facing the huts. What if Josephine convinced Brielle to run away with her? It would be for the best, and Brielle would be safe. However, he'd never find someone like her again. Someone intelligent, kind, eager to learn, and who wanted to work with him as his equal.

A lone figure walked toward him hauling a wheelbarrow filled with sacks. His panic faded. When Brielle reached him, she set the wheelbarrow aside and went up on her tiptoes, kissing his cheek. "It seems today is going to be the first day of the rest of our lives."

An idea occurred to him. "Would you like to marry at your father's house?" he asked. "It's only a few hours away. We can be there before supper." Declan was certain his father wouldn't mind. Especially once he saw all the money. A fortnight ago, he never would have thought any of this possible.

"That sounds like a wonderful idea."

"Can you handle the boat ride?"

"With you by my side, I can handle anything."

Brielle didn't feel any different, yet everything had changed. After she and Declan had married at her father's house, they traveled back to Sunder with the king and Orson. Now, she was standing before the mirror in a lavish wedding gown, about to have her second wedding. This one was for the people of Valdis.

Staring at her reflection, she found it hard to believe that not only was she a married woman, she was also a witch. Hiding it had been both easier and harder than she'd thought. The king didn't question the story she fed him about her powers being stifled and that she couldn't do much to help. She said it had been Mabel who aided her mother and who channeled all the power through her to end the curse which ended up killing her. Honestly, it was a lie bathed in truths.

Declan confessed that he didn't know the full extent of who was involved. Brooks had told him bits and pieces, the same with Orson. Even the queen admitted a few things. But as to who had concocted the entire thing, no one seemed to know.

"There," Jenice said, adjusting the veil on Brielle's head. "You're fit to be a queen."

"Let's hope that's not for a long, long time," Brielle said. While she might not mind it when Briar eventually passed, Brielle was in no way ready to be a queen. And Declan wasn't ready to take on the responsibility of being the king either. The two of them just wanted some time alone, getting to know each other in every way possible.

"You're blushing," Jenice teased. "That must mean you're thinking about the wedding night."

"You know we're already married."

Jenice elbowed her. "I know. That's why I said I knew what you were thinking about."

Brielle laughed. Since she'd been back at the palace, her things had been moved into a different wing. The queen had a few rooms redone in the wing adjacent to the royal chambers. That was to be Brielle and Declan's private space. She honestly didn't know if the queen just didn't want her around, or if Briar was being truly thoughtful and kind. Realistically, the queen probably didn't want to have to see Brielle any more than absolutely necessary.

"Since you're ready, I'm going to go and make sure everything else is done. I'll see you at the marriage ceremony." Jenice curtsied and left the room.

A knock sounded on the door. "It's just me," Brooks said as he came into the room. "Wow. You look stunning."

She turned to face him. "And you look quite dapper in your royal tunic as well." She knew he secretly hoped that once the blood oath ended, he'd regain use of his leg. However, that hadn't been the case, and he still needed the cane to walk.

"I'm glad we finally have a sane person in this family." Brooks kissed her cheek. "And someone who enjoys reading." He smiled kindly at her.

"I imagine you won't need to read quite as much as before." Now that the blood oath was over, she didn't know what he'd do to occupy his time.

"I'll just have to shift the focus of my reading. Make sure I'm up on the other kingdoms' politics and the like. There's more for me to do."

"If you need an assistant, I'd love to help you."

A look of sadness washed over his face.

"What's the matter?" she asked.

He shook his head. "Nothing. Another time, another place. I'll see you at the ceremony." He turned and left without giving her a chance to say another word.

She heard him talking to someone out in the hallway, and then Orson strolled into the room with outstretched arms.

"Look at my new sister," he said before wrapping her in a hug that lifted her off the floor.

"Careful," she chided him. "Jenice spent a lot of time making me look the part. She'll be furious if you mess up my hair or makeup."

He set her down. "Jenice's wrath I fear." He took a step back.

"To what do I owe the pleasure of this visit?" she asked.

"I want to let you know something." He rubbed the back of his neck. "General Sullivan was hanged today for his crimes."

She'd known it was coming, but it still shocked her. "I'm surprised they did it today of all days."

"I think they're trying to keep it contained. In any case, I'll be sworn in as general tomorrow. I expect you to be there."

"I wouldn't miss it." He was going to have his hands full with Valdis's army and being ready for threats from other kingdoms.

"I'm glad I won that bet and you helped us out," Orson said as he headed to the door.

"I didn't do much," she said, repeating the lie she'd told a hundred times since that day.

"Mabel, the blood oath, and my grandfather are gone. I'd say you did plenty." He winked and exited the room.

Looking back at the mirror, she barely recognized her own face. It wasn't the hair or makeup, but the eyes. When overcome with emotion, her eyes changed. Sometimes they went black, other times blue. She needed to learn to control herself. Otherwise, she'd need to wear the bracelet that blocked her powers. She had it tucked away somewhere. The one she currently wore on her wrist was a duplicate, but the metal was slightly different and a few of the marks were altered. No one seemed to know the difference. In the reflection, she saw Declan.

He came into the room, sliding his arms around her waist, setting his chin on her shoulder and hugging her.

She turned around to face him. He didn't let her go. "Are you ready to marry me a second time?" she asked.

"I am." He leaned in and kissed her. "And are you ready to rule by my side? To not be lost in a book all day long?"

She was ready to start living her life and seeing all the world had to offer. Not that she'd give up reading completely because she enjoyed it far too much. But at least she had her own adventures to go on now instead of living vicariously through her books.

"I am." She leaned in and kissed him.

THE END

ALSO BY JENNIFER ANNE DAVIS

TRUE REIGN:

The Key

Red

War

REIGN OF SECRETS:

Cage of Deceit

Cage of Darkness

Cage of Destiny

Oath of Deception

Oath of Destruction

KNIGHTS OF THE REALM:

Realm of Knights

Shadow Knights

Hidden Knights

ABOUT THE AUTHOR
JENNIFER ANNE DAVIS

Jennifer Anne Davis graduated from the University of San Diego with a degree in English and a teaching credential. She is currently a full-time writer and mother of three kids. She is happily married to her high school sweetheart and lives in the San Diego area.

Jennifer is the recipient of the San Diego Book Awards Best Published Young Adult Novel (2013), winner of the Kindle Book Awards (2018), a finalist in the USA Best Book Awards (2014), and a finalist in the Next Generation Indie Book Awards (2014).

Visit Jennifer at:

www.JenniferAnneDavis.com